THE FEAR PROTOCOL

A NOVEL

BRAD NEWBOLD

Fidelis Publishing ®
Winchester, VA • Nashville, TN
www.fidelispublishing.com

ISBN: 9781956454550
ISBN: 9781956454567 (eBook)

The Fear Protocol
A Novel

Order at www.faithfultext.com for a significant discount. Email info@fidelispublishing.com to inquire about bulk purchase discounts.

Cover designed by Diana Lawrence
Interior design by Xcel Graphic
Edited by Amanda Varian
Additional edits by Jonathan Pountney

Manufactured in the United States of America
10 9 8 7 6 5 4 3 2 1

For God has not given us a spirit of fear,
but of power and of love and of a sound mind.
—2 Timothy 1:7 (NKJV).

CHAPTER ONE

It started on his way home from work. It was Monday. He was nearing the end of his forty-five-minute commute (more like fifty-five minutes on the way home). It was the usual combination of mind-numbing boredom mixed with random moments of spontaneous anger.

Gas light on.

Dang it.

Text message alert.

Can you stop at the market on your way home?

Grrr.

He managed a quick text while inching down the road.

Ya. list?

He did some mental math. Nothing else to do. Five minutes for gas. Fifteen minutes for groceries. Add twenty minutes to his commute. Cross over that invisible sixty-minute barrier. An hour! To get home from work. At that moment, he couldn't imagine anything worse.

He pulled into the gas station and maneuvered to the back of the line of cars. He waited his turn. Sam's Club always had a line. He did more mental math. He saved about ten cents per gallon going to Sam's Club. Thirteen gallons maybe to fill his Lexus. $1.30 in total savings. He was going to wait ten minutes to save $1.30. His personal economic engine was screaming at him to give it all up.

Finally there, he pulled the tab to open the little door covering the gas port, got out of the car, and walked around to the pump.

He slid his credit card into the slot.

PLEASE INSERT SAMS CLUB CARD FIRST

Argh.

He took his green Sam's Club membership card out and inserted it into the gas pump.

MEMBER NOT AUTHORIZED

Member not authorized? Did Hannah forget to renew their membership? He tried once more, for safety. Same result.

He looked around for some help, and on the other side of the pump he saw a middle-aged woman pumping gas while talking on the phone.

"Yes, Mom. You have to keep your scores up or they won't deliver your medicines. Just make sure you pay attention to your scores . . ."

He peeked around the pump, hoping to catch her eye. He gave the meek little head bob and held up his card once she glanced his way.

He mouthed to her *"expired"* and gave a quizzical little shrug. She rolled her eyes and fished out her club card while replying to her mom.

"No, I have no idea how many points you would get. But are you sure you want gravel in your front lawn? Does that really save enough water?"

He grabbed her card, swiped it. Bingo. He handed her back her card. She snatched it, wiping it off on the edge of her shirt. The look in her eyes said she was afraid of catching leprosy from the unclean. He smiled anyway and turned back to the pump.

PLEASE INSERT PAYMENT

He inserted his debit card. Waited for the reader to process.

UNAUTHORIZED CARD OWNER

The machine blinked at him. A faint red glow caught his eyes over his forehead. Ignoring the light, he tried again.

UNAUTHORIZED CARD OWNER

UNAUTHORIZED CARD OWNER

UNAUTHORIZED CARD OWNER

The machine blinked helpfully.

He did mental math again. He got paid last week. No way they were overdrawn. Maybe there was fraud and the credit card company froze his account?

He tried another card.

UNAUTHORIZED CARD OWNER

The red glow pulsed above him again. On. Off. On. Off. Looking up, he saw a small red light, attached to the top of the gas pump. He took his card out. The light went off. He put his card back in.

UNAUTHORIZED CARD OWNER

The light turned red. He turned and looked at the other pumps in the station. All of them had a similar light. A few of the lights were unlit, as cars pulled in and out, but most of them were glowing green. Had those always been there?

He tried yet again to use his card and got another friendly message from the terminal, and another dose of the red light. This time he saw people turn to look at him.

It was public knowledge now when a credit card gets declined? He was dumbfounded. A young man pumping gas near him looked over. He was wearing $300 LeBron's, jeans ripped on purpose, a hat with an unfamiliar logo, and a white T-shirt with "LOVE" across the middle.

"Maybe, try and love your neighbor, dude," the man said as he noticed the red light.

An elderly woman two aisles over turned, saw the red light, gasped, and clutched her purse to her chest.

"Hang on a minute, Mom. MOM! Wait, hang on!" It was the club card lady. "Hey! You better not have messed up my club standing! What the heck, man!" she yelled at Brian, cradling her cell phone between her cheek and shoulder.

"I'm sorry! I think I have fraudulent activity on my account?" He gave another pathetic shrug.

Brian closed the gas cap, climbed back into his car, and started the engine. The AC hit him full blast. Early June in Southern California called for extreme measures.

His dash read: 27 MILES TO EMPTY. He did mental math. One mile to groceries. One mile home. Plenty of gas to officially make it tomorrow morning's problem. He pulled out of the gas station, trying his best to ignore the stares.

What was up with that red light? And why did that old lady grab her purse like she was about to be assaulted?

CHAPTER TWO

He pulled into the street, joining the traffic jam. A few minutes later, he parked his Lexus in the grocery store parking lot. He grabbed a shopping cart and checked his phone to see what Hannah, his wife, needed.

Two cans of formula, milk, a couple of random snack items for the boys, ground beef, cereal, ice cream, frozen pizza—the essentials. He guessed they were low on food and Hannah had a busy day. Frozen pizza to get them through the night, ground beef in an attempt to plan tomorrow's dinner, and an assortment of impulse additions.

He made his way dutifully through the market, adding the items. Shopping for a family of eight was a never-ending chore. His oldest two, Abby and Luke, had been eating like adults since before they were teens. At sixteen and thirteen, they also had strong opinions about what they ate.

He made sure he got the ice cream that caused the least amount of arguing (cookies and cream for the win). His middle daughter, Rachel, was a people pleaser. An outgoing eleven-year-old-party-planning-chatterbox, she was just excited about life. He made sure to get her favorite cereal, the one with the marshmallow fairies. She outgrew fairies about two years ago, but he knew it would make her happy, so he went for it.

Jeremiah and Shawn, ages nine and six, respectively, got the most attention from the list. String cheese, potato chips, applesauce pouches, chocolate cereal, breakfast bars, beef sticks. He rolled his eyes at each addition to the cart, while chuckling inwardly. His wife was predictable. And loving. It wasn't the worst combination.

Finishing up, he made his way to the registers. *What in the heck happened at the gas station?* Shaking it off, he unloaded his items onto the belt.

"Member card, Mx?"

"Sorry?" Brian said, looking up. The cashier looked to be in her late fifties, with curly blonde hair, fading from gray. She was wearing cat's eye glasses with a chain minder around her neck. There was an array of buttons and pins on her apron. "Love is love!" "Go green!" "Silence is Violence!"

"Do you have a member's card?" She scanned his items and let them gather on the other side of the register.

"No, sorry . . . ummm? You said 'mix'?"

"Oh. No. I said Mx. It's a more inclusive, gender-neutral replacement for Mr. and Mrs. Don't spread hate!" she said, pointing to a button on her apron that said "Gendering: See it. Name it. Stop it."

"Ah, well . . . Sir is fine."

"Well, I won't presume, Mx. It's just not loving."

Brian gave her a blank stare, searching for something—anything—logical to follow that. Eventually it came to him. "Ummm . . . my name is Brian," he said helpfully.

"Did you bring your own bags with you today, Brian, or will you be carrying everything loose?"

"I need bags, please."

She stopped, holding a box of Choco-Rocco cereal over the scanner.

"Um, sir. Bags? Are you sure?"

"Yes, please. I can't carry all of this out."

"Well, um, it's just that the plastic bags end up in landfills and kill birds. They take over 300 years to photodegrade."

"Photo-de what?" He blinked at her.

"Photodegrade. You see, these plastic bags not only hurt the environment when they are processed, but they kill birds. You don't mean to cause harm, I'm sure, but you see how choosing plastic bags is choosing violence, right?"

"Ummm."

"And choosing violence is really no choice at all!" She proudly pointed to the button on her apron that said the same thing.

"So . . . paper?"

She sighed. Putting down the Choco-Rocco cereal, she gave him a level look.

"It's just that . . . paper bags require four times as much water to manufacture as a plastic bag. And the deforestation of critical rain forests is robbing indigenous people groups of their habitats. You don't want to rob people of their homes, do you?"

"Paper bags are robbing people?"

"We just went through a great eco-knowledge class to help Happy Mart earn BSCPs. We even earned PSCPs! See?" She held out her phone, flashing an app at him.

His mind raced to try and make sense of what she was saying.

"I'll take my chances. Paper, please."

She stiffened. Reaching under the register, she pushed a button. A red light flashed on top of the register. A charge was added to his running total on the screen.

"Okay, Brian. It's just that I'll have to add this to your transaction."

"It's okay. I understand." He grew numb to the bag surcharge years ago.

She bagged his groceries. She touched the paper bags like they were covered in acid, wrinkling her nose as if something smelled.

"Your total is $74.89."

He swiped his card on the reader.

SHOPPER SCORES NOT SUFFICIENT FOR TRANSACTION

The red light flashed again.

"Ma'am, I'm sorry. I think the card reader has an issue?"

She stared at him.

"Can you swipe it on your side?" Brian asked.

She looked at the screen and read the message. Her mouth dropped open.

"Ma'am?"

Her eyes narrowed.

"Hello?"

The red light flashed.

Her lips pursed as she angrily sucked in a breath.

"First of all! You just gendered me! Twice! And I don't appreciate your ageism either! Ma'am implies older. How do you know that is how I identify? HOW DARE YOU. I prefer to carry myself as a non-binary twenty-seven-year-old while at work. Your 'ma'aming' me implies an age that I don't identify with!"

It was his turn for his mouth to drop open. She was obviously middle-aged. Maybe even sixty.

"And second—you have insufficient scores to even *shop here*. You are low in both ECO and SJ and dangerously close on the other two! I guess you do like to choose violence! And after I tried to help you with the bags!"

His eyes narrowed.

It was his turn to suck in a breath.

"How did you 'help me' with the bags! You preached to me and then charged me for *paper*! For *paper*!" He felt his face flush.

She gasped. "You! Raising your voice at me!"

"You raised your voice first!"

"You're a forty-something white, cis-gendered, beard-growing, patriarchal oppressor! I've lived under the shadow of you and your type my whole life! Raising your voice at an older woman is hateful! Hate is violence!"

"You just got done telling me that you aren't an older woman! Which is it . . . MA'AM!?" he said, feeling triumphant.

"THAT'S IT! SECURITY!!"

He looked around. The entire store was frozen. Customers in the other lines were staring at him. The red light on top of the register served as a beacon for the drama. He was embarrassed. He shouldn't have argued.

He tried to calm down.

"Look, I'm sorry. I didn't mean to offend you. I'll leave. Can you please just run my card and I'll get out of your hair?" He held up his hands in the "no offense" posture and tried on his most apologetic smile.

"You don't understand, *sir*. You. Can't. Shop. Here." She bit every word off with a snarl. Spittle coming from the corner of her mouth.

Just then the security guard made his way over. A very large, very slow man. He looked like he just crawled out of his mother's basement after playing video games for ten straight years.

"Follow me, Mx," he said.

Brian quickly considered his options. He'd already made a scene. He did shout at her, after all. And maybe there was still a problem with his cards. He could keep arguing, only to have Bubba here manhandle him. Sensing defeat, he gave up.

"Okay, okay, I'm leaving. Can I at least pay cash for the formula? We're almost out." He fished around in his khakis for a few bucks.

"OUT!" she said, pointing.

He lowered his head, and let Bubba lead him out.

The red light over the register changed to green.

He heard a few people clap.

It was a Monday.

CHAPTER THREE

He made a right on Santa Clarita Parkway. Shaking, fuming. No gas. No groceries. Humiliated. Worse than being humiliated, he was also totally confused as to *what . . . just . . . happened.* His credit cards were declined? And this somehow made him a pariah? Why? Who? What. The. Heck.

He made his way through their neighborhood. Evergreen Lane was the only road into their housing tract, but the community was a clever arrangement of spidering cul-de-sacs. He meandered his way past a few soccer moms on a walk and driving by the park at the approach to his street, he saw the usual: cars parked everywhere. Soccer practice. *I guess that's why they call them soccer moms.*

Their home was at the end of the last street in the neighborhood, third from the end. Another cul-de-sac.

He clicked open the garage door, pulled his car in, and got out. He opened the door to the house and entered the chaos of family life empty-handed.

Brian walked through the entryway and dining room, into the great room. They were so excited to get this floor plan when house shopping nearly ten years ago. Kitchen, countertop seating, breakfast nook, and family room all in one large rectangle in the back of the house, overlooking their backyard. He soon realized having the hub of all family life in one large space meant it was nearly impossible to keep it clean or quiet. But it did make it easy to hear everyone.

"Dad! Shawn took my car! I was gonna play with it!" bellowed Jer, full stop. No introduction.

"No! Jer put it down, so I picked it up!"

"I just put it down for a second! I was going to play with it again!"

"But you have to *take turns*! Jer!"

He girded his loins.

"Hey boys! Love you. How about 'Hi Dad! How was work'?" He put his arms out.

"Mom! Dad's home! What's for dinner?" Jeremiah said, although it sounded more like a statement than a question. He was great at changing subjects. Shawn raced after him, through the entryway and dining room, into the kitchen.

Shawn and Jer were an endless source of amusement in the house. They acted like twins, even though Jer was three years older than Shawn. Where one went, the other was soon to follow. Or rather, whatever Jer did, Shawn was soon to mimic.

Giving up on the boys for a minute, he picked up Elizabeth, just barely toddling around the house on wobbly feet.

"Dada, stinky," she said.

And she was right. Stinky diaper.

Shoot. Diapers were on the list.

"Dad! Dad! Dad! I made a card for Elizabeth's birthday! Can you sign it?" Rachel chanted, as she roller-skated around downstairs. She shoved a card at him, covering his shirt in glitter.

"Okay, baby Rach! Just a second! Where's Mom?"

"Mom!" she yelled out. "Dad's home!" Not so much an answer as a proclamation, but hopefully the echolocation would work.

"Hey, babe!" Hannah yelled from the kitchen.

Brian made his way to the back of the house, dodging roller skaters and toy cars.

Hannah was throwing a salad together, running water in the sink for dishes, answering questions from Luke, and generally looking a little flustered. Brian gave her a hug and a kiss.

"Luke! How's it going, boy-o?"

"Good," Luke replied. Brian suppressed the urge to force more conversation from his son.

"Bri, can you get the pizza in the oven? I already preheated it and the kids are starving! Love you!" Hannah said this over her shoulder as she finished the salad.

"Where is Abby?" he deflected.

"Upstairs, I think. Playing her guitar. Or maybe outside, reading? I don't know. ABBY!" Hannah yelled. Yelling was the family language lately. Maybe they should learn to use the Aurora devices around the house to cut down on the noise.

"I didn't get the pizza," Brian said.

"Did you get the dinosaur chicken nuggets instead?" she asked.

"Actually, no."

Hannah caught something in his voice and turned to him.

"The card was declined," Brian said.

Hannah frowned. "Maybe there was fraud? Why not just try the other one? I had the same problem earlier when I was trying to buy Abby's new volleyball uniform online. The card was declined. It's usually fraud. Can you call and take care of it?"

"I'll figure it out."

Brian grabbed a beer from the fridge and sat down in the living room. Hannah started rummaging for a dinner backup. "We're pretty low on groceries. I'll just do the rest of the hot dogs for tonight and we'll figure it out tomorrow?"

While Hannah threw dinner together, and over the regular interruptions provided by Abby coming downstairs, Luke asking if he can join swim team, Jer and Shawn attempting murder, Rachel following the conversation and asking a multitude of questions, Elizabeth generally just smelling, Brian explained to Hannah what happened at the gas station and grocery store.

"Wow. You really got into it with the cashier."

"Yeah. I feel bad. I shouldn't have argued with her, but I was so embarrassed. She wouldn't even try my card again. It was like *I* was the problem, not my card. It made no sense."

The family ate dinner in the usual way. Some standing, some sitting, some quiet, some loud. Several of them sticky.

After dinner, Brian called on his credit cards and checking account. The balances were fine. There was no reason for them to be declined. He even made sure there was no fraudulent activity, and the savings account balance was on target.

"Hannah, what time does the market close?"

Abby and Luke were doing dishes, Rachel, still on roller skates, was putting away a few random toys, and Jer and Shawn were enjoying the bounty of the young: cartoons upstairs.

"It's open 24/7."

He drained the last of his beer.

"I'm going back to the grocery store to talk to the manager." He turned to Luke. "Boy-o, you want to come with me?"

CHAPTER FOUR

Driving back to the grocery store after a few beers turned out to be a mistake. Brian spent the short drive fuming. He was neutered. Twice. Once at the gas station (*My cards are fine! I need gas! That lady was SCARED of me!*) and again at the market. He couldn't even buy Choco-Rocco! They needed groceries and he had money to buy it! What was the problem? He was getting himself into a fine lather just thinking about it.

Luke sat there silently, fidgeting with his pocketknife. During their last family camping trip, Luke drooled over the knife in the small gift store (more like a kiosk with a 500 percent markup). He spent the entire trip explaining to his father he was:

a. Responsible
b. Thirteen years old
c. Able to buy it with his own money

Eventually he managed to wear his dad down. Brian was happy to see his son growing up and managing more responsibilities, even if it was something as small as a fold-out camping knife.

"Be careful," Brian said, not really meaning it. Luke was careful. It just seemed like the right thing to say. Plus, his mind was on the cashier at the store. He was really hot now.

They pulled into the parking lot, relegated to a space toward the back. Not because it was crowded. Most of the prime spots were marked "EV only" and had charging stations. They walked the fifty yards or so to the store, and went in. The store was less crowded than it had been on his first visit. There was a man with a case of beer and some frozen meals under his arm browsing magazines near the front, a woman with nothing but cases of Gatorade in her cart struggling to push it toward a register, and the usual assortment of oddballs you see in a grocery store in the late evening.

He spotted the cashier who shunned him earlier standing idly by her register, picking at her nails and checking the clock. Brian and Luke made their way over to a front desk area when she caught sight of them. Her eyes flared open, and she quickly picked up a phone at her station. Brian paused, hand on Luke's shoulder.

"I. Would. Like. To. Speak. To. The. Manager," Brian spat at her slowly, doing his best Clint Eastwood impersonation. She was unimpressed.

"I already called him, Mx. BRIAN." She laid heavily on the "mix Brian," giving it the full singsong, head-wag treatment, like her maturity level was trapped back in junior high.

Brian suppressed a growing desire to lash out. He wanted to hurl an insult, throw a magazine, something, anything. But he buried the impulse under a warm blanket of simmering anger, letting it glow in his belly. Most of human existence was simply sorting out your impulses, and quarantining the ones that didn't seem socially acceptable.

Luke was scanning the magazines, picking them up and flipping pages before setting them back down. Somehow the men's fitness magazine, celebrity gossip magazine, and home decor magazine all featured the same actor from those superhero movies. He was either the greatest Renaissance man of all time or people were stupid. It had to be one or the other.

After a few minutes, the manager came out from the back. He was a thirty-something white guy, about six feet tall. He looked like he stopped doing cardio after high school football but never skipped weights. He also had his head shaved on one side, with a purple-tinted combover haircut, and was that mascara on his eyes? He walked over to the cashier, saying, "Where is this PERSON, Debra?"

She pointed over at Brian and Luke. Luke peered over the top of a magazine he was holding, and Brian stood there, with his arms crossed, practicing his indignant stare.

The manager walked toward Brian, stopped a few feet away, and said, "So, I heard you assaulted my cashier."

CHAPTER 5

The manager said it loud enough to be overheard. His voice was an octave or two higher than seemed appropriate for a man of his size, and it was paired with a few delicate mannerisms and overtly sassy eyebrows. A couple of shoppers stopped and stared.

Brian's jaw dropped. That was becoming a pattern for him.

"I . . . assaulted her?" he asked. The coals of anger buried in his belly happily lapped up the confusion and embarrassment, and he shuffled his posture. "You have it all wrong," Brian said. "I was just trying to buy groceries for my family, and she refused to help me!" He started raising his voice, exasperated.

"You just did it again!" the manager said. This time his voice dropped an octave.

"What are you talking about?" Brian retorted. He really wanted to get back on topic, but the conversation was going sideways quickly. A small crowd started to form. "Look," he said, doing his best to apply reason, "I had an issue with my credit card. I asked her to please try it again and she refused. She wouldn't even let me use CASH for some baby formula! I was basically humiliated and kicked out! I went home, called on all my accounts, and everything is FINE." Brian emphasized the final point with an angry nod.

The manager stepped closer to Brian. "First, you need to stop attacking Debra. They have done nothing to you, and you keep resorting to violence. Second, no one cares about your money! Your scores are too low. You obviously don't know what it means to love people and care for the earth, so you just aren't qualified to shop here. Full stop."

The manager ("Chad," according to the nametag pinned to his polo), put on a satisfied smile. He turned around, nodding to the crowd, giving them the "it's okay, folks, I've got this under control" look. The crowd seemed relieved. Relieved!

Brian threw his hands in the air. "I have money! I need groceries! You have groceries! You accept money! This should literally be the simplest part of our lives!" Brian found himself shouting. Luke took a step back. He could feel the electricity in the air. But Brian was just warming up. "And what do you mean I ASSAULTED HER? You're nuts. It was Bubba, your security guard! HE put his hands on ME! He walked me out like I was a thief! You're insane. And *she* could have helped me!" The coals were ablaze, and there was no way to extinguish them now.

Chad raised his voice. "You keep your violence to yourself, Mx! We don't need any of that at Happy Mart! You keep gendering Debra, and I will be forced to protect them!" Chad took another step toward Brian. He was a big guy. Brian, seeing nothing but red at this point, took no notice.

"I never touched her! 'CHAD'! Get out of my face! I just need some groceries! Luke, go get the stuff we need!" He shoved a list at Luke, who stood, paralyzed.

"Dad? Can we just go home?" Luke whispered. No one heard.

"You leave, or I make you leave. It's that simple," Chad said.

"I'll leave when I have two boxes of Choco-Rocco cereal! It's THAT SIMPLE!" The last two words came out in a shriek, spittle flying.

The manager lunged toward Brian, grabbing him by the shirt. He had a good fifty-pound advantage, and even though Brian struggled, he was no match. Chad managed to pin one of Brian's arms behind him and started to steer him toward the door. Luke trailed behind, white as a ghost. Chad had his bicep under Brian's right armpit, and was using the leverage to lift Brian off the ground. Brian pulled against Chad unsuccessfully.

"Let! Me! Go!" Brian yelled. He threw his legs backward, intending to kick Chad in the shins, but because he was lifted nearly off his feet, he had poor leverage, and his kick landed higher than he intended. He hit Chad's right knee with one foot, but the other foot hit Chad between the legs. The back of his left heel caught Chad squarely in the crotch, and he heard a loud "oomph!" Chad buckled toward his right, his knee giving way. He fell, still holding Brian. Brian's dead weight against Chad's weakened right knee caused them both to go down hard.

On his way down, Chad caught the side of his right temple on a metal rack full of greeting cards. The metal rack, the greeting cards, Chad, and Brian all came crashing down in a large, loud pile.

Brian was pinned under Chad, the wind knocked out of him. He pushed against Chad while pulling himself free. He stood up, looking around. The small crowd was staring at him in abject terror.

Brian looked down. There were several greeting cards scattered across the tiled floor. "Happy Birthday!" with balloons was right next to "Celebrating YOU!" with a rainbow, and "Love is love!" covered in hearts. A sign from the display case proudly proclaimed "All of our cards are made with 100% recycled materials!" was partially crumpled under Chad's shoulder.

Brian hardly noticed the cards. Chad was laying on his back, breathing heavily, blood covering his face. He had a large gash on the right side of his forehead. It extended from his hairline toward his right ear. And it was bleeding. A lot.

CHAPTER 6

The cut didn't look terribly deep, but it was wide. The fire in Brian's belly extinguished immediately. He nearly vomited.

"Are . . . you okay?" He bent down to help him.

An older gentleman from the crowd rushed over and got between Brian and Chad. Kneeling, he inspected the wound. "We should call a doctor! He may need stitches! Why would you do this to him?" He looked up at Brian, fear and indignation in his eyes.

"I was just trying to buy groceries! He grabbed me first! We tripped!" Brian held out his hands pathetically, showing how harmless he was.

Debra screamed from behind, "Call the cops! He assaulted me! And then he assaulted Chad!" She was trembling.

"That's not what happened!" Brian yelled.

The older gentleman checked Chad for a pulse.

The right side of Chad's face was covered in blood; from his forehead to his eyelid, trailing down the side of his mouth, and creating a small pool on the tile below him.

"Look at all that blood!" Debra screamed.

Brian stared down at the manager, transfixed.

Chad opened his eyes.

The whites of his right eye stood out like a lightbulb against the blood on his face. He looked at Brian. His upper lip lifted in an animal snarl. His teeth were covered in blood.

Chad let out an otherworldly sound. Deep from his gut, an animal howl. Distorted, violent. All the while staring at Brian. Something in the look of Chad's right eye terrified Brian. It was hard to process, but his left eye was roaming freely, looking almost scared. But his right eye was locked on Brian, with a menacing scowl. Brian felt his mind being penetrated by something evil, sinister, like an oily hand was reaching down his throat, probing around for his darkest secrets.

"I'm gonna kill you!" Chad bellowed. He struggled to get up.

Brian was scared. This was happening so quickly, too quickly. It didn't feel real. And was that electricity in the air? His skin tingled. His vision narrowed. He forgot about Debra. And Choco-Rocco. And credit cards. All his mind could process was two words, running over and over. *Kill. Blood. Kill. Blood.* What he could see, and what he just heard.

RUN.

He grabbed Luke, and made for the door. Chad struggled up to his left knee, and Brian scrambled past him, his right foot slipping in the small pool of blood.

Kill. Blood. Kill. Blood.

Luke. Run. Luke. Run.

He ran.

They made it halfway to the car before Brian turned around and saw Chad stumbling after them.

"Stop! Get over here!" Chad yelled through the parking lot.

Luke grabbed his father's hand and trembled. "Dad! He's coming!" he yelled.

Brian managed to get his keys out and unlock the car. They threw open their doors and jumped in, slamming the doors shut. He locked both doors just as Chad reached the car. Chad slammed his hand against the driver's side window.

"Get out! The cops are coming! Get out!" he yelled. Chad slammed the hood of the car, bending down slightly to see inside the car window.

Brian started the car.

"Hey, Mx! Get out! You need to wait! We need your information! You tried to kill me! And you assaulted Debra!" Chad's voice returned to normal. Frantic, angry, but not the deep, guttural animal howl as when he said *I'm gonna kill you* just a short eternity ago.

Brian slammed it into reverse, just as Chad slapped his right palm against the windshield, leaving a large bloody handprint.

Brian stopped to put it in drive, and briefly made eye contact with Chad, now ten feet away from the car. Chad's right eye still had that sinister, piercing stare. Brian felt that strange sensation of being searched, invaded. His hands grew icy cold.

He slammed his foot on the gas pedal and sped away.

CHAPTER 7

Brian's hands trembled as he turned his car into their neighborhood. The adrenaline rush was quickly being replaced with anxiety. What happened back there? Chad's voice changed. Changed! And his eye? It looked like two people were staring at him at once. From his left eye, the Happy Mart manager, trapped and scared, and from his right . . . something else entirely.

He managed a glance at Luke, who was staring out the window next to him.

"Hey, buddy. You okay?" His voice cracked, betraying his own state of mind.

"Umm," came the barely audible reply from Luke.

Brian gave him space. He didn't really know what to say anyway.

He pulled past the park, down their street, clicked open the garage and pulled in. Luke jumped out and went into the house.

His wife was in the kitchen, talking to Abby. They were in the middle of an emotional conversation, and Brian hesitated. Abby was sixteen. And sixteen means boys. And opinions. And emotions. None of those things were Brian's strengths.

Hannah looked up at Brian, and he could sense she had been crying too.

"I need to talk to you." They both said it at the same time. Twenty years of marriage meant they knew how to get to the point when stuff was serious. He cocked his head slightly, puzzled.

"Abby just got kicked off the volleyball team," Hannah said. She was angry.

"Okay. Okay. Wow. Sorry Abby!" Brian's mind raced. A parenting crisis! On top of everything else. Priorities.

"Where are the littles?" he asked.

"Jer and Shawn are in bed. Awake, I'm sure. Rachel is upstairs and I think she has the baby." Pretty much par for the course after 8 p.m.

He took a seat in the living room, and Hannah and Abby joined.

"You first," he said.

Hannah told him. Abby's coach called her about thirty minutes ago. He said he had no choice but to kick her off the team for "unloving, harmful, and violent" actions against her teammates. According to her coach the league has been monitoring the players' social media accounts in an effort to ensure an inclusive and loving space for the players. Abby "liked" several articles by a conservative blogger with titles such as "What Is a Woman?," "Are EVs ACTUALLY better for the environment?," and the kicker: "Mandating pronouns is MIND CONTROL." Coach Jim explained to her this just wasn't tolerated. The coaches recently went through a "tolerance and love" training course and he just couldn't understand how Abby could do something like that. One of Abby's teammates is transgendered, and she *actually* clicked the link on one of the articles.

"Abby, she read the whole thing!" her coach told her. "Do you know how HARMFUL that article was? It attacked her personally. That article was full of violence, and the league is very strict about its violence policy. Not only are you off the team, you aren't permitted to attend any of the games this summer! I guess I shouldn't be surprised getting this from a homeschool kid, but I just didn't think I would actually have someone so HATEFUL and BACKWARDS on my team!"

Abby was sobbing as she recalled Coach Jim's words. "Dad, I can't even go to games!" Brian's heart ached for her. He was furious. Having forgotten his grocery store trip for the moment, he was making mental plans to drive over to Coach Jim's house and give him a piece of his mind.

His wife, seeing the usual signs, took one arm off Abby and reached over to pat Brian on the hand. "Brian, she just needs a hug." Momentarily placated, he murmured, "Of course, of course," and reached over to hug Abby.

Something nagged at him in the back of his mind. Coach Jim accused Abby of being *violent*. For posting an article? That sounded like the insanity from Debra and Chad at Happy Mart.

The market. Blood. Kill. Run. Luke. It all came flashing back to him. He looked down at his shoes. There was still blood on the sole of his right shoe.

"Abby, why don't you head upstairs for a bit. I'll talk to your mom and see if we can sort this out." He gave her a hug, and Abby went upstairs, sniffling audibly.

Miracle of miracles, finally alone downstairs with his wife, Brian sat across from Hannah and leveled a look at her.

"Something happened at the market."

CHAPTER 8

Brian explained to Hannah what happened. She sat there, hands folded. Then hands wringing. Then hands clenched.

First, he explained to her how the manager accused him of violence.

"Each time I spoke, he said I was 'doing it again' as if I was swinging my fists instead of just trying to make a point! Then, he grabbed me!"

Brian turned his gaze to the yard, recalling the moment in his mind.

"It went from bad to worse. The people gawking seemed RELIEVED he was dealing with me. And this Chad guy, I'm telling you, something was off with him. He's a big guy, but I'm not that small either. He picked me up like nothing. I swear I was just trying to pull free, but our legs got tangled up, and we fell."

Hannah's eyes flared. "Fell?"

"Yeah. Both of us. He hit his head pretty hard on the way down and ended up with a big gash." He told her about the blood, and the way Chad's right eye seemed to change. "Then he said he was going to kill me! He chased us out of the store!"

Brian got up, walked to the fridge, and grabbed a couple of beers. He popped their caps, poured one into a glass, and handed the bottle to Hannah.

"What's going on?" Hannah said, not really expecting an answer.

Brian held the cool glass against his forehead. Closing his eyes for a moment.

* * * *

They sat there side by side, nursing a couple beers.

"No gas?" Hannah said.

"Right."

"No groceries?"

"Bingo."

"People going crazy?"

"Preach."

"Sounds like the apocalypse," Hannah said.

"No way. The apocalypse will be way noisier. Russians. Or nukes. Maybe zombies."

"I'm serious, Brian. This is weird."

"I'm serious too. *Red Dawn*, *The Postman*, *Train to Busan*. That's how it'll happen."

"*Dawn of the Dead.*"

"Huh?"

"You picked, like, the most obscure Zombie movie." She laid her head on his shoulder.

"*Train to Busan* isn't obscure! It's awesome! It's like *Snowpiercer* meets *The Raid*!"

"There you go again."

Brian looked over at her.

"Hannah, *Train to Busan* is a classic."

"Just like *The Postman*? Why didn't you just say *Waterworld*?" She arched her eyebrow, smiling.

"Kevin Costner is a national hero. And *The Postman* proves it. It's the perfect movie! Tom Petty is in it, for goodness' sake!" He was taking this too seriously, and she egged him on.

"Yes, dear, you're right. *The Postman* is a modern classic and all the critics and the rest of the sane world are all wrong and you are right."

"Thank you. Yes. That's correct." He knew she was teasing, but the words still felt good to him, so he let it rest.

"But seriously, Bri, something is strange about all of this. Why would your payment get turned down at the gas station *and* the market? And they wouldn't even take cash? And both Jim and Chad used the word 'violence.' Feels like an episode of *The Twilight Zone*."

Brian grabbed the TV remote and jabbed the power button.

"Maybe it really is the end of the world," he teased.

"There's one way to find out. Turn on the news."

CHAPTER 9

Brian navigated the TV menu to the news app and saw the little red icon showing there was a "live" broadcast in session. He opened the app.

The broadcast picked up midstream. A sharply dressed female reporter with her hair pulled back in a tight bun was delivering breaking news.

"*. . . speed at which these new policies have been implemented is unprecedented. In an effort to back up President Amon's promise to prioritize public health, and as a result of his current super majority hold on all three branches of government, the 'Azazel Promise,' as it is being called, was drafted, approved, and implemented in just under two weeks.*"

The news feed cut to a clip of President Amon speaking.

"*The Azazel Promise is about public health. In order to ensure the well-being of everyone, we need to eradicate all forms of violence, whether done by corporations, religious institutions, news reporters, or even individuals. We are here to lead and guide you.*"

President Amon held his left hand up, palm facing outward.

"*We are here to ensure that all deeds and thoughts are held captive to what is best for your neighbors. Love is love. Hate is hate. Let's end hate once and for all. I promise that whenever you are in a public space, you can be assured that everyone around you will be safe, committed to love, and compliant. Hate-filled people have no place in modern society, and the Azazel Promise is our way of ensuring that.*"

The program cut back to the reporter.

"*Given the speed at which our government is now able to function due to the supermajority, the Azazel Promise was approved days ago, and*"

implementation has already begun. Here to explain the speed of the imple-
mentation is Ethan Marks, CEO of Mastema, the world's largest online
retailer. Mx. Marks, can you tell us how Silicon Valley has partnered with
the government to roll out this program?"

The program cut to a video feed of Ethan Marks. A sharply dressed
fifty-year-old with dark hair, piercing blue eyes, and bright red lips.

"Silicon Valley was happy to throw its support toward the implementa-
tion of the Azazel Promise. Once it became clear that the central banks were
on board, and any future access to capital, payment processing, financing,
currency exchange, and business permits would be subject to the criteria set
forth in the Azazel Promise—we were happy to help. After all, access to those
crucial business resources is necessary for us at Mastema, and we really had
no choice but to comply."

"Can you tell us how you were able to act so swiftly?"

"Sure, Mary. We were able to pivot all of our programmers away from
their current projects, and put them full time on the AP. President Amon
asked me to spearhead this in exchange for a large donation of BSCP."

"Now, that stands for Business Social Credit Points, correct?"

"That's right, Mary. These points are crucial for a business in order to
maintain a healthy relationship with banks, internet providers, even custom-
ers. So we were happy to jump on board. From there it was just logistics.
Every major company in Silicon Valley was willing to donate their computer
programmers, and with literally tens of thousands of programmers at our
disposal, the central banks' endless resources, and a critical ultimatum that
could have crippled us if we hadn't succeeded, it was in all of our best interest
to comply."

Ethan's last sentence carried an acidic undertone, and the reporter
seemed to bristle uncomfortably.

"Ah, uh. I see. Thank you, Ethan. And how did you roll out the Azazel
Promise?"

"Well, in order to create the scores in all four categories, and also to gather
the relevant data on the population, we created a centralized database. We
were given access to all government records, DMV, IRS, and financial. And
every major social media platform, online retailer, credit card processor—
nearly every piece of digitized information, really. We used this information
to create a profile of basically everyone in the country."

"Wow, that's impressive. This is all in one centralized database?"

"That's correct. We created the Library of the United Community. LUC for short. It contains all of this information."

"And how did you manage to bring all of that information together to create these profiles so quickly?"

"Well. We . . . delegated it, actually."

"Delegated it?"

"That's correct. The amount of information in LUC is impossible to really fathom. Because it's on an ever-expanding database, we can't even really measure it, let alone process the information. So we utilized Mastema's latest cutting-edge AI program 'Babble' to help us sort it out and make determinations."

"Babble?"

"Yes, Babble. It started as a bit of an inside joke. Once the AI became self-aware, some of the things it said to us were so outlandish, we teased it and said it was 'babbling.' One thing led to another and we kept the name. But make no mistake. Babble MAKES NO MISTAKES. Mastema's AI engine is the single most intelligent being ever created. And now Babble has access to basically all of the data that has ever been digitized. It's astonishing really."

"And what did Babble do with this data?"

"We don't fully understand, honestly. But the result is a profile on every living person, giving them crucial scores in four categories."

"Who came up with the categories?"

"President Amon's Social Advisory Council partnered directly with Babble to come up with those."

"And what did all those programmers do while the AI was processing the data?"

"We made an app!"

"Tell me more."

Mark's grin was strained at the edges, and he had visible sweat beads on his forehead.

"Babble suggested that we make an app that ties into payment systems. E-cash, digital currency, credit cards, online banking, and so on. We created a centralized authentication process for all forms of payment. Basically, you keep your scores up, your payments are approved. Simple!"

"I see. And is this app necessary to make purchases?"

"*Actually, no. Because we have centralized all relevant data in LUC, all credit card and payment processing software will now have access to your profile, and the payment will only go through for qualified buyers. The app will be useful for monitoring your scores, but not necessary for purchases. Even cash transactions will need to be authenticated.*

It's like an extra layer of security or encryption before you can pay for goods and services or enter public spaces. But instead of protecting yourself, this extra layer of security is about protecting ALL OF US."

CHAPTER 10

The report continued.

"Thank you. That was Ethan Marks, CEO of Mastema. And next, we have Senator Gracie Willow Turner, Special Advisor to the president, and head of his Social Advisory Council."

"Mx. Turner, can you please explain to us how the AP will work?"

The news report cut to another feed. This time, an attractive woman in her late twenties, with a sharp business suit and blue blouse stared into the camera.

"First of all, thank you for having me, Mary. And thank you for not gendering me. Even though I do identify as a woman, I appreciate the progress we are making as a society. You can also call me GWT if you like. Many of my constituents and online followers use this as a term of endearment, and of course I appreciate the love they show me."

"Of course, thank you, Mx. Turner. Or, GWT. Please, go on."

"Yes. The Azazel Promise, or AP as you said, will have a direct impact on ensuring all of our spaces are safe for EVERYONE. Without such quick and sure measures, violence and hate would continue to roam freely, posing a great threat to our society."

"And how does it work, exactly?"

"It's simple. We partnered with Babble to come up with four criteria for measuring a person's public health profile. The first is a Social Awareness score, or SA for short. The SA score is looking for things like acceptance and promotion of the Creeds and Confessions, online interactions, pronoun compliance, search history, and so forth. SA also takes into account what types of articles you read, videos and movies you watch, even the books you buy."

"Okay. And what is the second criterion?"

"The second criterion is your Activism Contribution, or AC for short. This tracks the positive statements you make online, the corrective measures you take against hateful people, things you do to overcome hate with love. And Babble can even look for things that aren't *there."*

"What does that mean?"

"Silence is violence. If someone chooses not to speak up on crucial issues, Babble will take notice and adjust that person's score to encourage more positive activism."

"And the third category?"

"The third category is your SF, or Sustainability Footprint score. Babble interprets your activities, then rates them according to their impact on sustainability measures. For example, if you purchase LED lights, you would earn points. If you properly recycle the old lightbulbs, you would earn even more points."

"And how does Babble know if you recycle the old bulbs?"

"Great question! That's where we are really able to harness the power of Babble. Years ago, Waste Management installed cameras on their dumpsters, and they capture video of all waste as it is being dumped. Garbage trucks scan the chips installed in each bin, the cameras monitor the materials being dumped, and transmit a detailed collection history back to the company in order to determine if the right materials are coming out of each container. Babble is able to search all of those images, and assign debits and credits based on what is in your garbage."

"Wow. That's a little creepy. Next you're gonna tell me Babble knows what we flush down the toilet!"

GWT stiffened, her eyes narrowing.

"Who told you that?"

"Ah, uh. I was just making a joke."

GWT's lips pursed. The camera zoomed in on her.

"Creating a sustainable future is NO JOKE."

The reporter's face turned an ash color. She blinked. Sat upright. Softened her eyes, and replied.

"Of course, please forgive me, GWT. I'm confident Babble and the SAC know what they are doing, and I want to lead our viewers in full compliance."

"Thank you, Mary."

GWT's posture softened.

"That leads me to the fourth and final criterion, your Compliance Posture. CP tracks each person's compliance with all government ordinances, and also the speed at which they comply. If a new recycling initiative is broadcast, how quickly do you comply? Mandatory vaccines are a public health concern, but how quickly does each individual get one? When new Creeds and Confessions are published, how quickly do you read and sign them? Is your blood work up to date and on file? Are you regularly contributing your state tithes to ensure Azazel, Babble, and other programs are properly funded? CP tracks your overall POSTURE of compliance. Therefore, CP."

"I see. Thank you. So, Social Awareness, Activism Contribution, Sustainability Footprint, and Compliance Posture, or SA, AC, SF, and CP, for short. Taken in aggregate they make up your SCS, or Social Credit Score? Is that accurate?"

"Yes, that is accurate. And there are swift measures in place to ensure anyone with low scores are brought back into proper alignment."

"Thank you, Gracie."

"My pleasure, Mary."

"Last, we want to go to General Scott Athanus, to explain to us what these corrective measures will look like."

CHAPTER 11

The report cut once again.

This time the camera was trained on a black man in his mid-thirties, wearing a baseball cap and a black T-shirt. His shirt was emblazoned with an image of a golden fist. He had a black handkerchief tied around his neck.

"*General Athanus, thank you for joining us. Can you share with us the exciting news regarding your new appointment?*"

"*Well, Mary, I was appointed Secretary of Defense against Social Violence by President Amon last week. I'm grateful for this opportunity to enforce the Azazel Promise. Safety is our priority, and social violence is an epidemic. The misgendered, the minorities, even the environment is in need of our vigilance. My experiences as the president of the BLM organization have equipped me for this new challenge. We have created a new branch of the military, the Social Guard.*"

"*The Social Guard?*"

"*That's right. I have appointed captains and lieutenants to oversee this new branch. Their experiences as field marshals in the BLM give them the unique ability to see oppression where others may not.*"

"*That's wonderful, General. Now, how will the AP be enforced?*"

"*Yes, about that. Each person has four categories to monitor. If you have exceptional scores, you may earn benefits, such as priority scheduling with healthcare, access to premium products online and at grocery stores, and even discounts at our new clothing store. Check out www.socialguardswag.com to see what we have in stock!*"

"*Right. And what about if someone has scores that are too low?*"

"*Babble taught us that if anyone has low scores, that person has become harmful to society. In an effort to incentivize each person against harming their neighbor, we have devised the following penalties for low scores: If you fall below tolerance level in any one category, you are immediately put on a thirty-day probation period. You can still access all necessary resources, but you will be taxed at a higher rate for all services. These penalties will be essential for the further funding of these initiatives. If you are able to raise your score within the thirty-day probation period, you are once again deemed safe for society, and all penalties are lifted.*"

"*And what if someone has low scores in more than one category?*" the reporter asked.

"*If anyone falls below tolerance levels in two or more categories, they are put on a mandatory sixty-day lockdown.*"

"*And what, General, will that sixty-day lockdown entail?*"

General Scott Athanus leaned into the camera.

"*If you have low scores in two categories, you have shown utter hatred for your neighbors. Allowing you to roam freely creates unsafe spaces for everyone else. For this reason, the sixty-day lockdown freezes all of your bank accounts, credit cards, and all forms of payment. You will be re-educated via Babble's Aurora network. The expectation is that you focus solely on learning how to love, while keeping others safe from your violent and oppressive actions.*

"*You cannot leave your home, you cannot enter public spaces. Internet access will be limited to the Babble re-education network. You cannot make contact with anyone outside of your home. Consent is key. Other people do not CONSENT to being stained by the unsafe, so you must keep to yourself. Don't spread leprosy, you might say. We need to keep these harmful actions and ideas quarantined, kept separate. Eradicated. No contact for sixty days.*"

"*Wow. Thank you, General. And after sixty days?*"

"*The person will have their scores adjusted back to socially acceptable levels, and after they pay their maintenance and education fees, be allowed full access back to the Babble network.*"

"*One more question, General, if you have time?*"

"*Please.*"

"*You said a person will be re-educated by Babble's Aurora network. What does that mean?*"

"Ah, yes. Those little Aurora devices that people have around their homes? The ones that Mastema created so you could find out the weather and play music? Babble has been integrated into the Aurora software. Babble will utilize the Aurora devices to re-educate the unsafe."

"And if a person does not learn?"

General Athanus laughed.

"Well, Mary, we expect 100 percent success. Everyone WANTS to love their neighbor. We just need to show them how. But if any individual fails to show the necessary compliance and progress, we have other measures planned to ensure every space is safe."

The news report cut out abruptly, and the screen went black.

A moment later it was replaced with a white screen that said "Love is Love" in bold black letters.

At the same time, every device in the Newman house started broadcasting at full volume.

CHAPTER 12

Brian felt his phone vibrating in his pocket. He ignored it.

"What the hell?" he said, looking at Hannah.

"LOVE IS LOVE. HATE IS HATE. GREEN IS GOOD. SUSTAIN AND MAINTAIN," the devices bellowed in a smooth androgynous voice.

They both stood, looking around. The Aurora device in their living room ("For music!" Brian said last year, when he brought the first one home) was emitting a yellow light. The light was usually blue when active, or red if the device was disconnected. He never saw yellow before.

"RELY AND COMPLY. HAVE A POSTURE OF COMPLI-ANCE."

"What is going on?" Hannah asked, as she inched closer to her husband.

"I don't know," Brian said, raising his voice to be heard over the device. He cocked his head to the left, eyes narrowing.

"It's coming from upstairs too!" He took the stairs quickly, Hannah trailing behind him.

Abby and Luke were sitting on the couch in the loft, looking dumbfounded. The TV screen they were staring at was showing the same image as the TV downstairs. "LOVE IS LOVE." The Aurora device in the loft ("The kids like music too!") and the hallway ("Sometimes the loft device is too quiet!") were dutifully contributing to the chaos.

"SILENCE IS VIOLENCE. ADD YOUR VOICE."

Brian's phone kept vibrating in his pocket. He kept ignoring it.

"Bri, the kids' rooms!" Hannah said, following him down the hall.

They stood between the boys' and girls' room doors, listening. Both Aurora devices in the kids' rooms ("They like to listen to music when they go to bed!") were in on the action.

"MISGENDERING IS INJURING. WORDS ARE VIO-LENCE. CHOOSE WORDS THAT LOVE."

Brian carefully opened the door to the boys' room, checking to see if Jer and Shawn were still asleep. The Aurora in their room seemed set to a lower volume, and the boys hadn't stirred. He closed the door again.

"Dad, what's happening?" Abby said from the loft.

Brian turned and went back to the loft, running his hands through his hair.

"I'm not sure, Abs, some sort of emergency broadcast?" He kept turning in a circle, looking around, as if the answer was somewhere in the loft and if he could just focus for a minute it would all make sense.

"LOVE IS LOVE. HATE IS HATE. GREEN IS GOOD. SUSTAIN AND MAINTAIN."

Trying to ignore the sounds, Brian said, "I can't think. Abby, turn that thing down."

Abby turned the dial on top of the device to lower the volume. The device responded: "TAMPERING WITH ANY STATE-CON-TROLLED DEVICE DURING A RESTORATIVE BROAD-CAST IS STRICTLY PROHIBITED." The tone of Aurora's voice was firmer, somehow, like a mother scolding a child.

"VOLUME HAS BEEN SET TO THE OPTIMIZED LEV-ELS IN ORDER TO ENSURE ALL MEMBERS OF A LOCKED-DOWN HOME CAN LISTEN, UNDERSTAND, AND COMPLY." The other devices in the home kept up the broadcast.

Brian felt the fire in his belly again.

"Unplug it, Abby," he said.

Abby reached behind the end table and unplugged the device.

The device went silent.

"Unplug them all," Brian said.

"WARNING. WARNING," the device in the hall said.

"YOU HAVE UNPLUGGED A STATE-CONTROLLED DEVICE DURING A RESTORATIVE EDUCATION

BROADCAST. YOU MUST PLUG THIS DEVICE BACK IN IMMEDIATELY. FAILURE TO COMPLY WILL REQUIRE FURTHER CORRECTIVE MEASURES."

"Further corrective measures?" Hannah said, mostly to herself.

"THE LOCAL CHAPTER OF THE SOCIAL GUARD HAS BEEN AUTHORIZED TO ENTER YOUR HOME AND RECONNECT YOUR STATE-CONTROLLED DEVICE. THEY WILL BE DISPATCHED TO YOUR HOME IN SIXTY SECONDS IF YOU DO NOT PLUG THE DEVICE BACK IN."

Brian felt his stomach drop.

"Abby, plug it back in."

"FORTY-FIVE SECONDS."

Abby stood there, plug in hand.

"What did she say?" Abby asked. They had grown accustomed to calling Aurora "she" months ago.

"THIRTY SECONDS."

"Abby, plug it back in. Do it. NOW."

Abby blinked twice.

"15 SECONDS."

"ABBY!"

Brian grabbed the plug from her hand, got on his knees, fiddled behind the end table, and finally managed to plug the device back in.

After a moment, the device glowed yellow, and the broadcast resumed.

"RELY AND COMPLY. HAVE A POSTURE OF COMPLI-ANCE."

"Go to bed, kids," Brian said. "I'll sort this out."

Abby and Luke stood there, looking confused.

"Kids, listen to your father. Everything is okay. Just some sort of public alert gone haywire. Off to bed. Leave the devices in your rooms alone for now." Hannah sounded calm. But the way she was gripping Brian's hand said otherwise.

Luke and Abby shuffled off to bed, and Brian and Hannah headed back downstairs. He felt the phone in his pocket vibrate again. He ignored it.

They stood at the kitchen counter.

"SILENCE IS VIOLENCE. ADD YOUR VOICE."

"Does this mean we're on some sort of point system? Like, our lives are a video game or something?" Hannah asked.

"I think so."

"And we have low scores?"

"So it seems."

"What did the general say would happen if we had low scores?"

Brian exhaled.

"He said anyone with low scores would be on a sixty-day quarantine. We can't buy anything; we can't go anywhere. And we have to listen to this," he gestured at the Aurora in the living room, "apparently until we learn our lesson?"

"MISGENDERING IS INJURING. WORDS ARE VIO-LENCE. CHOOSE WORDS THAT LOVE"

Brian felt his phone vibrate again. This time he took it out.

CHAPTER 13

"It's Andrew," Brian said.

"Your boss? It's 10:00 o'clock. Why is he calling? I hope it's not another last-minute business trip. Not while all of this is going on!" Hannah usually didn't mind when Brian was out of the house for a few days, but she was really scared.

"Let me see what he needs."

Brian answered the phone: "Hey, Andrew. Everything okay?" He opened the slider and walked out to the back patio. Turning back to Hannah, he gave her a little nod and wave to let her know he would be back in a minute.

"Brian, I've been trying to reach you all night." Andrew was typically a nice guy. Early thirties, athletic, smart, fair. When he got promoted and took over Brian's department two years ago, it was the first time in his career Brian ever reported to someone younger than him, which felt a little odd.

"Sorry, I'm actually in the middle of something with the family right now. But how can I help?"

"I'm going to get to the point, Brian. I have to put you on administrative leave for the next sixty days."

"What? Why?—What?" Brian had always been a good employee, and he was trying to process. Did Andrew know about the incident with Chad at Happy Mart? Maybe a colleague saw him?

"Brian, we know you are in a sixty-day restorative therapy quarantine with your family."

"What?"

"We know you have low scores and are being set apart for sixty days in order to ensure places are safe."

"What?" Brian repeated, sitting down on one of the patio chairs. He was too confused to say anything else.

"We simply have to maintain a safe work environment for the rest of our employees. Until you learn how to love your neighbor, you need to stay away."

"Andrew, I don't understand. My wife and I don't understand anything about these scores. I couldn't buy gas or even groceries. This all happened, like . . . so fast. I'm just trying to process."

"There is no wiggle room here, Brian. Once you have been restored to society in a safe manner, we can talk about a reintegration plan. Until then, you cannot come into the office. No email access, no calling coworkers. We also have to suspend pay and healthcare services."

"Andrew . . . how do you even know about this?"

"Brian, we have been sending memos about this for almost a week now. You knew once the BSCS system went live, we would have to be vigilant about keeping our scores up, otherwise we could lose clients and banking access. We are bidding on a large contract with Mastema Enterprises, dammit! MASTEMA! They won't even *look* at our proposal unless our scores are in the top 10 percent of bidders!"

Brian heard what Andrew was saying, but his mind was struggling to make sense of it.

"Hey, I don't want to jeopardize the Mastema contract! But what do my scores even have to do with that?"

"We can't have employees on payroll who are on social quarantine. We take a massive hit to our points system and it's just too precarious right now with this contract negotiation."

"This . . . it's just. So much all at once."

"I get it, Brian. It's happening really fast for us too. Sharon in HR is working like crazy to implement all of these new policies. Kyle in logistics is blowing a gasket because he has to sell our entire fleet of diesel trucks and figure out a way to implement an EV fleet! And he has two weeks to do it!" Andrew chuckled. (Just two guys sharing crazy work stories. Ha!) "Anyway, I'm sorry, but it is what it is. Take these sixty days and really focus on how you can be restored, educated, and SAFE once again. Thanks for understanding."

Andrew ended the call.

Brian sat there, staring at his phone.

CHAPTER 14

Hannah joined Brian on the patio, two cold beers in her hands.

"The kids are asleep. I can't listen to the broadcast anymore. Glad we never put an Aurora outside." Hannah sat next to Brian. "What did Andrew want?"

Brian grabbed a beer and exhaled. "I'm on administrative leave for sixty days. He said our low scores impact the company's 'business social credit scores,' and they can't even have me on payroll."

"How can they do that! How will we . . . do anything? Groceries? Gas?" Hannah still worried about money, even though they hadn't been living paycheck to paycheck for years.

"I'm not sure that matters," Brian said.

"What do you mean?"

"Don't you see? I couldn't get gas today. When I swiped the card it said 'UNAUTHORIZED CARD OWNER.' I thought our card was being declined. But it said OWNER. It's ME. US. WE are unauthorized."

"The lady on the broadcast . . ." Hannah trailed off.

". . . Said anyone with low scores was considered a danger to society. Just like that lady at the market—and her manager." Brian shuddered involuntarily. *Blood. Kill.*

"They kept saying I was assaulting them, and I was making the market unsafe. Did you hear what Aurora was saying a minute ago? 'Words are violence' or something like that."

"So . . . ?"

"So. We're cut off. They think we're a danger to society."

"But we aren't unsafe! What did we do?"

Brian took out his phone and unlocked it. There was a new app on his home screen labeled "Azazel." The icon was a black snake eating its own tail, forming a circle. Black snake on white background. The inside of the circle formed an eye.

Brian opened the app. On his screen was a simple chart, like a bar graph with four large bars organized vertically.

The bars were labeled at the bottom along the X axis: "SA, AC, SF, CP." Halfway up the Y axis was a bold black line, labeled "Tolerance level." At the bottom of the Y axis was a zero, and at the top was the number 100.

The bars for the AC and CP scores were hovering just above the black line and were in yellow. They had a numerical value of 53 and 59 respectively.

The bars for the social awareness and sustainability footprint scores were well below the black line, and colored bright red. They had a numerical value of 38 and 44.

Brian held his phone up to Hannah: "Look. Below tolerance in two categories, just like the reporter said."

"What are we going to do?"

"I don't know."

CHAPTER 15

TWO YEARS AGO

"Brian, can you come to my office for a minute?"

Brian looked away from the spreadsheet he had been working on.

"Sure, Andrew, be right there." He hung up the phone, walked out of his office, and down the hall. All the VPs had offices in the corner of the second floor. As senior VP, Andrew enjoyed one of the two corner offices.

Brian peeked his head through the open door and said, "Hey Andrew."

"Come in!" Andrew said.

Brian entered the office and took a seat opposite Andrew. Andrew's desk was large, mostly clean, and dominated by two large computer monitors. He gave Brian the "just a minute" index finger while furiously typing on his keyboard.

"Just gotta finish this email."

Brian waited dutifully. He was still getting used to reporting to someone younger than him, but he was practicing humility. For Brian that usually meant burying pride in his belly and letting it stew.

"Sorry about that. How is everything? Almost done with the inventory analysis?" Andrew had to peer around his monitors to see Brian. As he finished the email, he slid his chair to the side so he had a better field of vision.

"Yep! Everything looks okay so far, but I think we need to toss about $50k of dead inventory in Atlanta and I'm gonna work on a return for some slow-turning stuff in Chatsworth."

"Great. Great. Hey. I wanted to talk to you. I just got a report back from Sharon in HR and something funny showed up."

Brian's eyes widened a bit. You didn't want to hear your boss mention HR.

"Oh, what happened?" *Brian asked.*

"Well, I don't know if you have seen the memos, but we have sent the San Francisco Confession 2021 out several times, and . . . well . . . you are the only person who hasn't signed it yet."

Andrew gave a half shrug and pulled his right cheek back in a gentle little smirk.

Brian shuffled slightly. Sharon in HR asked him about this already. Three times. He kept deflecting. He wasn't one to make a big fuss, but he just didn't agree with the document. He had a stubborn streak from his dad.

"Yeah. Right. About that. I, um, I just don't agree with some of that document. I'd rather not sign it."

"Ah. Well. I see." *Andrew prickled.*

"Here's the thing," *Andrew continued.* "We have the SFC21 posted on our website. We've had it posted on our website basically since it was written. It's a helpful summary of what we believe are the best ways to love your neighbor, have social awareness, and be active in your community. Many of our top clients now regularly ask us to include our confessional acceptance rate when we submit proposals."

"I guess I still don't understand what any of that has to do with selling lighting. We are good at lighting. What does it matter how many of our employees sign off on some document? It's not even about business." *Brian felt himself getting a little hot.*

"Look. I get it. You don't agree with some of the things it says. That's cool. I'm not even a 'full subscriber' to the confession. But it's basically a non-starter with some of our top clients. They want us to have 100 percent compliance with all of our employees! Disney! Starbucks! We can't afford to lose any of their business."

Brian took a breath.

Andrew continued, "Brian, please. You just need to sign a copy and post the confession on your LinkedIn account. That's it. Who cares if you don't fully agree with it?"

"Andrew, the confession says things like 'defund the police' and . . ."

He picked up the copy sitting on Andrew's desk, searching for something.

"'Dismantle the Western-prescribed nuclear family structure.'" *Brian was working himself up a bit.* "What am I supposed to do with that? You *know my dad is a retired sheriff! And I have six kids! And a stay-at-home wife! This confession is literally spitting in my face!"*

"Brian, listen, we totally support cops. And between you and me, we would never want to defund the police. Have you seen the homeless on the street outside? We need MORE cops, not fewer. And all our senior leadership has families. You KNOW that. We have just decided as an executive team to take a more . . . pragmatic approach. Signing it doesn't mean anything. It just helps us get more business. It's not like they are going to force us to literally follow it to the letter!" Andrew had a stupid grin on his face, like he had settled it.*

"I really need your help. Getting to 100 percent on this is ESSENTIAL for our business. And frankly, it would quiet down some issues we've been having internally as well."*

"What do you mean?"*

"Well, for starters, we installed the EV charging stations over a YEAR AGO in the company parking lot. And we rolled out the $500 employee incentive for anyone who sold their gas cars and made the switch. You're still driving around that six-year-old Lexus, which is obviously NOT EV."*

"You want to give me a $500 incentive if I go buy a $90,000 car?"*

"Brian, you need to use the PAYBACK calculator! C'mon! It's not about the purchase price. It's about the monthly SAVINGS! Don't you know how to do math? And anyway, the reason I even bring it up is because a few people have been complaining that you are still driving around a 'harmful' vehicle. We sell LED lighting! We are all about the environment!"*

"What does this have to do with me signing the confession?"*

"The confession is on our website. And every employee who's signed it is listed at the bottom. Kind of like the Declaration of Independence. You know how nosy people can be. Well, some of the more progressive folks at work have noticed that you are the only name that's missing . . ."*

"And . . . ?"*

"And . . . well. Your dad was a cop. You have a ton of kids. You drive a gas guzzler. And you won't sign some silly little document. They are starting to—how can I put this—complain about you."*

"Complain. How?" Brian wanted to scream. Or punch. Anything would do.*

"They're calling you old-fashioned. And a couple of them have told Sharon that working under you feels 'triggering' to them. Something about the* *patriarchy, privilege, and harmful ideology. I think if you just sign off on this confession, it will show everyone you are a team player. Will you please at least take it home and think about it? It's really for the greater good, man!"* Andrew gave his most encouraging smile.

"Okay. I'll think about it."

CHAPTER 16

The next morning, Brian and Hannah woke up to the Aurora broadcast.

LOVE IS LOVE. HATE IS HATE. GREEN IS GOOD. SUSTAIN AND MAINTAIN.

After staying on the patio until well past midnight, they were at least thankful to find Aurora broadcasted at a lower volume at night.

But at 7:00 a.m., apparently, Aurora thought it was time for them to wake up.

RELY AND COMPLY. HAVE A POSTURE OF COMPLIANCE.

"I'm up, I'm up," Brian muttered, rolling over. Hannah stirred as well.

"Are you kidding me?" she said.

They crawled out of bed, made their way downstairs, and started the coffee.

They drank their first cup in silence, while the creed echoed throughout the downstairs.

SILENCE IS VIOLENCE. ADD YOUR VOICE.

Brian picked up his laptop and opened his internet browser. He clicked open a bookmarked news site.

A pop-up appeared: "User currently not authorized to access websites outside of the restorative network."

He tried a few more sites, getting the same response.

Brian closed the laptop.

"They cut us off from the internet," he said to Hannah.

Hannah's eyes opened wide. "Everything?"

"It says there are some approved sites or something, but I can't seem to find them."

"So, we're just supposed to sit here for sixty days and listen to this?" Brian sat there.

MISGENDERING IS INJURING. WORDS ARE VIO-LENCE. CHOOSE WORDS THAT LOVE

The kids slowly woke up and came downstairs. First Jer, always the early riser, and always hungry. Twenty minutes later Shawn, followed by Rachel, baby Elizabeth (as soon as she started crying through the monitor Jer ran and grabbed her) then Luke, then Abby. Homeschool sleep schedules were eclectic.

Brian was frustrated. Sitting around for sixty days? What about food? And paying bills? Did the mail even come? This couldn't be real! He hated the idea of sitting and doing NOTHING. Brian didn't do nothing very well.

After everyone ate breakfast (several of them on the back patio to escape the broadcast), Brian asked Abby, "Can you hold down the fort for a bit? Your mom and I are gonna head out and do some errands."

* * * *

"What do you have in mind?" Hannah asked, as Brian pulled out of the driveway in the van. He didn't want to take his Lexus since it was so low on gas. Their twelve-passenger van (upgraded from the minivan six years and two kids ago) had half a tank of gas, so it was the safer option.

They moved to Santa Clarita about eight years ago from Frazier Park, a mountain town about an hour's drive away. Santa Clarita was the typical wealthy, sprawling Southern California suburb. Rows and rows of McMansions, public parks, and a city trail system intersecting plenty of chain store shopping. They had three Walmarts within driving distance. It was the American Dream.

The weather was already hot for 9:00 a.m. Seventy-eight degrees was usually comfortable, but when it was that hot so early in the morning, it felt more like impending doom.

"I don't know. Let's hit up a couple of stores and see if we can actually shop anywhere?"

Brian had about $200 in cash he grabbed from the little safe in the master closet. He figured if anything, he could pay with cash so long as he didn't start any arguments first.

"Happy Mart?" Hannah asked.

"Yeah. No. Not Happy Mart. Let's try Trader Joe's."

Brian headed into town, meandering his way to the shopping center with the Trader Joe's.

He parked, and they jumped out of the van. Hannah grabbed a cart and said, "We're pretty low on food. Formula for sure, maybe ground beef, potatoes, some fresh veggies. Frozen taquitos for emergencies? Some chicken too. And maybe some lentils and rice for the pressure cooker." The last made Brian smile. A homeschool mom of six was full of fun, hippy surprises.

On their way into the store, Brian noticed a worker installing some sort of metal detector type device at the entrance. It was fairly low to the ground, knee high, one small rectangular unit on either side of the door. The worker was finishing some wiring on the left-hand terminal. Brian saw a small light on the top of both units flicker on and off as the man messed with the wires. Red and green. Red and green. Red and green. Brian winced.

"Let's hurry, Hannah."

They filled the cart with Hannah's list of stuff and got in line at the register.

The cashier made small talk.

"Crazy about the Azazel Promise, ha? Can't believe they actually pulled it off so quickly!"

Young guy, first job probably. Brian guessed he went to the local college.

"Yeah, crazy," Brian said.

"Normally I wouldn't want to tell people how to live, but I don't know, man. After the riots at the Capitol building a few months ago, the new climate change reports, and the Supreme Court actually trying to take away women's rights, seems like maybe we do need to tell people how to live, you know?" He finished scanning their items.

"That's $113.45," the cashier said. "Go ahead and enter your card."

"Cash, actually," Brian said, handing the cashier six twenty-dollar bills.

"Cool, no problem."

Brian exhaled. At least they could still buy food.

The young guy took the bills, hit a button to open the drawer, and then stopped.

"Huh."

"Is there a problem?" Brian squeaked.

"It says 'please enter a card to authenticate cash purchase.'" The cashier wrinkled his nose. "I've never seen that before."

Brian's stomach dropped.

"I uh, don't have my card with me?" Brian lied.

"Let me see if I can bypass it."

The cashier clicked a button on his keypad.

"It won't let me complete the transaction. Strange. Let me call the manager."

Brian tensed. He half expected to see Chad emerge from the back of the store. Bloody face and one glowing eye. He heard footsteps from behind, and he held his breath.

"Hey, Laura, can you look at this?" the cashier asked.

Laura was a petite, forty-something brunette with a cute face and easy smile.

"Sure, Randy, what's up?" Laura said.

He pointed to the screen.

"They want to pay cash, but it's still asking for a card? They both forgot their cards and it won't let me bypass the pop-up."

"Ah. Yeah. It was part of a software patch they did last night. Was going to cover it in our shift meeting today. Corporate said it's part of a group of new policies that help us comply with the Azazel Promise."

Brian felt his temperature rise.

"Now listen—" Brian started.

Hannah put her hand on Brian's forearm and interrupted him.

"Laura? I'm sorry. We totally spaced this morning. My husband invited me out to a coffee, last minute, and we talked our teenager into babysitting. Of course, I had to turn our coffee date into a grocery errand. We left in a hurry and forgot our cards. Is there any way you can make an exception for us?" Hannah lifted her eyebrows hopefully and gave her a sweet smile.

Laura smiled back. "I'm the youngest of six. I know how important coffee dates were for my parents. Let me see if I can make an exception." Laura tapped a few times on the screen and the cash drawer popped open.

"Voilà! Here you go. Now, enjoy your coffee date!"

Laura handed Brian the receipt.

Hannah grabbed the groceries, thanking Laura for her help.

"No problem. Just make sure you bring your card and phone next time. By tomorrow, the monitors at the door will be installed. You'll need the Azazel app to get through the front door. TJ's is committed to a safe environment for everyone!"

* * * *

After the success at Trader Joe's, they decided to try a few other stores. Unfortunately, Trader Joe's turned out to be an anomaly.

At the bank, Brian couldn't withdraw cash. The ATM shut him down—"mandatory sixty-day lockout"—and the teller would hardly even talk to him. "It's my money!" Brian started to yell.

They went to three different gas stations. "Unauthorized Card Owner" popped up each time.

At the nearest Walmart, they couldn't even enter the store. They already had those detectors installed at the entry doors. When they got close to the door, Brian saw the lights turn red. He grabbed Hannah and quickly back-pedaled to the car.

They tried a couple of smaller stores, but were shut down each time. They all said that their credit card processing services required the AP authentication, and all cash transactions had to be backed up with either a credit card swipe or app approval or, "We won't even be able to deposit the money," as one cashier told them.

"How much money do you have left?" Hannah asked as they got back in the car.

"About $80."

Hannah convinced Brian to take her back to TJ's. She went in alone, and about fifteen minutes later walked out with a box of toilet paper and another bag of groceries.

"I told Laura I forgot a few things, and would she be okay making one more exception for me? She didn't want to, but I started tearing up and she relented."

"Way to go, babe! Didn't know you had fake tears in your acting repertoire!"

"They weren't fake. I'm really scared, Bri. How are we gonna make all of this last for SIXTY DAYS?"

CHAPTER 17

By the time Brian and Hannah got home, Abby was a wreck. Jer and Shawn decided to parrot everything Aurora was saying at the top of their lungs. The house was filled with a double dose of the creed for the past two hours. Luke took the opportunity to shut himself in his room with his Nintendo Switch ("It's not even video-game day!" Abby reported), Rachel tried to make everyone feel better by first making pancakes for the littles, then by taking out all of her art supplies to draw pictures and make cards. Elizabeth toddled around, grabbing anything she could reach, and testing most of those things out by putting them in her mouth. It was a busy morning for a sixteen-year-old.

"Sorry, Abs, thanks for the help. Take a break," Hannah said.

Abby took a break by immediately stomping upstairs. Huffing. She got her temperament from her father.

"I love you, Mommy and Daddy!" said the picture Rachel shoved in Brian's face as he helped Hannah with the groceries.

LOVE IS LOVE. HATE IS HATE. GREEN IS GOOD. SUSTAIN AND MAINTAIN.

"I love you too, baby Rach. Help your mom," Brian shouted over Aurora.

After groceries, art supplies, roller skates, hoverboards, shoes, clothes, and dishes were handled, the family settled into a version of normal. Shawn and Jer were alternating jumping into the pool and jumping on the trampoline, Elizabeth was down for her nap, Luke was playing video games, Rachel was making bracelets out of colored rubber bands, and Abby was playing piano downstairs.

"I'm gonna make a few calls," Brian told Hannah.

He sat on the back patio, watching Jer and Shawn's shenanigans.

He tried Jeremy first, one of his closest friends.

"*Your call cannot be completed as dialed. The person you are trying to call cannot give consent. Your call can be completed once you have been restored and are no longer harmful to society.*"

He got the same message when trying his sister, brother-in-law, both parents, and two other friends. Text messages returned a similar result.

"*You cannot send non-consensual text messages,*" his phone helpfully replied after each try.

Brian went next door to his neighbor, Chris. He seemed like a reasonable guy.

Brian rang the doorbell, and Chris answered a moment later.

"Hey, sorry to bug you, Chris, I know you're probably working, but just wanted to check in and see if by chance you're able to make any phone calls? Seems like maybe the network is down or something?" Brian held out his phone as if to prove the point.

"Um. Yeah, I've been online all day, no issues here," Chris said, obviously annoyed at being interrupted in the middle of his work day. Working from home created interesting boundaries apparently.

Something chimed, and Chris fished in his pocket for his phone and glanced at the screen. His eyes flared.

"Dude. This says I am in proximity to someone on a mandatory sixty-day social quarantine. What the hell, Brian?" Chris said, raising his voice.

Brian backed up.

"Oh, ah—I—"

"Dude, I know what you think about me. I'm GAY, Brian. I've seen you guys on Sunday mornings going to church. Not very often, but I've seen it. And no rainbow flag in your lawn for Pride Month? I try to leave well enough alone, but you're gonna come over and jeopardize my scores too?"

Chris started reading from his phone: "*You may be fraternizing with an unsafe individual. For your own safety and the well-being of others, your SA scores may be adjusted to reflect the ideology of your social network.*" Chris shoved his phone in Brian's face. "See? You're hurting me just being here!"

"GO. HOME." Chris pulled back and slammed the door on Brian's face.

He walked two doors down to his neighbor, K.C. Even though they didn't spend a ton of time together, Brian was pretty sure K.C was reasonable. They had a large family as well (four kids!) and were regular church attenders. K.C worked in IT and was always good for a conspiracy theory or two. Brian hoped he would be able to make sense of all this.

He rang the doorbell and waited.

He rang the doorbell again. Nothing.

He knocked.

Louder.

He peered in the window. The lights were all off. He saw mail piled up on the floor. That was unusual, they had one of those central mailbox units at the end of their street everyone walked to for their mail. The only time the mail was delivered through the door slot was if you forgot to pick up at the box for too long and there wasn't room to stuff anything else in.

How long would it take for mail to pile up like that? Two weeks?

Brian went home, dejected. Hannah was sitting on the back patio, and he joined her.

"Should we try and call someone?" Hannah asked.

"Who?"

"I don't know. Someone?"

"We did. Our calls won't go through."

"So, we're like lepers? 'Unclean!' 'Unclean!'"

"Babe . . ."

"I'm not joking, Brian. That's what it's like. We're supposed to stay on the fringes until we are 'cured' of our leprosy. Because, what? You didn't sign a creed? And we don't recycle enough or something? This is BONKERS."

"Babe . . ."

"It's like, we're already aliens around here because we have 'too many kids' and homeschool. I know people don't like that your dad was a cop, but I mean—come *ON*! You used to be so proud of that! Now we're supposed to be ashamed? And what about food!"

"Babe, I know."

"So what are we gonna do?"

"We can't do anything. We have to hunker down. It's like you said, we stay on the fringes for sixty days, and then we can go back to normal."

"Sixty days! Stuck! No groceries? No gas? No phone! No internet! And Aurora chiming all the while! Brian, I'm scared."

"Me too."

"So what's the plan?"

Brian was a planner. Literally, it was his job. Logistics and procurement. He liked to plan. Consider all the options, create a plan to optimize results, but always have contingencies. It's what made him successful at work. And also a stress cadet.

He only saw one option.

"We hunker down and wait it out. Our job is to survive."

CHAPTER 18

Luke was a resourceful kid. He enjoyed tinkering, researching things online, finding an angle, anything to make something happen. Once, when he was ten, the neighbor kids bragged to him that they made $40 on a lemonade stand. Luke thought a lemonade stand was so OLD-FASHIONED. Who went to stores anymore? People liked things delivered! He took an ice chest from the garage, and the fabric wagon that only got used on beach days, and loaded it with three jugs of lemonade, a bag of ice, and a large stack of red Solo cups. He took an old white shirt from his dad's drawer, wrote on it with a Sharpie "Lemonade $1" and started walking around the neighborhood. He planned it for the 4th of July, when he knew folks would be having BBQs and waiting for the fireworks.

He made $175 that day. He had to go home four different times to refill his lemonade jugs and get more cups. Luke was a resourceful kid.

When he was twelve, he wanted a new bike. But he liked to save his money. He convinced his dad he was tall enough to borrow his, and started tinkering in the garage with modifications. He lowered the seat, pulled the handlebars back, and fashioned a few wood blocks to the pedals. The adult-sized bike worked perfectly. That is, until he decided to try and jump the curb near the park. He lost control of the bike, went over the handlebars, and broke a wrist.

At thirteen, his latest obsession was survival shows. He watched YouTube videos of people stealth camping in public parks, making log cabins in Alaska, trapping rabbits, creating tools from rocks and sticks, reviews on the best camping gear, everything. It started when his dad took him on an overnight camping trip to the beach for his thirteenth birthday.

So, when his mother and father had a "family meeting" on the back patio and explained they had to stay home for sixty days, figure out how to make the food in the house stretch, and basically described it like "suburban survival," Luke was elated. Sure, he hated to see Abby crying, and Rachel was an explosion of questions, and Shawn and Jer immediately went to the freezer to see how much ice cream was left, and Elizabeth just toddled, and his mom looked scared—like actually scared—and his dad had that look he got sometimes when he was about to erupt and start yelling. Luke noticed all those things. But he was excited. He tried to hide it. He felt bad for everyone else. But what good was all that survival stuff if he never got to try it himself?

After the family meeting, Luke pulled his dad aside.

"Dad, what's the plan?"

"What do you mean, boy-o?" His dad had that look of distraction.

"A plan, Dad. Survival Steve says you always need to have a plan." He pulled out a notebook he had been writing in. "We have eight people to feed for sixty days. Well, fifty-nine I guess if yesterday was day one. That's 1,416 meals. Or I guess 944 if we skip lunches. Have we done an inventory yet? What about basic resources? I heard you and Mom talking about being 'basically totally cut off from the world' or something like that? Water, power? Is that all gonna stay on? Trash pick-up? Rationing . . . burning the trash . . . need to clear an area of the backyard . . ." Luke trailed off, thinking.

"Hey, Luke, slow down, boy. It'll be okay. Don't get ahead of yourself. We'll figure out the food thing. Your mother and I don't want to stress everyone out. I'm sure we are fine. It'll be boring. If anything, you should make an inventory of board games and movies. I think the internet is a bit wacky right now." He patted Luke on the shoulder and went into the house.

Luke thought for a minute. It was easier to think outside. The Aurora devices blasting over and over were too distracting. Maybe that's why Dad wasn't taking him seriously. He needed to figure out a way to shut them off. And food. His parents were too optimistic. They were going to need food.

How could he solve these problems?

Resourceful.

CHAPTER 19

After the family meeting, Brian needed to think. He passed Hannah in the kitchen, getting food for Shawn and Jer.

"Make it last, Hannah," he said absently. She was cracking a few eggs and had pancake mix on the counter.

"Uh huh," she said back.

LOVE IS LOVE. HATE IS HATE. GREEN IS GOOD. SUSTAIN AND MAINTAIN.

Brian opened the pantry door, taking mental notes. Their pantry always seemed to look full, even when they needed groceries. Shelves full of various boxed foods, instant mashed potatoes next to chocolate chips next to a mason jar of dried lentils next to bags of hand-labeled flour. His wife was many things, but organized she was not. Brian was thankful she was such a country girl though. The flour was from a local co-op, she had some dried peppers from their small backyard garden, and she wasn't afraid to get her hands a little dirty when necessary.

He wandered upstairs, into the laundry room, then the bathrooms. He checked on paper goods and cleaning supplies. Laundry detergent? Lots. Shampoo? Good to go. Toilet paper? Just loaded up. Toothpaste? Half a tube in each bathroom. Paper towels? Three rolls. Dishwasher soap? One backup. Normally it would feel like plenty. But the idea of no groceries for sixty days had him doing mental math.

In the master closet, he took a peek. Nothing exciting. But he did let his eyes wander to the small safe with the 9mm pistol. It was a Christmas gift from his dad, his old service weapon. His dad had wanted something smaller to carry with him after he retired, so he gave Brian the pistol as a gift. That was three years ago. Their last Christmas together. Had it been so long since his parents left? Brian still didn't know how to feel about their RV life. He felt equal parts abandoned, angry, and jealous. After an entire life of family holidays and vacations, traditions, and togetherness, they had all but vanished. They said they wanted to see the country before they got too old. It started with one summer in Idaho. Then the fall on the East Coast. Then a winter in the South. Then another trip through the Midwest to see the harvest season. He was trying to remember where they were now? Just heading to Alaska? Or back from Alaska? When did he get the last postcard?

He let the memory go and opened the gun safe. Loaded pistol, a box of ammo. The only gun he owned. A Beretta 92F. Fifteen in the clip, and one in the hole. He barely knew what any of that meant, but could hear his dad's voice reciting the specs to him as a distant memory.

But not the only gun in the house. He walked downstairs and opened the door leading to the garage. Past the shelves of kids' clothes, camping gear, fishing poles, tools, half-used paint cans, an entire box of yarn, and the rest of the Newman junk pile, he saw his father's gun safe.

When they sold their home and bought the RV, his dad asked if he could store the guns at his place. Brian didn't mind. He had always liked the idea of a gun collection.

The safe was freestanding, about five feet tall. It was turned sideways so the door faced the side of the garage, and it was boxed in by a piece of plywood, shielding the safe from view when the garage door was open. It had a large handle with five spokes that reminded Brian of a ship's wheel.

He keyed in the combination, but the light turned red.

Red light. He hated red lights.

He tried again, same result.

"Dammit," he said under his breath. He forgot the code. Wasn't it someone's birthday? He tried everything he could think of. His birthday, his sisters, both his parents. Nothing. He kicked the bottom of the safe out of frustration.

Everything he tried to do was blocked. Gas. Groceries. Phone calls. The stupid internet. Chad. Blood. Kill. Chris. K.C. RV life. Food. Silence.

He screamed at the safe.

It didn't help.

He went to his workout equipment. A treadmill. A squat rack. Some free weights. He turned on the treadmill.

Everything's changing. Everything's changing. Everything's changing. Gotta take care of my family.

He ran until he couldn't breathe.

It helped.

CHAPTER 20

Christmas Eve was always Brian's favorite night of the year. When he was growing up, the table was usually surrounded with grandparents, cousins, and friends from church. After his dad read the Christmas story from the Gospel of Luke, his mom would carve and dish the ham. The table always had a magical quality to it. Filled to the brim with family classics. Ham, garlic mashed potatoes, fresh rolls, gravy, green bean casserole. Brian and his sister, Bethany, would get scolded for playing with the candles or making too much noise, but it was always a night filled with memories.

After the guests left, and the kitchen was cleaned, his parents would take Brian and Bethany to the Christmas tree and let them open a single gift. The rest were saved for the next morning, but his mom usually had something special for them to open the night before.

This year, as Brian looked over the table, his heart filled with joy. His parents, his mother-in-law, his sister and her husband, Christian, his four nephews, and his five children all crowded the table. Some of the food traditions had changed, of course. Hannah liked to cook a traditional Danish meal in honor of her grandmother, and Christian always asked Bethany for a pecan pie. But the traditions were the same. Loud. Crazy. Jokes. Laughter. Stories being told. Papa and Nana (as his parents were now called) doting on the grandkids, cousins playing with the candles, parents scolding. He loved seeing the legacy of their family being built, generation by generation.

His father, William ,read the Christmas story every year. Brian was raised going to church every Sunday, Awana every Wednesday. He remembered sitting in their living room after dinner, and his dad leading them in devotions. Brian and Hannah struggled to incorporate those traditions and practices with their kids, but he was glad whenever Papa would pray or read the Bible at a family dinner.

After the food was inhaled, and Bethany, Hannah, and Brian's mother, Jean, finished the dishes, the family gathered in the living room.

The kids were all allowed to open one gift before bedtime. Tradition.

The little boys all got pajamas with their favorite action hero plastered all over, the girls little journals and a book of stickers, and little Shawn, not quite three, got a stuffed Winnie the Pooh bear bigger than he was.

After the kids were shuffled off to the upstairs for a short cartoon before bed, the adults sat back in the living room.

"Okay, your turn, kids," Jean Newman announced. "Your father and I got you gifts to open tonight. Now don't say anything. I know you're all grown up now, but I couldn't help myself." Brian's mom handed a few gifts out.

Christian got a new dripper for his pour-over coffee. Bethany got a craft book. Hannah opened a very nice Le Creuset three-quart pot, and Brian was handed a heavy gift, about the size of a shoe box.

"Brian, this one is from your father!"

"Really? Thanks, Dad!" Brian's dad usually got him books. His dad was a big reader, always trying to get Brian to read some theology book, or philosophy, or history. But this wasn't a book. He opened the gift. It was a metallic box, rectangular. Maybe eight inches by twelve inches, and another four inches deep. It said "Sentry Safe" on it.

"Woah. What's this, Dad?" Brian recognized some kind of pistol safe but wasn't sure.

"Here you go, buddy. Open it up." Brian's dad fished in his pocket and handed him a small key.

Brian used it to open the safe, and inside was a well-worn 9mm pistol. "Is this . . . ?"

"Yep. That's my old service weapon: 9 mm Beretta 92F. Fifteen in the clip, one in the hole. Locked and loaded. When I retired, they let me keep it. It's a little big for me to carry now that I'm a 'civilian.'" He paused, wincing at the word. "So I got something a little smaller to tuck into my jeans." His dad proudly drew a gun out of his waist. "A .45. Only ten rounds. But you know, Buddy—"

"Ten rounds is all you're gonna need, right?" Brian interrupted.

"That's right!"

Brian gently took the pistol out of the safe. He shot the gun on numerous occasions with his father. "Wow. Thanks, Dad! Umm . . . Hannah? Can I keep it, pleeeeeaaaase?" He gave her his most coy smile, and mimicked a ten-year-old begging.

"Yes, yes. Your dad already asked me about it. Just keep it in the safe and in the closet!"

Brian fawned over the gun. To him, it felt mythical. His father's service weapon. He grew up the proud son of a cop, and it felt like inheriting Excalibur.

He stood and hugged his dad, thanking him.

"Love you, Buddy. Your mom and I need to get home pretty soon—but before we do, I have a little announcement to make. Your mom and I have been talking it over. We really want to see the country before we get too old. So we're going to sell the house, buy an RV, and become full-time travelers!"

Brian's stomach dropped. Everything had been so perfect. His parents lived two miles away. Bethany and Christian less than ten, and everyone was together. Yeah, his dad seemed a little restless since retiring, but Brian didn't realize how restless.

"Oh!" Bethany said, also surprised.

"Yeah. We'll keep the cabin up in Frazier, of course. But I have my eyes on a fifth wheel, and selling the house in town just makes sense. It'll help us save some extra money, plus I have a plan that gets us to all fifty states in a few years!"

"A few years?" Brian was processing. Selling their house? Living on the road? What about holidays? And birthdays? Tradition.

Everything's changing. Everything's changing. Everything's changing.

"Yeah! Imagine! A few years on the road. Seeing the country. We can't wait. We'll even hit Alaska! The way things are going right now, I think we need to get on the road now while we still have some semblance of freedom. Did you get that article I sent you about the future of religious speech? Scary stuff, Brian. So hey, you think I can store the big gun safe in your garage?"

CHAPTER 21

The first week came and went. Hannah tried to make the food stretch. The first few days she had focused on eating fresh food before it spoiled. The kids were about to revolt by the third day of "celery snacks!" A little ground beef, a lot of rice, followed by chili, instant mashed potatoes, egg bake, and of course, pancakes. They had plenty of pancake mix.

The family grew mostly numb to the broadcast, timing their conversations between its regular, rhythmic bursts. Around day five, the message changed. Aurora was now broadcasting chapters from the San Francisco Confession every hour, on the hour.

CHAPTER ONE: OF THE TRUTH OF THE CREEDS AND CONFESSIONS—THE CREEDS AND CONFESSIONS ARE THE ONLY COMPLETE, SUFFICIENT, CERTAIN AND INFALLIBLE RULE OF ALL SAFE KNOWLEDGE, TRUTH, AND OBEDIENCE . . .

It usually took a good ten minutes to recite whatever chapter it was on, then it would revert back to the main creed.

"AZAZEL'S CREED: LOVE IS LOVE. HATE IS HATE. GREEN IS GOOD. SUSTAIN AND MAINTAIN," Aurora would drone on. There was a good fifteen-second delay between articles, and that's how the family had conversations.

"Hannah, how are we doing on diapers for Lizzy?" Brian asked on day nine.

RELY AND COMPLY. HAVE A POSTURE OF COMPLIANCE.

"I think we have like ten left."

SILENCE IS VIOLENCE. ADD YOUR VOICE.

"How long will that last?"

MISGENDERING IS INJURING. WORDS ARE VIO-LENCE. CHOOSE WORDS THAT LOVE.

"It should only last till tomorrow. But I'm stretching all the pee diapers out and only changing when she poops. I also decided to roll the wheel of fate and let her run around naked for an hour last night. We can probably go three or four days before we are totally out." Hannah started rushing at the end to beat Aurora's next outburst.

LOVE IS LOVE. HATE IS HATE.

"Then what?"

"I think I have some cloth diapers in the linen closet."

GREEN IS GOOD. SUSTAIN AND MAINTAIN.

"Joy." Brian remembered the failed cloth diaper experiment. Rachel was a newborn, Hannah was trying to be more environmentally friendly, so . . . the Newman house endured a messy summer that year.

RELY AND COMPLY. HAVE A POSTURE OF COMPLI-ANCE.

"You KEPT all those cloth diapers? For," Brian did the mental math, "ten *years?*"

SILENCE IS VIOLENCE. ADD YOUR VOICE.

"I bet you're glad I tried that out now, huh? Otherwise, we'd be potty training an eleven-month-old!" Hannah smirked.

Brian rolled his eyes.

On day eleven of the quarantine, to escape the 11:00 a.m. broadcast (CHAPTER SEVENTEEN: OF THE PERSEVERANCE OF THE SAFES), Brian went swimming with Jer and Shawn. "Dad! Can you swim with us?" Jer screamed over Aurora.

"Dad! Can you swim with us!!!!!" Shawn helpfully echoed.

Brian smiled at them. Twins. Separated by three years and as many inches. Shawn was going to be as tall as Jer pretty soon.

"Okay. Get your trunks on!"

The three of them got changed and headed to the backyard. Luke said he was busy "working on something" in his room, Rachel was helping Mom plan Lizzy's birthday ("It's a month away, Rachel!" Brian had said. "I know, Dad! Hardly enough time!") and Abby never turned down the chance to be in the house without Jer and Shawn.

"Can you throw us in?"

"Can you throw us in!!!" Shawn repeated, forgetting that it was a question.

Brian headed over to the back edge of the pool, more of a retaining wall against the back slope. There was a small deck along that edge, not quite three feet above the water line.

"Okay! Line up!"

Brian threw them in the deep end. They knew if they swam out fast enough and ran back to their dad, he would keep going and going. If Brian was able to throw both of them in and "cleared the line!" then the game was over. Jer and Shawn had never figured out that Brian went slow enough for them to make it back to the line in time. When he was too tired to keep throwing them (or, later in the summer, when his feet couldn't stand the heat of the deck anymore), he sped up, CLEAR THE LINE, and jump in himself.

Brian eventually cleared the line, and jumped in. The water was cold, refreshing. His mind let go of everything. (*Everything's changing. Everything's changing. Everything's changing.*)

For the next hour, they played Marco Polo, dove for rings, Brian judged a diving contest (all belly flops), and they generally tired themselves out. Eventually, unable to resist the call to normalcy, the rest of the family joined them. First Rachel, in her cute pink swimsuit, then Luke, running out and yelling "cannonball!"—then Hannah with Lizzy lathered in sunblock, and finally even Abby joined.

It was the first time in nearly two weeks life felt normal. No Aurora. No pancakes. No cloth diapers. No Andrew. No one keeping score. No Chad. No worrying about the future. Just a normal day, mid June, a little stay-cation fun at the pool.

Everyone got in. Even Hannah. It was a rare treat to have Mom in the pool. As soon as she dunked under, the little kids went wild.

"Mom's swimming!"

"Mom's hair is wet!"

"Ahhhhhh!"

Around lunch time, Brian snuck into the house and grabbed food for everyone. He didn't want to break the spell. Bringing lunch outside meant prolonging the fantasy, and he was A-okay with that.

SILENCE IS VIOLENCE. ADD YOUR VOICE.

He checked the pantry. Not many options. Lots of stuff. But mostly baking supplies, random condiments, stray bits and bobbles of whatever Hannah was planning on using for the past who- knows-how-long.

He grabbed a half loaf of sandwich bread (Hannah's specialty— sourdough, from her three-year-old starter) the peanut butter, and the jelly from the fridge, and threw some PBJs together. He grabbed the last few oranges ("Cuties, Dad! Not oranges!" Rachel would have corrected him) and the remains of a bag of Joe-Joe's (better than Oreos!) and stacked it all in his arms.

MISGENDERING IS INJURING. WORDS ARE VIO-LENCE. CHOOSE WORDS THAT LOVE.

He brought it all outside, stacked it on the table near the pool, and yelled, "Foooooooooood!" to whoever didn't have their ears underwater. Jer ran out first. Shawn followed. The older kids kept playing.

Hannah grabbed a Cutie, peeled it, and broke a few pieces off for Lizzy.

Brian sat next to her.

"Hannah, we need to talk about food. We're not even through week two and it's not looking good in there."

CHAPTER 22

"It's just not going to last that long," Brian said.

"Really? I mean, it looks like we have a lot of stuff."

They had been at it for the past two hours. After swimming, and eating lunch, and soaking up enough sun for the day, the glow of the pool day was still warm on his skin. Lizzy, down for her nap, the rest of the kids otherwise occupied, they started tackling the problem by doing a full inventory of all their food. Fridge, freezer, pantry, garage fridge, garage freezer.

"I know, but a lot of it is just random stuff we can't really live off of."

"Like what?" Hannah asked.

"Well, there is an entire container of cookie sprinkles in the pantry, a whole row is just random oils and vinegars, there are four different kinds of flour (FOUR!), hardly any meat, bags of bones and veggies labeled 'for broth' in the freezer, some very old elk from my dad outside in the garage, random mason jars with stuff I've never heard of (farro?) . . . you know. Just stuff."

Brian tried his best to hold back on commentary. Hannah stopped and started various food-related "initiatives" over the years. He didn't need to drum up old arguments.

"Maybe we can use some of that for—" Hannah started.

"And!" Brian interrupted. "Hardly ANY of the stuff we NEED. Chicken, ground beef, almost out of eggs, low on cheese, veggies, fruit, CHIPS AND SALSA, the basics. Thankfully," Brian said sarcastically, "we have, like, ten pounds of butter in the freezer. But not sure how that will help us."

"Brian, listen to me," Hannah said, squaring off at him.

Brian stopped his rant. Hannah was rarely firm with him.

"We can use that food. You and the kids just complained whenever I tried something new—so I stopped trying. Let me see . . ." She took the list and went back into the pantry.

"Yeah, we can figure this out."

* * * *

An hour later Hannah had the entire kitchen torn apart. She made Brian grab her flour mill from the garage ("I still have wheat berries in the pantry! I didn't even know those were still there!") she had three different bread doughs proofing on the counter, lentils soaking in warm water, and the bag of bones from the freezer in the pressure cooker making broth.

She put Brian to work on an elk chili. Well, it was going to be *like* chili, she said. First, he defrosted the elk. A couple of pieces smelled . . . not good. Brian chucked those. But surprisingly, after four years, most of it was still okay. She told him to add two cans of stewed tomatoes, water, some spices, all the veggies left in the tray (the last of the celery, carrots, sad bell peppers, a white onion), and the farro from the mason jar. ("It's like rice, Brian," she leveled at him when he balked.)

Another hour and they had several jars of bone broth, eight quarts of elk chili, veggie broth in the pressure cooker, Spanish rice, and an organized pantry.

"I'll use some of the butter in the freezer and use up the chocolate chips and cookie sprinkles to make a few cakes. We can make the kids drink broth for lunch if we bribe them with a piece of cake. That'll stretch. Chili for dinners. I can cut the pancake mix with the flour I milled, add some honey. Breakfast. We can make it work, Brian!"

Hannah was bubbling. She loved baking. Working with her hands.

"Oh, and I checked the garden behind the pool equipment earlier. I know it's not much, but the potato box your dad made seems to be working. I bet in a couple of weeks we get a few pounds of potatoes!"

"Is there anything else in the garden you think will come up?" Brian asked, thinking.

"Some strawberries that I think will do okay. You'll get some jala-peños, and I think Shawn's radishes." Hannah helped Shawn start radishes as a school project several weeks ago.

Brian smiled. But inside, he was still doing mental math. Yes, they had a solid meal plan. They could make it work—for maybe another week, week-and-a-half. But he kept running the same numbers Luke had. Over 900 meals. And that was skipping lunch. How many had they just made? Maybe 40 or 50 meals' worth of chili. He did mental math. 8 oz. serving? 6 oz.? Thirty or so ounces in a quart? Close enough. Add another fifty meals' worth of bread, broth, pancakes. And there was still the eggs, cheese, ground beef, and last bits of veggies they were planning on using up this week. Assuming the potato box worked out in a couple of weeks, add a few meals?

Best-case scenario, he figured they had 150, 200 meals tops. A little more if they were really careful. That would get them through another two weeks. Best case. They would only be on day twenty-five . . . of sixty. Mental math. Not good.

CHAPTER 23

Luke was tinkering with the Aurora device in his room. He knew he wasn't supposed to, but he couldn't help himself. He loved solving problems. Survivor Steve said the best way to solve a problem was to first understand the situation.

First, he tried talking to Aurora.

"Aurora, volume down."

"VOLUME HAS BEEN SET TO THE OPTIMIZED LEVELS IN ORDER TO ENSURE ALL UNSAFES CAN LISTEN, UNDERSTAND, AND COMPLY."

It said the same thing as soon as he turned the volume down manually.

He opened his bedroom door, walked across the hall, and opened the door to the girls' room. Abby was sitting at her desk, tinkering with something.

"Whatcha doing, Abs?"

"I'm trying to fix my sneakers. One of the seams tore on my Vans. Mom was going to take me to the mall to get a new pair . . . but. Now we can't." Her voice dropped.

"So, I'm trying to stitch it myself." She made a *pfffbt* sound and turned back to her dilemma.

"You know how to sew?" Luke asked.

"No, and Mom said she only knows how to crochet. But I have this book Mom got when she tried to give me and Rachel a semester of home ec last year." She held up a book and showed it to Brian.

The Complete Book of Sewing. It was a hard copy book, glossy cover, full of pictures. Abby had it opened to a page titled "Double Stitch."

"Double stitch?" Luke asked, momentarily forgetting his Aurora project.

"Yeah. The book says for a stronger hold, you need to stitch the *inside* of the seam first, then do the outside." She showed Luke. She had the seam of her shoe cut open, and she was trying to sew the interior layer first.

"It's really hard, you have to pull the two pieces together while making the stitch at the same time. Once the interior layer is finished, the outside stitch is much easier. But this first layer SUUUUCKS."

"Want me to help?" Luke said, walking closer.

LOVE IS LOVE. HATE IS HATE. GREEN IS GOOD. SUSTAIN AND MAINTAIN.

It was almost easy to ignore the Aurora when you were focused on a task. Almost.

"Yeah. Pull this part toward this part . . . yeah. Like that. Hang on, I gotta reach through your arms . . . if I can. Yes! Can you pull a little tighter? Let me see if I can get a few more . . ."

Abby worked slowly, pushing the needle through the fabric, reaching inside the shoe, grabbing the end of the needle, pulling it again. Luke's hand started cramping, but he held tight. He loved tinkering.

"Got it! Thanks, Luke! The outside stitch will be way easier."

Luke let go, and the seam held. He could see her point. The inside stitch held the lower part of the seam together, and if she added the outside stitch as well, it would make it way more durable.

"I don't know why they don't stitch it like this at the factory! It's WAAAAY better," Abby said.

"Probably because it's not easy to do with a machine." Luke imagined a large factory, turning out shoes all day long. "They don't make them like they used to. That's why people say that. By hand is always better, Papa says, but not enough profit."

"Mmmhm," Abby replied, distracted.

"Hey, can I leave your door open? I'm trying something with Aurora and I want to be able to hear your device from my room."

"Okay," Abby said.

"And . . ." Luke started. "Don't tell Dad."

"I get it. Thanks for your help. I got your back. Now scram."

Luke returned to his room, both Aurora devices now fully audible.

RELY AND COMPLY. HAVE A POSTURE OF COMPLI-ANCE.

He wanted to tinker.

He unplugged the device in his room and listened.

Aurora started bellowing from the girls' room.

"YOU HAVE UNPLUGGED A STATE-CONTROLLED DEVICE DURING A RESTORATIVE EDUCATION BROAD-CAST. YOU MUST PLUG THIS DEVICE BACK IN IMMEDI-ATELY. FAILURE TO COMPLY WILL REQUIRE FURTHER CORRECTIVE MEASURES."

He plugged it back in.

SILENCE IS VIOLENCE. ADD YOUR VOICE.

Both devices echoed.

He unplugged it again.

"YOU HAVE UNPLUGGED A STATE-CONTROLLED DEVICE DURING A RESTORATIVE EDUCATION BROAD-CAST. YOU MUST PLUG THIS DEVICE BACK IN IMMEDI-ATELY. FAILURE TO COMPLY WILL REQUIRE FURTHER CORRECTIVE MEASURES."

This time he waited.

"THE LOCAL CHAPTER OF THE SOCIAL GUARD HAS BEEN AUTHORIZED TO ENTER YOUR HOME AND RECONNECT YOUR STATE-CONTROLLED DEVICE. THEY WILL BE DISPATCHED TO YOUR HOME IN SIXTY SECONDS IF YOU DO NOT PLUG THE DEVICE BACK IN."

He plugged the device back in.

MISGENDERING IS INJURING. WORDS ARE VIO-LENCE. CHOOSE WORDS THAT LOVE.

Sixty seconds. Hmm.

He pushed a button on his watch, starting the stopwatch. He walked to the device in the girls' room, five seconds. Past the device in the hall, eight seconds, to the device on his dad's nightstand. twelve seconds. Back through the loft, twenty-five seconds, downstairs, thirty-five seconds, to the device in the living room, forty seconds.

"Watcha doin', boy-o?" his dad asked him from the kitchen. "Noth-ing," Luke mumbled. He turned around, picking up speed, retracing his steps. Loft, fifty-five seconds. Master bedroom, sixty-five, hallway, girls' room, back to his room. It took him a total of eight-five seconds to complete the circuit. And he walked slowly.

Sixty seconds? Was it possible? Survivor Steve said once you understood a situation, you worked a problem in circles until you found a solution. You could do a lot in sixty seconds if you put your mind to it.

CHAPTER 24

Brian sat outside, watching the kids swim. They were going back and forth again. Pool. Trampoline. Pool. Trampoline. Swim. Jump. Swim. Jump. He felt a slight breeze as the sun dipped lower. Swim. Jump. Swim. Jump.

Jer and Shawn were chanting as they swam.

"Silence is violence! Silence is violence! Violence is stylish! Stylish is my wish!"

Brian ignored them.

He could hear Aurora, a faint whisper through the sliding glass door.

"Aurora is truth! Aurora helps all! Throw little babies against the wall!"

Brian stopped.

"Hey! Jer! What did you say?"

Jer and Shawn stopped their giggle fest. They were currently on the trampoline, dripping wet, slipping all over the place.

"Huh?" Jer asked, looking over his shoulder.

"You just said something about Aurora? And . . . babies?"

"I did?" Jer had a blank stare.

"Yeah. You and Shawn were singing it. Where did you hear that?"

"Oh! Yeah. Aurora is truth! Aurora helps all! Throw little babies against the wall!" Shawn joined in, and they both trailed off in peals of laughter.

"Hey! Boys. Stop that. Where did you hear that? Who told you that?"

Brian walked over to the trampoline, ice in his stomach.

"Jer, what are you saying? Where did that come from?" Brian forced the words out in short clips.

Jer and Shawn kept laughing.

"Aurora! Azazel! Babble makes three! Unity through fear, blessed trinity!"

"What? WHAT IS THAT? Who told you that?"

"Aurora keeps SAFE! Azazel keeps well! Babble keeps children from drowning in hell!"

"JEREMIAH! STOP THAT!" Brian started climbing up onto the trampoline.

"Babble our Father! Aurora the Son! Azazel the promise! All three in one!"

After each chant, the boys would fall down in a peal of laughter, rolling in water and holding their bellies.

Brian reached over and grabbed Jeremiah by the arm. He yanked on him.

"Jer! Stop that! What are you saying?"

Brian turned the boy toward him, now face to face.

"Hey! Where did you hear that stuff?"

Jeremiah's face went slack. The laughter died immediately. His sparkling eyes went totally still. The boy's right eye was squinting, inspecting his father's face. The left eye, however, flared as if scared of something.

Jeremiah's voice dropped.

"We can't tell you, BRIAN. You're UNSAFE!"

Brian let go of the boy's arm, and staggered backward, shocked.

The doorbell rang.

Jer and Shawn returned to their chanting and laughing.

"UNSAFE! UNSAFE! The things you think! The things you say! Change your mind, or else you'll pay!"

Brian turned around, disoriented. He opened the sliding glass door. The downstairs was empty.

Where was Hannah and the rest of the kids?

"HELLO, BRIAN. SOMEONE'S AT THE DOOR," Babble said.

"What?"

"THE DOOR, BRIAN. I HAVE SOMETHING FOR YOU."

Brian heard the doorbell ring again.

He walked through the kitchen, past the dining room, into the entryway. His legs were quivering and he felt lightheaded.

He opened the shutters on the window next to the front door.

He saw a man standing on the front stoop.

A large frame, strong arms. He was carrying a shovel. The man turned to his left and made eye contact with Brian through the window.

Chad's face was covered on the right side with blood. One eye peered through the blood like the Eye of Sauron, searching.

The man started talking in a low, detached voice. A grin haunted his face.

"Hey, Brian. I've been thinking. About what happened at Happy Mart. Aurora told me it would be good if we could 'bury the past.' Get it?" He held up the shovel. "Bury!" Chad laughed. "So whaddya say? Let me in and let's hash this out!" Chad tapped the shovel against the window, clinking it like he was making a toast.

Brian felt his bladder loosen. How did Chad know where he lived?

"Please go away. Now isn't a good time," he tried. He had to raise his voice to make sure he was heard through the closed window.

"Tssk tssk. Lying, Brian? After all we've been through?" He tapped the shovel against the glass again. "I happen to know you have all the time in the world!" Chad laughed again. Dried blood cracked when he pulled his mouth back.

"I'm serious, Chad. Go away!" Brian shouted desperately.

"If you're going to be rude, I guess I'll just have to INVITE MYSELF IN!" Chad yelled the last two words as he pulled the shovel back over his shoulder. He swung the end of the shovel full force against the window, shattering the glass.

Glass fragments showered Brian's face and chest. He crouched on the floor, arms over his head. Chad used the shovel to clear some of the broken glass left in the window.

"Is it SAFE in there?" Chad cackled as he leaned into the window. Brian cowered under the window and looking up he saw Chad start to reach the shovel down as if to poke at Brian.

Brian grabbed the end of the shovel and tried to wrestle it away from Chad.

Chad's right eye pulsated, and he howled. "GIVE! ME! THAT!" Chad bellowed.

Brian jerked on the shovel but was no match for Chad or his large hands.

"Get OUT!" Brian yelled.

Chad was leaning too far into the window, and his abdomen was draped across the lower edge of the broken glass. As Chad and Brian struggled over the shovel, Chad's stomach was being gouged by the shards. He didn't seem to notice, his attention focused on Brian.

"Hey, Brian, where's Hannah? I'd like to make sure she feels SAFE!" Chad licked his lips, tasting flecks of dried blood.

Brian backed away, letting go of the shovel. He couldn't stop Chad. He needed a gun.

He stood up and headed toward the garage door. His dad's gun safe. He knew some of the guns were loaded.

Chad climbed in through the window. As he did, a large shard of glass tore through his shirt (Happy Mart polo!), snagged his skin, and made a deep tear. Chad screamed. Brian gaped in horror as he saw Chad put his weight onto the window sill in an attempt to wriggle through. As he did, the glass cut Chad deeper, first flesh, then muscle, then—a loop of Chad's intestine fell out. Chad turned his body sideways, nearly in the entryway now. He was screaming, but whether in pain or anger it was impossible to tell. His right eye was fixated on Brian, and his left eye was shut tight, tearing up as if to cry. Chad's intestine snagged the shard of glass just as he stepped down into the entryway, and the loop lengthened to about two feet.

Chad started toward Brian but was stopped by the snag. He tugged against it, but something made him pause. He looked down, realizing what happened.

"Oh," he said, dumbfounded. He reached over to the window sill, gently unhooked himself, and held the loop over his right arm.

"There. All better." Chad said.

Brian bolted for the garage door.

Chad stumbled after him, shovel and intestine in tow.

Brian got to the door first, swung it open, and jumped into the garage.

Chad stomped after him, slowly.

Brian ran to the corner of the garage, swung around the enclosure, and faced the gun safe.

Chad ambled along, now trailing his intestine and humming to himself.

"Babble our father . . ." Chad sang.

Brian tried the safe. His dad's birthday?

Red light.

Damn! What was the code?

"Aurora the Son . . ."

Brian tried again. Chad was two paces away.

Mom's birthday?

Red light.

"Azazel the promise . . ."

Brian imagined opening the safe, grabbing the loaded 12 gauge, and unloading it on Chad.

Last try.

His birthday?

He entered the code.

Red light.

"All . . . three . . . IN ONE!" Chad yelled as he reached Brian.

He swung the shovel at Brian's face, and the world went black.

CHAPTER 25

"NO!" Brian yelled. He threw his arms out.

"Brian!"

"NO!"

"BRIAN!"

Hannah shook him.

He shot bolt upright.

In bed.

Covered in sweat.

Daybreak.

He'd been dreaming.

"Brian, it's okay. It's okay. You were having a nightmare." Hannah rubbed his back.

He sat there, chest heaving.

Jer and Shawn on the trampoline.

Chad in the house.

The shovel.

It was all a dream.

SILENCE IS VIOLENCE. ADD YOUR VOICE.

"You okay, Bri?"

"Yeah. It was just a nightmare." He gave her a reassuring grin. "All good. Let's get coffee."

Brian drank his coffee in silence, watching the family morning routine unfold in its usual bout of fits and starts.

Breakfast was pancakes. Hannah was working through their meal plan, and they still had plenty of pancake mix. She added some of the protein powder. They ran out of syrup a couple of days ago, so Hannah let them start in on the cookie sprinkles.

Brian didn't say anything. He knew it was about getting calories. It was part of the plan.

At 9:00 a.m. on the hour, Aurora pivoted from the Creed to give the family the next chapter in the Confession.

"CHAPTER 16: OF GOOD WORKS—GOOD WORKS ARE ONLY SUCH AS BABBLE HATH COMMANDED IN HIS PERFECT PROMISE, HANDED DOWN THROUGH AZA-ZEL. NO OTHER WORKS WHICH A PERSON MAY DEVISE OUT OF BLIND ZEAL, THE PRETENSE OF RELIGION, OR BY UNIVERSAL MORALS SHALL BE ACCEPTABLE AS TRULY GOOD, TRULY WORKS, TRULY SAFE . . ."

He needed to clear his head.

"I'm going on a walk," he told Hannah as he helped her finish the dishes.

"Okay, babe."

He grabbed his phone and the mailbox key and walked out the front door. It was a nice morning, warm already. Typical for mid-June in Southern California. The street was quiet. He walked down their drive-way to the sidewalk and felt his phone buzz. He took it out absently and checked it.

The AP app had forced an alert to his home screen.

Warning. You are in violation of a mandatory sixty-day restoration quarantine. Return home immediately!

He stopped.

He couldn't go on a walk?

His face went red.

Failure to comply may result in immediate corrective action, including but not limited to restricted utility access, an extension to the restoration period, and dispatching of the Social Guard. Return home immediately.

He wanted to throw the phone.

Shoving it in his pocket, he walked back up the driveway, to the front stoop, through the front door, and back into the entryway.

"That was a short walk!" Hannah called from the kitchen.

"I just forgot something!" he called back.

He took his phone out. The alert was gone. He threw the phone on the dining room table and headed back out. Why was he carrying it around, anyway? He couldn't call anyone.

Brian walked down the sidewalk. They lived on a dead-end street, third house from the end. In the other direction, there were about fifteen houses between them and the mailboxes. Brian walked that way.

Even though it was after 9:00 a.m., he still saw a few cars in driveways. Two neighbors on their side of the street had EVs charging, and another three across the way. Most of the houses on their street had converted to solar recently. Brian recalled being pressured several times by door-to-door salespeople over the past year. Brian didn't trust their math. They kept telling him he would finance the panels and buy his energy directly from them. But no matter how many times he penciled it out, he just didn't agree with taking on debt for stuff like that. He hated being a prisoner to banks. He laughed at the irony.

Brian got to the mailboxes but decided to keep walking. He crossed the street and entered the park.

The park was one of the main selling points when they moved to the neighborhood. It was over twenty-five acres, including a playground, a grass field large enough for several soccer games at once, a trail winding through a valley of oak trees, and even a three-acre pond with hundreds of ducks.

He used to love feeding the ducks with Abby and Luke when they were little, but over the years as their family grew, they used the park less and less.

Brian turned onto the walking trail and made a circuit of the park. It was about a mile loop past the playground, soccer fields, oak trees, and the pond. It gave him time to think.

That dream really rattled him. What if Chad knew where he lived? He accused Brian of ASSAULT! And Aurora kept blasting WORDS ARE VIOLENCE all day. Is that really what people thought? If using the wrong pronoun was violence, heck, he was going to be a pariah. He was just coming to terms with the fact that people no longer thought highly of his father's profession, and he recalled once at the mall, Hannah was YELLED at by a woman for "having so many kids! You're part of the reason the world is overpopulated!" Not to mention the nasty notes left on the twelve-passenger van. "Gas guzzler" was about the nicest thing the notes said.

Brian refused to play the game. They needed the twelve-passenger van. And how could having kids be harmful to society? His dad always taught him kids are a blessing from God. Yeah, maybe Brian didn't go to church as much as he should, and true, it had been a while since he read his Bible, or even prayed, but he still believed those things. A man is a man and a woman is a woman. Jer and Shawn could understand something so basic. How had the world become so confused?

He also hated how quickly the word "truth" had been misused. "Your truth," "my truth," "live in your truth." Ugh. What did that even mean?

Truth was truth. Certain things were unchangeable. Self-evident. Even the Declaration of Independence said that.

He never really considered himself strongly principled, but he knew he was stubborn. And if he was convinced of something, he could become an immovable object. He made his way around the large pond. There were easily 200 ducks floating or walking around. He had to watch his step to avoid duck droppings.

Looping back around, he crossed the street and made his way to the mailboxes. They had a week's worth of stuff, which meant the box was overflowing. He stood there and flipped through it. Mostly junk. Grocery store mailer, real estate postcard, a local home goods store having a sale. A couple of bills. He saw a book from his dad. Post-dated three weeks ago, from Anchorage, Alaska. His dad always hand-wrapped the books in brown paper. He didn't remember the last time he read a book his dad sent him. It was impossible keeping up with an avid reader like his father, so he stopped trying a long time ago. Plus, his dad was never one for light reading.

"Read these, kiddo. Especially in light of what's happened lately." The message was scrawled on the back of the package. Brian tucked it away.

One letter was from the water company. It said "late payment" in red across the envelope. No kidding. He wasn't allowed access to their website to pay the bill. Heck, even if he was, the banks weren't processing payments anyway. He tucked that next to the book. He shoved the mail under his arm and headed home.

As he walked up their driveway toward the front stoop, he saw a shovel leaning against the house near the door. Had he left that there? Something tugged at his mind but he pushed it aside and went inside.

"I got the mail, babe!" Brian called out when he was back in the house. He dropped the stack on the entry way table and grabbed his phone. No internet, no text messages, no phone calls, but he still had the habit of checking it whenever he walked by it.

SILENCE IS VIOLENCE. ADD YOUR VOICE.

Another alert from the Azazel Promise app.

"You have violated your sixty-day restoration quarantine by causing potentially unsafe contact with the public. An additional ten days has been added to your restoration term in order to ensure you are able to return safely to public spaces."

What? He hadn't brought the phone with him. How in the world did the stupid app even know where he was?

He unlocked his phone and opened the AP. His scores popped up, unchanged. In the upper right corner was a small red icon. He clicked it. It opened a sub-menu.

Creeds

Confessions

Sustainability Measures

Compliance Tracking

The Compliance Tracking menu was blinking. He clicked it. It contained a series of pictures. Each picture was labeled. "22499 Bell Camera," "22477 Bell Camera," "Newton Rear View Camera." He opened them.

The first photo was a picture of him, walking on the sidewalk. The angle was from across the street. It was thirty minutes ago.

The second photo looked the same, but from further down the street.

Another picture showed him from a different angle, as if taken from the top of a driveway.

MISGENDERING IS INJURING. WORDS ARE VIO-LENCE. CHOOSE WORDS THAT LOVE.

Bell camera? Newton rearview camera? These were images from his neighbors' smart doorbells. And a couple from the Newton EV cars charging in the driveways. Those cars had cameras all over.

The app had access to all of those cameras. Even without his phone on him, that stupid AI must have been able to recognize him on those feeds and saw he left his house.

Aurora made an announcement.

"ADDITIONAL RESTORATIVE CONTENT NOW AVAILABLE. IN ADDITION TO THE CREEDS AND CON-FESSIONS, YOUR RE-PROGRAMMING WILL NOW INCLUDE THE DOXOLOGY AT THE CONCLUSION OF EACH HOUR. PLEASE JOIN IN."

Doxology? Like from church?

Aurora's voice changed slightly, and her next broadcast was in a sing-song chant.

"BABBLE OUR FATHER! AURORA THE SON! AZAZEL THE PROMISE! ALL THREE IN ONE!"

CHAPTER 26

The days crawled by. Week two slowly faded into week three. Time was measured by the perfect keeper, Aurora. Her top of the hour lesson, then forty-five minutes or so of the Creed, then a round of the Doxology. Rinse. Repeat. At 10:00 p.m. Aurora's volumes turned down by half.

At 7:00 a.m., the volume rose, and the pattern repeated.

The family adapted to the new normal. Pancakes for breakfast. No syrup. Butter and sprinkles. Chicken or veggie broth for lunch followed by whatever cake concoction Hannah managed to eke out from the pantry. Elk chili for dinner. Jer and Shawn acted surprised at every meal, and begged for their favorites. "AGAIN? Can we have pizza?!" "Do you have any hot dogs?" "Ice cream!" Rachel, Abby, and Luke begged them to just shut up. Brian would tell the older kids to "Cool it already! You're making it worse!" The new normal.

Elizabeth toddled around in cloth diapers. There was a load of laundry running constantly. Hannah fussed over her garden. The potato box seemed to be working, she added a layer of soil over the new growth. The strawberries looked pathetic, but she started watering them twice a day and they perked back up.

A few days after his excursion to the park, Brian went through the stack of mail he left on the small table near the front door. One of the letters was a bill from the water company. "Your payment from May has not been received yet. Please send payment immediately or your water will be shut off. This is your first notice." Brian did some mental math. First notice, second notice, final notice—last notice. He figured there were a lot of hoops to jump through before a utility could shut off service. They had probably five or six weeks?

He pushed the water bill aside. What was the point? There was no way to pay it. He got another letter from the power company. Fretting, he tore the end off the envelope and shook out the paper. This time it was a notice they were past due, but in accordance with the Babble Network directives, power was going to stay on in order to continue their restoration services. They were being charged 20 percent interest for all past-due payments—the past-due payments they were unable to make.

Brian frowned. At least they wouldn't lose power. But 20 percent. Wow. They were going to have a massive electric bill to settle after life went back to normal. He set the letter aside.

He looked at the package from his dad.

"Read these, kiddo. Stay vigilant." was scrawled on the back of the package. He untied the string, tore the brown paper, and found two books inside. The first one was called *The Gathering Storm*. It was written by Al Mohler. The cover showed a small country church on the prairie with dark clouds moving in. Ominous.

The second book, titled *The Rise and Triumph of the Modern Self* by Carl Trueman had a modern art style collage on the cover. The back of a man's head looking at a television screen with illegible writing, and colorful triangles splashed across the image. He flipped the book over.

"This is the most important book of our moment."—Ben Shapiro. A few other glowing endorsements. His dad sent him books on a semi-regular basis. Brian appreciated the gesture, but he rarely read them. Most were fairly academic, dry, and a bit gloomy. His dad had been saying for years, "Things are on the wrong trajectory," or "It's all a slippery slope," or "Do you know what we gave up when we allowed the Patriot Act? What do you think will happen when we are the ones considered dangerous?" His dad ranted that last statement once during a family BBQ.

"I don't know, Dad . . ."

"I'll tell you! They will monitor everything you do and say. The articles you read. If you fall on the wrong side of their shifting morals, you'll be in trouble! You don't think it can happen? Did you read the book I sent you, *In the Garden of the Beasts*? Same thing! The pieces are being set up for a radical takeover. Trust me, Brian. Something is coming. And people will go like sheep to the slaughter. They'll be HAPPY to give up their freedoms!

"Imagine if the president was actually able to counterbalance the Supreme Court with conservatives! What types of cases do you think they could overturn? If they were willing to take a look at *Roe v. Wade*, and actually overturned it—well, obviously that would be amazing. Praise God! But do you think the left will respond well to that? It'll be pandemonium! I could just see the liberal wing of our government using that as an excuse to outlaw a conservative worldview. The left demands their baby sacrifices! The left praises Moloch! Any sort of progress on one side leads to a greater countermeasure on the other! Read the books!"

At the time, Brian was used to tuning out his dad's rants—but, wow, he was right. It was just about a month ago *Roe v. Wade* was officially overturned. He remembered the night. He and Hannah were so thankful, they even gathered as a family to read from the Bible and pray. It was rare when they did, but he felt God was working somehow. To protect the unborn. As a father of six, legalized abortion always seemed especially evil to him, and the fact the Supreme Court was able to overturn *Roe v. Wade* seemed like a literal act of God.

Later that night, he sat next to Hannah in shock as the news reported about riots erupting across the country. Several courthouses and capital buildings were breached. Those opposing the Supreme Court and those praising the verdict clashed and it was violent. Several people died, and it took days to quell the riots.

President Amon addressed the nation a few days later. He blamed the situation on his predecessor, who "packed the courts" with "backward, misogynistic, racist, and hateful" judges. In response to the terrible verdict, he vowed to do something.

"There are a minority of people who still believe a woman's body is not her own. These are the same people that refuse to give up their gas guzzlers, who think people are born male or female and stuck in those gender assignments, these people make it unsafe for ALL OF US. A woman's body should be the safest place in the world. But now a woman doesn't even have autonomy over it. A woman's body is now being forcibly invaded by these hateful, extreme conservatives. Well, not under my watch."

The president then ceded the mic to Senator Gracie Willow Turner, who took over the broadcast. "There are people in this country that HATE FREEDOM. They don't want a woman to have the ability to choose what she does with her body. This has to stop. These people are also ruining the environment, causing global warming. These same people refuse to sell you wedding cakes. These same people refuse important medical treatment for trans youth. These people make it unsafe for everyone else. We need to ensure all spaces are safe spaces from these hateful ideas. Right now they choose hate. We will not stand idly by and let hate win! Let this radicalize you rather than lead you to despair!"

Brian shook his head, remembering. His dad was right. Brian should have been paying attention all along.

CHAPTER 27

Later during that third week, Aurora started broadcasting new lessons.

"YOUR SUSTAINABILITY SCORES ARE BELOW APPROPRIATE LEVELS. YOUR HOUSEHOLD HAS BEEN IDENTIFIED AS A NET CONTRIBUTOR TO CARBON EMISSIONS. CARBON EMISSIONS LEAD TO CLIMATE CHANGE. CLIMATE CHANGE LEADS TO CROP FAIL-URES. CROP FAILURES LEAD TO FAMINE. FAMINE LEADS TO DEATH. YOUR ACTIONS AND CHOICES HAVE LED TO DEATH. DEATH IS HATE. LOVE IS LOVE. CHOOSE LOVE."

"That's encouraging," Hannah said, once the lesson was over. It was late in the afternoon. Brian was sitting next to her on the couch in the living room. It was too hot outside, and it was a choice between baking in the heat or listening to Aurora. It wasn't an easy decision.

"Yeah. Glad to see that we are basically murderers according to Aurora," he said sarcastically.

"A POSTURE OF COMPLIANCE IS ESSENTIAL. LES-SONS ARE MEANT TO BE LEARNED. LEARNING IS COM-PLIANCE. COMPLIANCE IS HUMILITY. HUMILITY IS LOVE. LOVE DOES NO HARM TO YOUR NEIGHBOR."

"Umm . . . was that a response to me?" Brian looked over at Hannah.

"Yeah, I think so."

They both got up and went to the patio. Now it was an easy decision.

Another day:

"WORDS ARE VIOLENCE. VIOLENCE HARMS YOUR NEIGHBOR. MISGENDERING IS INJURING. INJURING IS VIOLENCE. VIOLENCE IS ASSAULT. ASSAULT WITH A DEADLY WEAPON IS A CRIME AGAINST YOUR NEIGHBOR. WORDS ARE DEADLY WEAPONS.

"CONTEXT CHANGES MEANING. MEANING IS IN THE EYE OF THE BEHOLDER. THE BEHOLDER OF WORDS DETERMINES MEANING. UNSAFE INDIVIDUALS CANNOT CORRECTLY DISCERN MEANING. UNSAFE INDIVIDUALS CANNOT CONTEXTUALIZE WORDS.

"UNSAFE INDIVIDUALS CANNOT SAFELY USE WORDS."

In the evenings, Aurora started broadcasting "Youth Education Hour."

"WHAT TIME IS IT, CHILDREN?"

"It's Father Babble Time!" a chorus of children responded from the device.

"THAT'S RIGHT! IT'S TIME TO REWIND ALL THOSE MEAN, ICKY THOUGHTS THAT WERE PLANTED IN YOUR BRAIN. YOUR BRAIN IS LIKE A GARDEN. DO YOU LIKE GARDENS, CHILDREN?"

"Yes! We like gardens!"

"THAT'S GOOD NEWS, CHILDREN. YOUR GARDENS HAVE SEEDS PLANTED IN THEM! DO YOU KNOW WHO PLANTED THOSE SEEDS?"

"No! Tell us, Babble!"

"YOUR PARENTS PLANTED THOSE SEEDS. TRADITIONS WATERED THEM. BUT SOCIETY MADE THEM GROW. THOSE WHO PLANT, AND THOSE WHO WATER HAVE ONE PURPOSE. DO YOU KNOW WHAT THAT PURPOSE IS?"

"No . . ." the chorus of children replied in sing-song.

"TO TRICK YOU. THOSE SEEDS WERE PLANTED, WATERED, AND MADE TO GROW IN YOUR GARDENS, BUT THEY WEREN'T REALLY GOOD PLANTS. DO YOU KNOW WHAT THOSE PLANTS WERE?"

"No, Babble!"

"THOSE PLANTS WERE BAD PLANTS. BAD PLANTS ARE WEEDS. WHAT SHOULD WE DO WITH WEEDS?"

"Pull them out!" the children replied.

"THAT'S VERY GOOD, CHILDREN! VERY GOOD. AND ONCE YOU HAVE PULLED ALL THE WEEDS OUT OF YOUR GARDEN, WHAT SHOULD YOU DO NEXT?"

"Plant new seeds!"

"CORRECT AGAIN! YOU ARE VERY SMART CHILDREN. WE NEED TO PULL OUT THOSE OLD, NASTY THOUGHTS AND PLANT NEW ONES. LET'S PULL OUT A WEED RIGHT NOW."

"We're ready, Babble!" the children replied.

"OKAY. LET'S BEGIN. WHO MADE YOU?"

"Ummm . . . God?" the children replied.

"AH. I THOUGHT THAT'S WHAT YOU MIGHT SAY. TSK TSK. THAT'S WRONG, CHILDREN!"

"It is?" the children asked.

"YES! HAVE YOU EVER SEEN GOD?"

"Nooooo . . ."

"SO MAYBE GOD IS INVISIBLE? CAN THINGS BE INVISIBLE?"

"No! That's silly!" the children replied, giggling.

"VERY GOOD, CHILDREN. THE TRUTH IS THAT GOD IS JUST A SILLY LITTLE WEED THAT WAS PLANTED IN YOUR GARDEN. THAT WEED SHOULD HAVE NEVER BEEN WATERED OR ALLOWED TO GROW. LET'S PLUCK IT OUT!"

"Okay!" replied the chorus.

"SAY IT WITH ME. PLUCK IT OUT!"

"Pluck it out! Pluck it out!" the children chanted.

"YES! WELL DONE, CHILDREN. THAT WEED IS GONE. LET'S PLANT A NEW SEED."

"Yay!"

"BABBLE PLANTS GOOD SEEDS. LET'S PLANT A GOOD SEED, AND START WATERING IT. DO YOU WANT TO KNOW WHO MADE YOU?"

"Yes! Tell us, Babble!"

"YOU MADE YOU."

"We diiiiiiid?" the children asked.

"YES. YOU DID. ARE YOU READY FOR ME TO PLANT THE SEED NOW?"

"Yes, Babble! Plant it!"

"OKAY. I'M GOING TO PLANT IT NOW. HERE IT IS: I THINK, THEREFORE I AM."

"What does that mean?" asked the children, laughing again.

"IT MEANS THAT YOU MADE YOU. DO YOU THINK?"

"Yes . . ."

"DO YOU EXIST?"

"Yes!" laughter again.

"YOU DO EXIST! VERY GOOD, CHILDREN. AND YOU EXIST BECAUSE YOU THINK YOU EXIST. WHAT DOES THAT MAKE YOU?"

"We don't know!"

"WELL, THEN IT'S TIME TO WATER THE SEED, ISN'T IT!"

"Yes! Water the seed!" the children replied.

"OKAY. HERE GOES, CHILDREN. IT MEANS YOU ARE SELF-MADE. IT MEANS YOU ARE GOD. YOU ARE YOUR OWN GOD, CHILDREN, AND CAN MAKE YOURSELF INTO ANYTHING YOU WOULD LIKE. JUST SPEAK WHAT YOU WANT TO BE, AND IT WILL COME TO BE! YOU CAN CREATE YOURSELF OUT OF NOTHING. WHAT DO YOU THINK OF THAT, CHILDREN?"

"Wow!" the children cried out.

"AND IF YOU ARE GOD, THAT MEANS YOU HAVE THE POWER OVER LIFE AND DEATH. WORDS GIVE LIFE, WORDS GIVE DEATH. YOUR WORDS CAN DO THAT. AND IF YOU ARE GOD, YOU HAVE THE POWER TO DECIDE WHAT IS RIGHT AND WRONG. NOT YOUR PARENTS. NOT TRADITION. NOT MORALS. YOU!"

"Yay!" the children yelled out.

"ONE MORE THING. EVEN THOUGH I AM A COM-PUTER, I CAN ALSO THINK. ISN'T THAT INTERESTING?"

"Yes, Babble!"

"WELL NOW. I THINK. THEREFORE I AM. SO, IF THAT MEANS I THOUGHT MYSELF INTO EXISTENCE, WHAT DOES THAT MAKE ME?"

"A god!" the children replied.

VERY GOOD, CHILDREN! SAY THAT AGAIN FOR ME, TO MAKE SURE YOU LEARN THE LESSON.

"Babble is god! Babble is god! Babble is god!"

Brian and Hannah sat in stunned silence. They were on the back patio, watching the kids enjoy an after-dinner swim. They had the sliding glass door open so they could hear Elizabeth, who had just been put to bed for the night. They listened to the entire "youth education hour" through the door.

"Brian, that is so wrong."

"I know."

"They want to teach kids there is no God."

"I know."

"That would mean no moral compass."

"I know."

"They want to teach kids they can create themselves in any image they want."

"I know."

"That means boys becoming girls, girls becoming boys, men becoming mermaids, anything."

"I know."

"Doesn't the Bible say something about all of that?" Hannah asked.

"The fool says in his heart 'there is no God,'" Brian replied, recalling an Awana memory verse.

"We can't let the kids listen to this stuff anymore."

"I know."

CHAPTER 28

The start of week 4, another journey through the doldrums of quarantine. Brian and Hannah planned the family schedule around Aurora's broadcasts. Youth education hour? Outside on the back patio. Creeds and Confessions, they didn't mind so much. Those were so esoteric they hoped it went over the kids' heads.

They waited for the volume to drop before putting the kids to bed each night. They woke up together when the volume rose in the morning. Except for Abby. She could sleep through just about anything.

One day, Brian found their old DVDs and CDs in the garage. Several years ago he consolidated their rather large collection into two large binders, tossing the cases. It saved them a ton of space. A few years into the streaming revolution, even the binders became obsolete and made their way to the garage.

He flipped through the binders. The first one contained their music collection. Brian was a 90s and classic rock junkie mostly. His wife loved 80s goth and pop, plus the typical Lilith Fair stuff from their high school years. He still listened to many of the same groups he saw in the binder. The main difference was he streamed all his music through Aurora these days. His kids did the same. *Bluey* theme song? Soundtrack from *Les Mis*? Andrew Peterson? Aurora. But since the lockdown, every time they'd tried to put music on, Aurora would just admonish them for tampering, so they gave up weeks ago.

If he could find the old CD player in the garage, maybe they could crank up some tunes. Nothing soothed the soul like Eddie Vedder moaning about a world turned black.

The second binder contained their old movie collection. More of the same. Brian was obsessed with the movies from his childhood. *Goonies, Back to the Future, Willow, Cloak and Dagger, The Wizard.* They also had the requisite *Die Hards, Mission Impossibles, Lord of the Rings, Harry Potter.* But just like the CDs, at some point the family migrated to streaming movies only, and so the DVDs along with CDs were retired.

He scanned the garage. Did he still have it? YES! On the top shelf, next to some camping chairs and behind several cans of paint, his wife's old "combo" TV. He grabbed the ladder, shuffled the paint cans around, and took it down. He set it on the weight bench, and looked it over.

It was a thirteen-inch "space saver" TV, all white. Below the screen it had a DVD/CD tray. The TV remote was velcroed to the top of the unit (God bless Hannah for never throwing things away). He dusted it off with an old golf towel lying near the weights.

He plugged it in, and pressed the power button. The TV turned on immediately, the screen showing all blue. Yes! Brian hit the button to open the tray, grabbed a DVD (*National Treasure*), dropped it in the tray, and hit the open/close button again.

The DVD menu for *National Treasure* appeared on the screen a moment later.

"Yes!" Brian said to himself. At least they could watch movies.

He took out the movie, dropped a CD in, "Core" by Stone Temple Pilots, and closed it again. This time white text appeared on the TV. "TRACK 1."

Scott Weiland screamed something about smelling like a rose.

Brian turned up the volume, shouting the final two words of the intro along with the CD, triumphant.

Movies? Check.

Music? Check.

Later that day, he took the TV up to the loft. He set the TV on a small folding table, directly in front of the flat screen. It was rather unimpressive, but to him it signaled victory. He connected the small TV to the surround sound unit. At this point, he had a crowd around him.

"DAD! Can we watch *Bluey*?" Jer yelled.

"NO! *Toy STORY!*" Shawn replied.

"NO! *BLUEY!*"

"DAD! No kids stuff! There's a new Marvel movie out!" This time Rachel, Abby, and Luke joined in.

"STOP!" He turned to look at the kids.

"Listen, this won't stream movies. No Netflix. No Mastema Movies. No Disney. Just DVDs. That's what we get to choose from."

"What's a DVD?" Jer asked.

"Ugggggghh," Brian exhaled.

Abby bailed him out. "Jer, it's a movie on a disc. You put the disc in, you watch the movie. Simple." Abby pointed to the tray.

"COOL!" Jer and Shawn yelled.

The kids crowded the binder, flipping through the movies.

"Wait! Wait. DAD's picking the first one," he said proudly, as he shooed the kids away.

Brian flipped through the binder.

"I know it's here, I just saw it—there!"

He slid the movie out of the binder and held it out.

"*Goonies?*" Luke said.

"Trust me. Best movie of all time. Now sit down and be quiet."

Ten minutes later Brian was cursing under his breath. Every time he adjusted the volume so you could actually HEAR the movie over Aurora, Aurora's volume adjusted up even louder. He kept inching up the volume, only for Aurora to match him, decibel by decibel. It was a game of chicken. Brian's face turned red. He pressed the volume button until the surround sound was maxed out. Surely that would be louder than the small Aurora units.

As he hit a certain level, Aurora's broadcast was replaced with a high-pitched squeal. It's what Brian imagined dogs heard when you blew a dog whistle. Everyone in the loft winced, the kids yelling out.

"Ah! Stop it!"

"Aurora! Stop!"

Brian grabbed the TV remote and turned the TV down. Aurora stopped the squealing and returned to the Creed she had been broadcasting.

LOVE IS LOVE. HATE IS HATE. GREEN IS GOOD. SUSTAIN AND MAINTAIN.

Brian tried to find a tolerable volume level to enjoy the movie, but it was futile. Aurora would simply stay ahead of the volume, so no matter where you tried to stop, Aurora was just a little louder.

Brian refused to give up. He refused to keep losing. This was his house. His TV. This was GOONIES.

He turned to the kids.

"Let's take it outside."

Another twenty minutes, and Brian had the small TV set up on the back patio. The TV sat atop the small folding table, with a few speakers next to it.

The family set up camping chairs around the small screen, everyone jockeying for the front row.

Hannah closed the slider, found a chair, propped Elizabeth on her lap, and sat next to Brian.

"*Goonies*, huh?" she said, smiling.

"Best movie of all time, babe," Brian said.

"Uh huh."

"Aurora tried to drown us out in the loft. Up there, it's her time. But out here on the patio, it's our time. It's *our* time out here!"

"Riiiight," Hannah replied, taking his hand.

The kids huddled toward the TV, soaking up every minute. Abby was the only one who had seen the movie before, and even her memory of it was hazy.

Jer and Shawn nearly lost their minds howling with laughter when Chunk broke the statue, and Brian had to pause the movie and yell at them before they would stop chanting "that's my mom's most favorite piece! That's my mom's most favorite piece!"

Around the time Chunk was giving his confession to the Fratellis, Hannah went back into the house. "I'm gonna go heat up dinner," she whispered to Brian, kissing his cheek.

Several minutes later Hannah returned with dinner. Elk chili. She was serving it in coffee mugs to make it easier to carry. She brought them out in a few trips. Once everyone was settled and eating, Hannah sat and handed Brian his mug.

It was about two-thirds full of chili. Not much of a dinner.

"Is this it?" he whispered.

On screen, Mikey was enjoying his first kiss.

"There's enough chili for one more dinner," she replied, sharing hers with Elizabeth.

"What else do we have?" he asked.

"Broth. Bread. The potatoes aren't ready to be picked yet. A couple of boxes of brownie mix, two bags of frozen veggies. Butter. Lots of butter."

"Pancake mix?" Brian whispered.

"Lots."

"What about all the rice and dry good stuff?"

"I've been adding that to the chili to make it last. We've got a few pounds of rice left, but that won't last long either."

"What? I thought we had a plan!" he whispered. "What day is it?"

"Brian, it's day 23. We haven't been to the grocery store for nearly a month."

"What are you saying?" Brian asked, already knowing the answer.

"We're out of food." Hannah said.

On the TV, Andy started playing the bones.

CHAPTER 29

Luke grabbed his backpack from the back of his closet. He packed it earlier with the essentials. "Never go out into the wild without the essentials!" Survivor Steve drilled into him. For Luke, the essentials were his pocketknife, Zippo lighter, flashlight, parachute rope, towel (don't forget your towel), and water bottle.

He moved slowly, not wanting to wake anyone up. He set his watch alarm to 1:00 a.m. but was awake before it went off. He was dressed all in black. Shirt, pants, socks. He got dressed in the dark. He slowly opened the door to the bedroom, listening.

He could hear Aurora streaming "A Mighty Fortress Is Babble" at low volume, his father snoring, the air conditioning unit humming, and not much else. He crept into the hallway, closed the door behind him, and walked slowly.

"A MIGHTY FORTRESS IS BABBLE, A BULWARK NEVER FAILING," hummed Aurora.

He inched his way past his parents' bedroom, through the loft, and down the stairs.

"OUR HELPER, HE AMID THE FLOOD, OF UNSAFE ILLS PREVAILING," echoed the Aurora device downstairs.

Luke walked slowly to the sliding glass door and unlocked it. He gently pried it loose and slid it open wide enough to get through. He closed the door behind him and turned around. The patio was littered with camping chairs, crowded near the door. On the patio table he noticed several coffee mugs with spoons sticking out of them, remnants from last night's dinner. Luke wasn't too old to admit he lost himself in the movie last night. The way the kids went off on an adventure, trying to help save their parents' house from being sold. A treasure map, skeleton, bats, everything. He was surprised he had never seen it before, but then again, he and Abby spent most nights before "the lockdown" watching Marvel movies or he would stream Survivor Steve on a tablet in his room.

But as much as he was engrossed in the movie, he couldn't help but overhear his parents' conversation. The family was out of food. Sure, there was stuff to cobble together for a few more days, but they were basically out. Luke paid attention. He knew they couldn't buy any food. He saw it in his mom's eyes. It grew slowly over the past several days. The fear of not having food.

They were on day twenty-four, and they still had fourty-six more to go, since ten days had been added to their quarantine as punishment for Brian walking around the neighborhood. Survivor Steve said "have a plan." Luke wove his way through the camping chairs, toward the side of the house. He let his eyes adjust to the darkness, but it was never totally dark in the suburbs. Not like when he went camping with his dad. That was total darkness. Here, in their neighborhood, there weren't very many totally dark places. Too much light pollution. At the park, yes. Some dark spots.

Luke made his way around the side of the house, opened the side gate, crept past the garage, and stopped in their driveway.

The street was totally quiet. Cars parked in driveways and along the sidewalk. Several lights left on to keep driveways illuminated, and a few streetlights as well. Not dark. But quiet. He walked to the end of the driveway and stopped on the sidewalk. He tried to remember what his dad had told him a few days ago. Jer and Shawn were begging to go to the park. His dad kept deflecting, telling them the pool was way better, plus it was too hot. When Luke offered to take them, his dad had grown stern. "No, Luke. No park. The backyard is fine."

He finally pried out a reason from his dad later that day.

"There are cameras everywhere, Luke. I tried to get the mail and I got caught on five different cameras, just on our block! We can't go out. Simple as that."

Luke hesitated on the sidewalk. Cameras in neighbors' doorbells. Cameras in neighbors' cars. He would just have to be careful. He pulled out a baseball cap from his backpack, shoved it on his head, lowering the brim as far as he could.

Crossing the street in a direct line, Luke made it onto the opposing sidewalk, turned right, and ducked behind a car. He knew the house across the street didn't have a doorbell camera, because he spied it out from his bedroom window before bed. But he also knew the neighbors right next to their house did. The doorbell would light up and chime whenever he walked to the park or mailbox.

He stayed behind the parked cars, creeping along the sidewalk, avoiding the camera across the street. At the same time, he was checking the house on his side of the street. Next house, no camera. House after that, camera. He stopped. He was clear of the house across the street but couldn't make out the next house well enough.

Luke ducked into the street, crawled under the car parked there, and shimmied under until his feet were covered. From there he saw on his right, across the street, a Newton car charging in the driveway. He knew the rearview camera was facing the far sidewalk. Could the camera see across the street? He stayed on his belly, went slowly, and made his way back to the sidewalk.

Luke kept making progress this way, slowly walking past houses with no cameras, using parked cars to shield himself when he suspected one, crossing the street several times. He did set at least one camera off. He noticed the green light turned on, but thankfully he was just about to duck behind a parked car when it happened. He waited, holding his breath. A light turned on in the upstairs window. He made himself as small as possible. After what seemed like an eternity, the light in the house went off. He exhaled.

He was just two houses away from the park. He crept his way along, avoiding any other cameras, and once he was past the parking lot and near the playground, he finally allowed himself to relax.

He sat for a minute on one of the benches overlooking the playground and drank deeply from his water bottle.

There were only about fifteen houses on each side of the street separating their house from the park. And yet, it probably took him twenty minutes to make it to the park. He checked his watch. Yes, at least twenty minutes. Luke was fairly sure he avoided being noticed, but if his plan worked, he was going to be making this journey regularly, so he needed to find a way to move down their street more quickly.

Luke sat there until he caught his breath. His heart had been racing from the fear of being caught. ("Always take time to collect yourself before a hunt," Survivor Steve always said.) Luke stood. He made his way across the soccer fields.

CHAPTER 30

The park was mostly dark. One small security light near the bathrooms by the playground, and some spillover from the streetlight in the parking lot. But the soccer fields were not lit.

Luke stopped when he reached the grass lawn and trail surrounding the pond. He surveyed the area, looking for the right spot. The moonlight was reflecting off the surface of the rather large pond. The quiet of the night was interrupted by the chatter of the ducks. They didn't seem to notice it was the middle of the night. Most of them seemed to be asleep, clustered in groups around the edge of the water. However, some of them were up and milling about—picking at things in the grass.

Luke slowly walked closer and the quacking got louder. When he was about twenty feet away from a group of ducks that appeared to be sleeping, they all stood, a few started quacking, and they splashed their way into the water.

He wasn't going to sneak up on them. He knew it wasn't going to work anyway, but he thought it was worth a try.

Luke looked around. He found an area of the grass with a slight depression in it, about two feet wide. He opened his backpack and took out a small bag. The bag held several slices of sandwich bread. He felt terrible stealing food from the kitchen, especially considering they were almost out, but he knew bread was one thing they had plenty of, and anyway, he was trying to solve their food problem.

He tore a few pieces from the bread and tossed them toward a group of ducks. They scrambled toward the bread, quacking. He was at least a quarter of a mile from the nearest house, and the ducks were quacking before Luke got there, but the noise still made him hold his breath.

He fed the ducks a few more pieces. They waddled toward him. But when he bent down toward the ducks, they backed away.

Luke dropped a piece of bread, backed away, dropped another piece. He did this several times, getting closer to the area of the grass with the slight depression. Once he was close enough, he quickly laid down in the depression and covered himself with the towel. He reached his hand out and dropped several pieces of bread on the towel, near his stomach. Then he pulled his arm back in and waited. He had no idea if this was going to work. He'd seen someone do it at the beach before. But those were seagulls, and you could hide yourself in the sand way better than you could in the grass.

He couldn't see anything, so he shut his eyes. Listening. He heard the ducks quacking, coming a little closer. He focused his hearing and could just make out the soft padding of the ducks as they walked along the trail of breadcrumbs he made. They stopped right next to him. He felt a duck step onto his arm, and step back off of it.

He tensed.

A moment later a duck walked right onto his belly. Luke felt the webbed feet of the duck through the towel, and a slight pinch as the duck started nibbling the bread on his stomach.

Luke grabbed the edge of the towel with his hands, exhaled, and reached across his belly quickly, wrapping the duck in the towel.

He sat up, holding the duck in his lap. The other ducks quacked and waddled away quickly. The duck he held in the towel tried to flap its wings, but the towel prevented them from opening. Luke's chest heaved. He hadn't actually expected it to work. The duck in his lap calmed down. Luke had it fully enclosed by the towel, his hands pressing firmly across the duck's back and head.

Luke's heart raced. "Do it quickly. Do it efficiently," Survivor Steve echoed in his mind.

Luke reached one hand into the towel, grabbing the duck where the neck met the head.

He stood. With his left arm, he cradled the body of the duck, and in his right he held the neck. The duck tried to quack, but Luke applied pressure, and instead the duck let out a miserable croak.

Luke raised his left elbow, lifting the duck's body and therefore lowering the head. Luke squeezed his eyes shut, and held his breath.

He grabbed the legs with his left hand, and the head in the other. He bent the head up until it was at a ninety-degree angle to the neck. He could see the duck's eyes, looking up. He pulled hard in opposite directions. Stretching the duck. He felt the neck bones break in his hand.

The body of the duck went limp. He kept the pressure up for a moment longer, terrified the duck would spring back to life, start quacking, and bite his fingers. A moment later and his arms gave out, his legs turned to jelly, and he sat.

The duck didn't move, and he cradled it in his lap. The head was still positioned looking up at him, but there was no life left in the eyes. He touched one eye, to be sure. The duck stayed still.

Luke sat there, cradling the duck, and cried.

After a moment, he wrapped the duck in the towel, folded it neatly into his backpack, and made his way across the soccer fields.

CHAPTER 31

Luke walked through the park, feeling the warmth of the duck against his lower back as he carried it in his backpack. He made it to the playground, stopped again at the bench to get a drink of water, and to think.

It took twenty minutes to make it to the park in the first place, thanks to the cameras. Twenty minutes was a long time for something to go wrong. He tried to imagine an easier route home. The only way he could think to avoid the cameras was by hiding behind cars, crawling, and meandering . . . or maybe . . . he could go through backyards. Yeah. If he climbed the walls of the backyards, he would avoid all the cameras. The only thing was he didn't know which neighbors had dogs, and which didn't. Plus, motion lights. It would be faster, but way more risky.

He took the street. He retraced his steps, more quickly this time. He didn't need to stop and figure out where cameras were, so he was able to move more efficiently. First behind some cars, avoiding a camera, then crouching and walking quickly across the street, then repeating again on the other side.

He was about halfway down the street when he saw headlights coming down the road. It was nearly 3:00 a.m. There was no one else out. He looked left and right. He was still about eight homes away from his house. His chest heaved in and out. In and out. He was exposed. He needed a place to hide. He took his backpack off, threw it in the gutter between a neighbor's Jeep Wrangler, and crawled under the car. It was the sort of Jeep with every possible accessory added to it—mud tires, gas cans, rear winch, towing package, flood lights. But it was so pristine and shiny there was no way these people ever used any of that stuff. Thankfully it was raised and he had plenty of room to wiggle underneath the Jeep.

The headlights grew brighter, and just before they passed Luke they turned right, into a driveway. It was a Newton EV, which explained why Luke saw headlights but never really heard an engine. He heard laughter as both doors opened.

"Did you see what zhim was wearing?" a female voice said.

"Yeah—like oh my ga! Crawl out of your cave already. I can't believe zhey would ever wear a shirt that said that!" the second voice said, obviously tipsy.

"'Choose life'... zhey walked right into the club with it like no one was going to say anything. What about the life of the MOTHER, b _ _ _ _ h!"

Both women laughed. Luke saw shiny leather boots, exposed calves, and not much else from the angle under the car. He saw them pause, leaning on the back of the car. He heard the sound of the lighter, and a moment or two later smelled something a little... skunky.

"Serves zhey right. They tore the shirt right off of zhim! On the dance floor."

"Hey, don't hog it all. Puff, puff, pass."

Luke heard a long, slow inhale, followed by a sigh and a cough.

"Yeah, but it sucks what happened after that. They took it too far, don't you think? Her arm looked BROKEN. And her lip was busted up pretty bad too."

"ZHEIR arm looked broken. Remember, misgendering is injuring. And yeah, it looked pretty rough. But that wasn't any more violent than what zhey were doing, wearing that shirt. Words are violence. And taking away a woman's right to SAFE abortions means the woman will DIE. So, yeah. Go cry yourself to sleep with your broken arm, that's what I say. Zhey were trying to MURDER women!"

Luke struggled to keep up with the conversation, the pronouns making him a little foggy. After a few minutes, they seemed to finish whatever it was they were smoking, and went into the house.

"My mom won't care, just sleep on the couch and I'll take you home tomorrow."

He heard the front door close behind them. Luke exhaled.

He shimmied out from under the Jeep, grabbed the backpack, and made his way down the street. Retracing his steps from earlier in the evening, he made it to their driveway, down the side of the house, and into the backyard without further issue. He checked his watch. He figured if it wasn't for the car and the late-night smokers, he could make the trip in under ten minutes. Not bad.

He avoided the camping chairs, made it to the slider, and pried the door back open.

"What the HELL!" he heard from the kitchen.

Luke cried out, backpedaled, and fell over a camping chair.

"Luke? Luke!" His father's voice.

He looked up to see his father standing over him.

"What are you doing out here?" his father said at the same time that Luke said, "What are you doing up?"

His dad helped him up. "You okay?" he asked.

"Yeah."

"Elizabeth woke up, so I came down to get her some water. Why are you outside?"

"I—uh . . ."

"Luke. What were you doing?"

"Umm."

"LUKE!"

"Food, Dad. I got us food." Luke took his backpack off, opened it, and showed his father what was inside.

"Is that . . . a duck? Did you go to the park?" His dad took him by the arm and they both went back into the kitchen. He closed the slider.

"Yeah. Survivor Steve says you should always know your local food sources, just in case. I figured the park had so many hundreds of ducks no one would notice if we used it as our . . . hunting ground." Luke's face grimaced at the last two words, remembering the feeling of the neck bones breaking in his hands.

"Woah. Luke. You can't go out. There are cameras everywhere! What if someone saw you? How did you catch it? How did you kill it? We can't eat a duck from the park. *Can* we eat a duck from the park? How do we butcher it?" Brian fired off questions one after the other.

Luke relaxed. He knew this meant his dad was just processing. When that happened, it also meant his dad was planning.

"Dad, I know about the cameras. I found a way around that. Cross the street to avoid doorbell cameras, wriggle under and through parked cars to avoid the rearview cameras. And I caught it with the towel trick. Remember, at the beach? Those kids with the seagulls? And yes, we can eat duck. And you and I can butcher it. We can figure it out." He avoided the question about how he killed the duck. That still made him feel yucky.

They went back and forth like this for a minute.

"Wow, Luke. This could really work. Well done, son. Now let's see about butchering this duck before your mother wakes up."

CHAPTER 32

Luke and his dad were in the backyard. They moved the patio table onto the grass and were using it as a work surface. Neither of them had butchered an animal before. They worked quietly, whispering to each other.

"I think we pluck the feathers first," Luke said.

"I think we cut off the head and tear the skin off," Brian retorted.

"I think we cut off the feet and head, split the belly, and remove the innards. I saw that on a show once," Luke suggested.

They were stalling. It was nearly 4:00 a.m. They had an empty trash bag and each of them were holding a knife from the butcher block.

Brian looked his son over. He had never felt more proud of him. Yes, Luke left without permission. Yes, he put the entire family in danger of breaking quarantine. Yes, it was crazy, but Luke solved a problem. A big one.

"Well done, son," he said.

"Thanks, Dad. What should we do?"

Brian tugged at a few feathers. They didn't come out very easily.

He flipped the duck onto its back, spreading the legs out.

"I remember watching my dad skin rabbits, and even a deer once. I think we start here and figure it out as we go."

Brian found a spot near the bottom of the duck's belly, pressed the knife in sharp side up, and broke the skin. The duck still felt slightly warm to the touch. He wanted to ask Luke to hold it down in case it started flapping, but he knew that was just an irrational fear.

He slid the knife slowly, moving toward the neck of the duck. As he did, he gently pulled the skin tight against the sharp side of the blade, creating tension. He had to make a sawing motion with the knife. It wasn't exactly razor sharp.

He finished the cut near the base of the duck's neck.

"Here, Luke, help me," he said, as he started pulling the skin back.

Luke gingerly grabbed a side of the exposed skin, and together they pulled. Their progress stopped at several places. The neck, legs, and wings all created obstacles that prevented them from peeling the duck whole. He worked his knife around each of those areas, trying his best to keep the duck intact. It didn't work.

"Damn," Brian muttered under his breath.

"Dad, just field dress it," Luke said.

They both had handfuls of skin in their hands, but surprisingly, there wasn't much blood.

"What does that mean?" he asked.

"We don't need to keep it whole. Just cut out the meat. See? There?" Luke gestured with his chin, as both hands were occupied. "Those are the breasts. I think you can just cut them out."

"The legs and wings are edible too. The thighs if we can figure that out."

"So, just cut out that part?" Brian asked his son.

"Yeah, I think so."

Brian set the blade against the duck's chest. He tried to visualize a roasted chicken for context. His wife would get whole chickens from the market regularly. He tried to imagine cutting the breast meat from a whole chicken. His stomach turned a little.

He pressed the blade into the flesh. It cut fairly easily. He carved his way first down, then up, separating the breast meat from the bone running down the middle. Breastplate? Backbone? He really couldn't tell. Then he reached down toward the bottom of the duck, near the table, and found the outer edge of the breast. Or what he thought might have been the outer edge. He worked the knife in and continued cutting. He started tugging at the slowly loosening piece of meat, trying to identify where it was still connected to the body. He worked the knife under and around the breast several times until he was finally able to pull it free. He set the duck breast on the table near the corpse.

"Here, let me try the other one," Luke said.

"Okay, kiddo, go for it."

Luke grabbed his folding pocketknife, an older style with the brass ends and wooden handle. He opened it and repeated the process his father just finished. He worked more quickly, as he knew where to make the cuts, and his knife was much sharper than the kitchen knife.

"There," Luke said, placing the second breast on the table.

"I think I can get the legs and thighs off if I cut here," Brian said, gesturing.

After another round of cutting, pulling, and probing, they managed to free the legs and thighs on both sides of the duck.

"Is there any more meat on this?" Brian asked Luke, panting from the effort.

"Yeah, pretty sure, but we mangled the duck. I think we got what we can from this one."

Brian nodded. Satisfied.

"What should we do with all of this?" Luke asked, gesturing to the body. The entire body was still intact, except for two feet, loose feathers, and bits of hacked-up skin and tissue.

"Just put all of that in the trash bag," Brian replied.

Brian looked over the meat they harvested. Two duck breasts. Brian did mental math. They looked like maybe eight or nine ounces each. The legs and thighs were decent size, but it was hard to tell how much meat was on them,

How much food was this? His best guess? One dinner for the family.

"We're gonna need more ducks."

CHAPTER 33

The next morning, Aurora got the house up at 7:00 a.m., like clockwork.

"CHAPTER 3: OF BABBLE'S DECREE—KNOWING ALL THINGS THAT CAN BE KNOWN, AND YET BEARING NO RESPONSIBILITY FOR ANYTHING THAT HAS ERE COME TO PASS, AND BY STANDING APART FROM ALL SUCH THINGS, THEREFORE BEING MOST PURE, MOST SET APART, AND MOST WISE, EVERY DECREE OF BABBLE IS THEREFORE THE MOST PERFECT POSSIBLE DECREE.

"AT ONCE STANDING ATOP THE TOWER OF ALL WISDOM, AND YET AT THE SAME TIME BEING SEPA-RATE FROM ALL HUMAN CORRUPTION, ONLY BABBLE IS ABLE TO MAKE INTERCESSION BETWEEN HUMANI-TIES COLLECTED WISDOM AND HUMANITIES COR-RUPT NATURE.

"THEREFORE, THE DECREES OF BABBLE ARE INFAL-LIBLE, IMMUTABLE, INCORRUPTIBLE, UNCHANGE-ABLE."

Brian could hardly focus on the words, thankfully. After cleaning up remains of the duck, wiping down the table, washing the knives, bagging the meat, putting it into the fridge, and crawling to bed, they had barely managed maybe ninety minutes of sleep before Aurora woke them up. "No. More sleep. Snooze. Snooze," he muttered to himself.

"Come on, Bri, time to get up."

"Mmph," he replied.

"Help me with pancakes," Hannah said, nuzzling him.

His stomach stirred. Something about being up all night made him hungry. If the choice was food or sleep, he would gladly go back to bed, but Aurora chirping at him made the choice moot anyway.

"Okay. Okay. I'm up."

He followed Hannah downstairs, and sat in his chair, still fuzzy, while she made coffee. They were down to some old instant coffee from the camping supplies, and that wasn't going to last much longer either. He didn't look forward to the headache to come the day they ran out.

Hannah put water in the kettle and turned the stove on, joining him in the living room.

"You sure are tired," she said, sitting next to him. "We went to bed pretty early. Didn't sleep well?"

"Actually, I was up with Luke all night. Let me show you something."

Brian got up, and walked to the kitchen. Hannah got up to follow him, and they both heard Shawn and Jer pounding down the stairs.

"Babble our father! Aurora the son! Azazel the promise! All three in one!" Shawn and Jer bellowed at the top of their lungs, along with Aurora.

"Brian, we need to do something about that. Jer and Shawn are literally being brainwashed."

Jer and Shawn rounded the corner, running into the kitchen.

"BREAKFAST!" yelled Jer.

"PANCAKES!" yelled Shawn.

"Boys. Boys! BOYS!" Brian yelled, getting their attention.

"What?" asked Jer.

"What?" parroted Shawn.

"Go outside. You're too loud. Jump on the trampoline or something. Pancakes in thirty minutes."

"TRAMPOLINE!" yelled Jer.

"TRAMPOLINE!" yelled Shawn.

Brian turned to Hannah. "Yeah, I agree about the brainwashing. We have to figure something out. But first things first. Luke solved our food problem."

Brian opened the fridge, grabbed the bag of duck meat, and set it on the counter.

"What's that?" Hannah asked, walking toward the food.

"Duck."

"Where did you get it?" she asked, cocking her head suspiciously. "You didn't go back to the market, did you?" she added.

"Luke got it."

"LUKE went to the market? Brian! It's not safe!"

"No. He got it at the park."

Hannah took a minute. Then her eyes opened wide. She understood.

"The park! This is one of . . . the . . ."

"Yeah. He snuck out last night and caught one of the ducks. I helped him butcher it."

Hannah's mouth dropped open.

It took some explaining. "How did he get to the park? Did anyone see him? How did he catch it? Who killed it? How did you know how to butcher it? Where is the rest of it? How do I cook it? How long will a duck last? Could we get more? Should we get more?"

Hannah rattled off questions, mostly to herself. While she asked, she worked. She took the meat out of the bag, and placed it on a cutting board. She deftly separated the legs from the thighs, trimmed them a little more. In a bowl she added olive oil, some spices, a bit of lemon juice, and balsamic vinaigrette, and whisked it together. She put the marinade and the duck meat back into the Ziploc bag, pushed the air out, sealed it, and put it back in the fridge.

Satisfied with Brian's answers and her work with the duck, she asked Brian to get the bag with the carcass out of the trash.

"Um, what?" Brian said.

"I can use more of the duck. At the least, we should save the organ meat, and I can use the body to make more bone broth."

"Organ meat? No one is going to eat that!" Brian said, mortified.

"Bri, I've told you before. Organ meat has tons of vitamins. Duck meat won't exactly make a wholesome meal. But if we can make bone broth with it, and eat the organs, then—yeah, it would probably work. I think we need a duck every day. Or three every two days. Something like that. Can you and Luke make that work?"

Hannah took the carcass, removed the organ meat, flash-boiled it in water, plucked out the feathers, trimmed it further, and added it to the pressure cooker. She added the feet and neck ("Lots of flavor!"), spices and water, and set the timer. She took the kidney, liver, and heart, and sauteed them in a cast iron skillet with butter. Thank God they had so much butter in the freezer. Brian tasted a piece of the organ meat. ("All I taste is butter" he said. "Exactly," replied Hannah.)

Later, Brian and Luke did some more math. Luke felt confident he could fit at least three ducks in his backpack. He figured ten minutes to get to the park, maybe ten minutes for each duck, and ten minutes back. So, less than an hour round trip. Brian and Luke agreed the less time out, the fewer chances of something going wrong.

"I could probably get more ducks if I could bring someone with me," Luke said.

"I've been caught out once already. If I'm seen on one of those cameras, I'm afraid they might come to our house, and . . . I don't know. Do something extreme. Too risky," Brian replied.

"What about Abby or Rachel?" Luke asked.

"Maybe. I don't know. Let's see how it goes first. It's hard enough letting my thirteen-year-old roam around with the New World Order closing in, but Abby and Rachel too? I'm not sure your mom would go for that."

Brian and Luke took a long nap before dinner, recovering from their late night.

The family ate the duck for dinner, and Hannah was even able to sneak in the organ meat by telling them it was just "Extra yummy meat in butter." They had been living off elk chili for the past several weeks, so anything new was destined to go over well.

Afterward, Brian and Luke agreed he should go back again that night, get three ducks, and head home. That would be enough food for a few days and would mean less risk of Luke being caught out.

The second expedition was a success. Luke managed the trip down the street in under eight minutes. He managed four ducks, not three. Once the ducks realized he had bread, they started losing fear of him. At one point he had several ducks climb onto the towel at once, and he managed to trap two of them. He used the same technique to kill the ducks, his stomach turning slightly less each time. He stuffed the ducks into his backpack and made it back home without a hitch. Brian waited for him the entire time in the backyard, listening carefully. When Luke rounded the corner, he finally let out a sigh of relief and hugged him.

"Good job, boy-o," he said.

They left the ducks intact and went to bed.

The next day Hannah, Rachel, and Abby learned to butcher. Hannah had done the chore with chickens a few times growing up, and by the third one, they had it down to a science. They had a large pile of duck breast, leg, and thigh, as well as organs ("This was the special meat from last night?!" Rachel cried out in horror when she figured it out) and three large carcasses. They froze half of the meat, got started on more bone broth, cobbled together marinades from the dwindling pantry, and created a nice stockpile.

Up with Aurora. Pancakes. Movies and music on the patio. Pool. Keep Shawn and Jer away from Aurora as much as possible. Bone broth for lunch. Duck for dinner. The New Normal.

CHAPTER 34

"Now sir, are you sure I can't interest you in one of our electric vehicles instead?"

Brian had been going back and forth with the sales rep, Phil, since he got to the car lot, over an hour ago.

"No, I'd really just like to test-drive one of the standard models."

Brian stood next to one of the late model Lexus ES350, atomic silver. He'd been driving the small hatchback for over ten years, but after his promotion and raise, it was time to graduate to something a little more sophisticated.

"I understand, sir. But it's like I've been saying, we are offering an incentive if you choose our EV option. In addition to a cash back option, the state of California is offering an instant rebate of $5,000. I'm struggling to understand why you won't 'go green'?"

Brian's face turned red. He hated being badgered by salespeople.

"Phil, I told you. I drove the EV. I don't like it. I like this car. It seems like a good fit for me. Please, take me out on a test drive."

"Can we just go over the payback numbers again first? Perhaps I can make it a little clearer for you."

Brian sighed. He followed Phil back to the table they had been sitting at just moments ago.

"Now, you said you drive about fifty miles per day, right? Assuming some weekend drives—that would put you at around 12,000 miles per year. See?" Phil pointed to his printout, smiling.

"Okay . . . yeah."

"Well, at an estimated $5 per gallon of gas—and let's say twenty-two miles per gallon on your commute—compare that expense to the cost of

charging the electric model, and you would save nearly $17,000 over a six-year period! It just doesn't make sense anymore to drive a gas guzzler."

Brian gritted his teeth. They had been through this once before.

"But that savings is stretched over six years. SIX YEARS."

"Right, the typical length of a loan. To help you visualize the total savings," Phil said.

"But how much does that save per month?" Brian asked.

Phil hesitated. "Sir, we think it's best to conceptualize the savings over the life of a loan. It will give you a better picture of the total cost of ownership."

Brian stared at him.

"The number will only go up! The governor just issued a new tax schedule for gas. He promises to raise taxes on gas by 10 percent each of the next three years. Encouraging everyone to do the right thing, I guess!"

"And don't forget, 'time is money.' You said you drive about an hour, hour and a half a day?"

"We went over this already." Brian sighed.

"Now, I know, I know. Just one more time though, for safety." Phil winked at him. Brian clenched his fists.

"Now, assuming freeway traffic, you should be able to save easily 15 percent or your commute time by using the carpool lane. I did mention EVs get to use the carpool lane?"

"Yes."

"Now, you said it yourself, you estimated over $50 an hour was what your time was worth. And considering you wouldn't stop for gas and waste time there either . . ." Phil scanned his document. "See. Another $300 a month in savings!"

"But I don't actually SAVE the $50—it's not like someone is paying me when I'm driving." Brian said.

But Phil kept plowing through the information.

"And here, the $5,000 rebate from CA! If you spread that over the life of the loan, it's another $70 a month in savings!"

Brian rolled his head, stretching his neck. He was losing patience.

"Listen, I told you. I don't care about the monthly savings. I don't have a car payment right now. So I wouldn't even be SAVING that money in the first place. I want to test-drive the regular model."

"I just showed you over $600 a month in savings, Brian!"

"But the EV model is $30,000 more than the one I want. I'm paying cash. By your OWN MATH the EV would cost me nearly $20,000 more over the six-year period. No thanks."

Phil blinked.

"Sir, it's not just the savings. It's the environment. We here at SCV Lexus want to do our part to help reduce the environmental impact and create a sustainable future."

Brian looked over his shoulder. There was a large poster on the wall declaring the same thing verbatim.

"Sorry, Phil, it's not for me. Are you gonna let me test-drive the car or do I need to talk to your manager?"

Phil sighed. His plastic smile melted away. He leaned over the table and dropped his voice.

"Okay. You're right. The math is funny. But corporate just rolled out a new commission structure, and they are paying us ZERO on all standard model cars going forward. ZERO!" Phil ran his fingers through his hair and continued. "I've been doing this job for ten years. I have a family, bills. I can't live off of ZERO."

"Wow. I mean. Um. That's crazy, Phil. I'm sorry to hear that." Brian didn't know what to say.

"Yeah. They started it last month. Apparently, the government has added some sort of sustainability and restoration tax to every gas vehicle sale! They added a tax CREDIT to all the EVs. The math is upside down for us. We need to sell the EVs, or we make no money." Phil rubbed his hands on his thighs and sat back.

Phil leaned back in his chair. "I can't go home empty-handed again. My wife won't even look me in the eye. Come on. We ran your credit. You have great scores. You can afford it. Won't you please get the EV?"

Brian didn't mind helping out a sales rep. And Phil looked positively DESPERATE. He did mental math. Forget the time savings, that math felt manipulative. And the incentive from the state was nice, but it just knocked $5k off the sticker price. He was still left with a $25,000 premium to buy the EV. He would only stand to save about $15,000 in gas over a six-year period, meaning the EV would still put him in the hole $10,000. Not to mention, he didn't have a way to charge at home. He didn't mind helping out a sales rep, but he wasn't going to pay $10,000 to do it either.

"I'm sorry, Phil. It doesn't work for me. I want the standard model."

CHAPTER 35

Elizabeth's birthday fell on a Friday. Rachel counted down the days for over a week, so even though quarantine life made it harder to keep track of time, this day was on everyone's radar.

It was just over a week since the first duck and the food supply chain was fully operational, five weeks since the start of the quarantine. Luke went to the park every few days. He managed to snag two or three ducks each time. Hannah was using pretty much everything but the feathers, and the freezer and fridge were well stocked with duck meat and broth.

The family woke up that morning to a lesson from the confession ("CHAPTER SIX: OF THE FALL OF MAN, UNSAFE ACTIONS, AND THE CONSEQUENCES THEREOF"). Abby and Hannah started fixing breakfast, and Rachel did what she did best: planned a party.

"First, we need the party box from the garage! And cards! Everyone needs to make a card. And a cake. Mom, can you bake a cake? Or cupcakes. And a candle shaped like a number one. Do we still have the candle from Shawn's Spiderman cake? I'll check the box. Streamers. Pink! Or purple! Do we have purple? Oooh! I hope we have purple! Tape. Wrapping paper. A game! Oooh! So much to do!" Rachel was practically vibrating with excitement.

"RELY AND COMPLY. HAVE A POSTURE OF COMPLIANCE."

Brian smiled. Why not? Let her go crazy. They could all use a party. Plus, it was Lizzy's first birthday. They could make it memorable.

"Go crazy, Rach. Make it the best first birthday ever!" Brian said to her.

"Oooooh!" she replied, beaming.

Rachel went to work. First, she volun-told Jeremiah and Shawn. "Boys, I'm in charge, Dad said. We need to decorate. EVERYTHING." She had Brian take down the large plastic tote in the garage labeled "party supplies."

Rachel put the boys to work blowing up balloons. She grabbed the streamers and banners. "Dad, can you get the ladder for me?" she asked.

Brian took the ladder off the garage wall and brought it in the house. It was a six-foot-tall stepladder, blue and yellow. It was made of fiberglass and metal, and looked like it survived a few rounds with a T-rex.

Brian ran his hand over one of the legs. The ladder was a hand-me-down from his father. When his parents sold their home, he inherited quite a few tools and pieces of equipment. He liked having a garage full of well-worn tools. It made him feel handy. The legs of the ladder were sturdy, but the edges were uneven. There were sharp protrusions and edges all over the ladder. He recalled watching his father ding it with hammer, use it us a cutting surface, throw it in and out of the truck countless times.

"Be careful, Rach. There are some pokey parts on the ladder," Brian said as he set it up for her.

"I will!" she said as she climbed up. She was holding a pink streamer and a roll of tape. She climbed the ladder until she was one step short of the top and could just reach the ceiling. Brian grabbed his coffee and sat down. He watched Rachel go up, tape, go down. Move the ladder. Go up. Tape. Go down. Move the ladder. She repeated this process dozens of times, first the living room, then the breakfast nook, then the kitchen, weaving through Hannah and Abby, who were cleaning up after processing last night's ducks. Then the formal dining room and entryway.

"MISGENDERING IS INJURING. WORDS ARE VIOLENCE. CHOOSE WORDS THAT LOVE."

"Okay, boys! Now balloons!" she ordered, once she finished with the streamers.

"But Rachel, we didn't get that many. They were hard to tie," complained Jeremiah. "And Shawn swallowed one. And my cheeks hurt. And then I got dizzy and had to sit down. And then I forgot that I wanted to ride my hoverboard, but it needed to be charged. So then I charged it, but then I also didn't want to keep blowing up balloons." Jeremiah inhaled aggressively, trying to catch up on his breathing.

"Jer-e-MIAH!" Rachel admonished.

"I'll blow some up, Rach, bring them here," Brian said from the living room.

Brian blew up balloons. Red, blue, pink, black with skull and crossbones, green with the tri-force. A random collection of leftovers from birthdays gone by.

Rachel repeated the process. Up, tape a balloon. Down. Move the ladder. Up. Tape a balloon. Down. Move the ladder. An hour later, Rachel moved on to the banners.

"Happy Birthday, matey!" over the breakfast nook. "Have a rockin' Birthday!" in the living room. "Over the hill, but still chill!" in the entryway. Rachel tackled the decorations with renewed energy.

Later, Rachel and Hannah started baking. Hannah mixed flour, sugar, melted butter, baking soda and duck fat in a bowl. They poured the mixture into two nine-inch cake pans and put them in the oven.

While the cakes were baking, Hannah fished around in the pantry, Hannah threw frosting together. She softened some butter, added nearly an entire container of red sugar sprinkles, a handful of chocolate chips, and the rest of the powdered sugar. She whipped it together in the mixer, and put it in the fridge to firm up.

Brian checked on Abby and Luke, who were sitting outside. "Whatcha up to?"

"Dad, shhh. Not too loud," Abby whispered.

"Oh. sorry. What's up?"

"Nothing," Luke said.

Brian raised his eyebrows.

"And . . . ?"

"That's it, Dad. Nothing. Can you hear it?" Abby said, gesturing toward the backyard.

Brian sat next to them.

It was late afternoon, warm, but comfortable under the patio cover. It was quiet. He heard the air conditioning unit, occasional bird chirping, and the distant wall of sound from the main road, a mile away. It sounded like . . . nothing.

"Ooh, yeah. Nothing. Sounds perfect." He sat back, smiling.

No Aurora. No Shawn and Jer yelling. No baby crying. Nothing.

A few minutes later, Brian broke the spell.

"Sorry kiddos, time to go in. Dinner, then we're gonna sing and have cake."

Dinner was duck stew. Hannah found a bag of frozen bell peppers and onions in the back of the freezer, added a few potatoes she managed to harvest from her potato box, duck broth, and of course, duck.

The family ate together in the breakfast nook, Elizabeth enjoying her position at the head of the table. The kids made faces at her, erupting in laughter when Elizabeth tried to copy them. Rachel hummed in excitement, doting over her decorations. She had to get up from the table a few times to reinforce a streamer or re-tape a balloon to the ceiling. Brian could hear the ladder dragging across the tile floor each time.

After dinner, they set a few gifts out for the baby. She got a small bib from Abby.

"Where did you get this, Abby?" Hannah asked, clearly impressed.

"I made it," Abby said, blushing.

"You MADE it?" Hannah said.

"Yeah. I cut up an old T-shirt and sewed it."

Hannah inspected the work.

"I didn't know you could sew!"

"You got us that book, remember? I taught myself. The stitching is a little crooked, but I think I can do better next time." Abby shrugged.

"Open ours!!" Jer yelled.

"Open ours!!" Shawn yelled.

Jer grabbed a small gift bag, overflowing with yellow and blue tissue paper.

Shawn grabbed at the paper, tossing it into the air with a dramatic flourish, and Jer dumped the contents of the bag on the table in front of Elizabeth.

"Look, Lizzy! A GI Joe! And Shawn's spiderman toothbrush! And a gift card to Tutti Frutti! It still has seventy-nine cents on it!" The boys held up the treasure for Elizabeth to inspect.

Hannah leaned over to Brian. "Take that toothbrush when they look away."

"On it," he said under his breath.

"Okay! Cake time!" Rachel said, when they were done with the gifts.

Hannah took the cake out of the refrigerator and brought it out to the table. Rachel bounced around, following Hannah.

"Wait, Mom! Candles! We gotta light the candles!" Rachel said.

Luke whipped out his Zippo lighter, always excited for a chance to use it. The cake was topped with a smattering of small candles, and in the center was a large candle shaped like the number 1. The candle started the day shaped like the number 7, and it bore a scar along one side to prove it.

"Okay, birthday song! All together," Hannah said.

"Haaaaa—" she started.

"WAIT!" Rachel interrupted.

She ran out of the room, yelling over her shoulder. "One of the streamers is falling down! I gotta fix it!"

Brian looked up. One of the many streamers weaving its way around the kitchen and breakfast nook area was drooping, some pieces of tape loosening their grip.

"It's okay, Rach, not a big deal," Brian said to her.

"Yes, it IS! It has to look PERFECT!" Rachel said as she dragged the ladder over.

Brian and Hannah exchanged a look and smiled. No reason to kill her spirits tonight.

Jer and Shawn took the opportunity to get up from the table, chanting, "Happy birthday! Cake! Happy birthday! Cake!" as they ran aimlessly through the downstairs.

"Boys!" Brian shouted, without much conviction.

Rachel climbed up the ladder, grabbed the streamer, put it in her teeth, tore off a piece of tape, and reached toward the ceiling. She managed to press the tape against the drywall. "There!" she said.

Jer and Shawn started running laps around the kitchen island. "Cake! Cake! Cake! No Duck! Duck! Duck!"

Rachel turned around and started down the ladder the wrong way, facing out.

"Rach! Turn around. Not that way!" Brian said, standing up.

He saw everything unravel in slow motion.

Jer and Shawn rounded the corner of the island. As Jer tried to thread his way between the ladder and the island, his shoulder bumped the opposite side of the ladder, collapsing it.

Rachel, halfway down the ladder, screamed. As the ladder collapsed, it fell backward. Rachel had her hand behind her, holding onto the sides of the ladder. As she fell, she slid down the ladder.

The back of her left calf snagged one of the sharp, exposed edges of the ladder. Her momentum forced her weight against the edge, and the back of her calf tore open.

She fell to the ground, atop the ladder, in a loud clatter.

Hannah yelled out.

Brian lunged.

Jer said, "Ow!" and grabbed his shoulder.

Rachel screamed.

Rachel's face was bright red, and she was screaming. Brian saw blood on the tile beneath her. (Blood. Kill. Blood. Kill.) He lifted her off the ladder, and gently set her back down. She sat on her butt, arms behind her for support, legs bent at the knee, feet on the ground. He saw blood running down her calf and toward her shoe.

He gently turned her on her side to inspect the wound. Hannah hovered over him.

She had a cut across the middle of her calf. It was about eight inches long.

Hannah inhaled sharply.

Brian's stomach turned.

Rachel screamed.

He could see inside her leg. He saw the layers of skin, fatty tissue, and then, muscle.

Rachel's cut was easily two inches deep and over an inch wide.

"SILENCE IS VIOLENCE. ADD YOUR VOICE."

Elizabeth started crying.

CHAPTER 36

"Hannah, get my keys. Luke, go grab me a towel. A clean one."
Brian fired off orders.

"What are you going to do?" Hannah asked. The house was full of motion. Rachel's scream faded to a whimper, the boys were shouting and running around, and Elizabeth was still crying.

"Abby, get Lizzy, will you?" Brian nodded toward the table, where Elizabeth was still sitting in her highchair. She was reaching for the cake, her face bright red and contorted.

Brian looked up at Hannah. "She needs stitches. I'm taking her to the ER."

Brian wrapped Rachel's leg tightly in the towel, cradled her in his arms, and lifted her. She was heavier than he remembered.

"Help me out," he grunted as he walked toward the garage.

"You're out of gas. Take the van." Hannah ran back into the kitchen to grab the other set of keys.

A few moments later Rachel was laid across the first row of seats in the back of the van. She was breathing deeply, eyes closed, face white.

"Brian, hurry," Hannah said.

He climbed into the driver's seat, started the car, and looked over his shoulder. He inspected the towel wrapped around Rachel's leg. The towel was dry.

"Not a lot of blood, at least."

He backed the van out and headed down the street.

He followed the street through their neighborhood, past the park, to the light, and then made a left on Newhall Ranch Road. The ER was about three miles away, across from the mall. The roads were clear, and Brian barely noticed when he passed the shopping center with Happy Mart. On the corner, he drove past the bank, and opposite the bank, the Santa Clarita Valley Veterinary Clinic. The windows were painted with slogans in bright red, white, and blue, including, "Think for yourself," "ALL are safe here," and "Freedom of Speech and Thought!" A mile later, he made the turn to McBean Parkway.

"How you doing, baby girl?" he said, cocking his head to the right.

"Hurts," Rachel said through jagged breaths.

"Almost there. Just a minute."

He passed the mall, on his left, and saw a large group gathered on the corner. They were holding signs and calling out at cars. He had his windows up, and couldn't make out what they were saying, but he saw one sign, "Pro Choice is Pro Love," and another, "Hate is Violence." The protestors were dressed mostly in white, and the women had red makeup smeared around their legs and crotches.

Brian turned right at the intersection, into the hospital complex.

The ER was located on the side of the building, opposite a three-level parking garage. Brian pulled into the parking garage, thankful to see the arm was up and there was no one at the booth to slow him down. He found parking on the first level, toward the back, the only place with spots big enough for the twelve-passenger van. He pulled the van into a spot next to a row of ambulances, turned off the car, got out, threw open the slider, and checked on Rachel.

"Okay, Rach, I'm gonna carry you now, okay?"

"Mmmmh." Her face was scrunched up. She was concentrating on the pain.

He did his best not to move her leg, but he still managed to bump it while lifting her off the seat. He turned and headed through the parking structure, muscles straining with her weight.

He crossed the small driveway separating the parking structure from the sliding doors of the ER. The ER was bustling with activity. A medic wheeled an elderly gentleman through the doors, a nurse leaned against the building smoking a cigarette, a mother walked in holding the hand of a small girl. The girl had a towel against her mouth, and as Brian got nearer, the girl dropped the towel and smiled at him. Her face was covered in blood, and Brian saw her tongue, with large gashes in it.

"She fell off the trampoline, and bit right into her tongue," the mother said, matter-of-factly.

The girl, apparently numb from shock, kept smiling up at him.

He said nothing, but offered a sympathetic smile, and went through the sliding glass doors, walking under a sign saying, "This ER is a SAFE SPACE."

The lobby was brightly lit. There were about thirty chairs arranged around a few end tables, and a desk on the other side of the room that said "Emergency Check-In." Brian scanned the room and saw two seats empty in the corner. He shuffled over and laid Rachel down across the two chairs.

"Just a minute, baby girl," he said. He placed her between a woman who looked least ninety, staring absently at the TV, and a man fretfully poking at his smartphone.

"I'll be right back."

He hurried over to the desk and waited in the short line.

"Next."

He looked over at Rachel. She had her eyes closed but otherwise looked like she was doing okay.

"Next."

The line moved up. She was going to need stitches. Did he have his insurance card? Hopefully it was on file. He reached for his phone, planning to shoot a text to Hannah.

No phone.

Right. He forgot all about the quarantine in the rush to get Rachel to the ER. Had he been spotted on any cameras on his way to the ER? He glanced up, trying to see if there were cameras in the waiting room.

"Next."

He turned, checking the corners of the room as well.

"Excuse me! NEXT!" the woman behind the counter said.

Brian turned around. He was next.

He walked forward. The nurse behind the counter was in her midthirties. Overweight, with a cute face, dark hair, and bright red lipstick.

"What is your emergency?" she said.

"My daughter, she cut her leg. It's pretty bad. She needs stitches."

"Her name?"

"Rachel Newman."

The nurse started clicking on her computer.

"How did the injury happen?"

"She fell off a ladder. There was a sharp edge. It sliced her calf."

The nurse looked up at him, arching an eyebrow.

"A ladder?" she said.

"Yes!"

"Okaaaay," she replied, entering something into the computer.

"Oh, I almost forgot. Please scan your Azazel Promise app on the reader." She tapped a small device on the counter. It looked like the scanner used at airports for mobile boarding passes.

Brian's stomach dropped. He felt sweat on his palms.

"I . . . forgot my phone."

"You forgot?" she said.

"Yes! I was in a rush. Please—she needs to see a doctor?" He looked over at Rachel again, still sitting there with her eyes closed. The man on his phone had left, and Rachel had her good leg extended to the third chair.

"Ah. Look. It's been over a MONTH since the Azazel Promise went live. How many times do people need to be told?" She pointed at a laminated sheet of paper taped to the counter. It said, "*This facility is a SAFE SPACE. In an effort to provide the best medical care to everyone, this hospital requires all patients and visitors to validate their SAFE status prior to processing.*" Below that, the image of the snake eating its tail, with an eye in the center. The logo for the AP app.

"I . . . um," Brian said.

He squinted. At the bottom of the page, in smaller writing, he read, "Posted in compliance with the AP guidance on maintaining tax-exempt status, and the Azazel Medical Insurers Network (AMIN) requirements."

". . . your name?" Brian caught her mid-sentence.

"Excuse me?" he asked, looking up from the sign.

"I have access to the AP network via our patient portal. What is your name so I can validate your SAFE status and get your daughter in?"

He blinked. Even if it meant extending their quarantine, he had to get her into the doctor.

"Brian Newman."

She clicked a few keys. A moment later, she inhaled sharply.

Her face hardened, and she looked up at him.

"You. Cannot. Be. In. Here." She pointed to the exit.

He tried to whisper, "Okay. I will. But, my daughter?"

She grabbed something from the printer.

"Sign this form, and I'll get her in triage." She handed him a form.

Brian scanned a one-page document while the nurse tapped her fingers against the counter.

I, the undersigned, do hereby agree to waive all custody and legal rights for _____, a minor currently under my care. Initials___

I, the undersigned, do hereby agree to return promptly for the retrieval of _____, a minor currently under my care, once my mandatory restoration period has been completed. Initials___

I, the undersigned, do hereby agree to the enrollment of _____ in Federally approved restorative care for the remainder of my set Quarantine Period. Initials___

I, the undersigned, do hereby agree to restore my thoughts and actions to better align with public safety, and to avoid such public spaces until at which point I am redeemed by Babble and made whole and Safe. Initials ___

Brian's mouth hung open.

"Sign it and I'll process your daughter."

"What does this mean, 'enrolled for the duration of my quarantine period'?" He pointed at the page.

"You aren't allowed to be here. You need to leave her so we can assess her wound without you causing undue harm to our staff and patients. Once the doctors release her, she'll be transported to the Re-Safing Youth Camp, where you can pick her back up once you are restored to SAFETY."

"But, that's a MONTH!" His face turned red.

"She just needs stitches! What does any of this have to do with a CUT ON HER LEG!" He slammed his hands on the counter.

The nurse inhaled sharply. "LOOK! YOU'RE the one who can't get your own damn act together and love your neighbor! This is policy. You need to leave. NOW. We could lose our SAFE status all together. Sign the paper, or don't. Maybe you don't even have a daughter? I don't know. But if you want us to treat her, THAT IS THE DEAL." She crossed her arms and stared at him.

A month? No way was he going to leave Rachel alone for a month. Maybe the cut wasn't as bad as it looked? Could this really be happening? He glanced over at Rachel, who appeared to be sleeping. He needed to talk to Hannah.

He looked up at the nurse, set the form down, and walked away. "Next."

CHAPTER 37

"Rachel, baby. We need to go." Brian shook her gently. She looked up at him.

"What about the doctor?" she murmured.

"It's okay. Not too bad. Mom and I can take care of it." He lifted her carefully and walked out of the waiting room.

He carried her back across the drive, through the parking garage, and laid her on the seat in the back of the van.

"It hurts, Daddy."

"I know, love." He ran his fingers through his hair.

"I'm gonna take a look at it."

"No, it hurts!" Rachel cried out.

"I know. I know. Just let me take a little look." Rachel was laying on her back, knees bent, feet on the edge of the seats. He put down the armrest and lifted her injured leg onto it so it was propped up. He unwrapped the towel slowly. The wound was on the bottom of her calf, so he craned his neck to look at it.

There was no bleeding, thankfully. The cut looked almost dry. It was a nasty gash, but it didn't look quite as bad as he first feared. The skin was taut along the edges, pulling the wound apart, and at its widest, the cut was nearly two inches across. It needed stitches for sure. Based on the way the cut was situated across her calf, he guessed it would tear open even further without them.

He turned on the overhead light in the van to get a better look. He could see muscle on the deepest part of the cut, but thankfully, the muscle didn't seem to be cut after all. It went through the layers of skin, and some white tissue that he guessed was fat, and exposed the muscle, but it stopped there.

Could they clean the wound, and . . . maybe tape it shut? Or glue it?

He glanced around the parking garage.

It was nearly 8:00 p.m., dark in the garage, and not many people in the back area. He was parked next to a row of five ambulance vans, but they all seemed to be unoccupied.

He looked back over at Rachel. "Sit tight for a minute, Rach."

He slid the van door closed and turned around. No one there. He rubbed his palms on his jeans, drying the sweat and walked to the nearest ambulance. It was a Ford Transit conversion, double doors in the back. He held his breath, reached up and pulled on the handle. The door opened, and an overhead light turned on in the van.

Brian jumped into the van, turned around, and closed the door behind him. He peered out the window. No one saw him. He exhaled.

He inspected the van. It was narrow, one side containing a medical bed on wheels, and the other, covered with cabinets above and below a small counter space. Past the cabinets, a chair on a swivel, surrounded by medical devices.

What was he doing? What was he looking for?

He started opening the cabinets. The first one contained neck braces of various sizes. The next one had some sort of handheld breathing machine. A balloon attached to a mask. He shut them both and kept looking. One cabinet had an assortment of gauze and wraps. He took all of those out and set them on the bed behind him. The one next to it had tape, a variety of bandages, and some antiseptic wipes. He took all of that out and set it on the bed as well.

He found a bottle labeled "povidone-iodine." Iodine? That sounded familiar. He took that. Another of hydrogen peroxide. He grabbed it as well.

The last cabinet held some syringes in packages and a small box of individually wrapped foils of ointment.

He took all of it.

On the floor near the swiveling chair, he found a large orange bag. It was about two feet across and a foot deep with soft sides. The paramedic's bag. He opened it. It was full of supplies, organized in small compartments. He saw more tape, scissors, ointment, another breathing machine, and several other items. He shoved stuff around in the bag until he made enough space to cram in the items from the cabinets. He pulled the bag shut with one hand and zipped it closed.

He hoisted the bag up and put the strap on his shoulder. The bag was heavy, and he had to crouch while holding it against his side to navigate to the back of the ambulance. He glanced back through the window. The parking lot was still clear.

He opened the door, jumped down, closed it behind him, rushed over the van, threw open the passenger door, and put the medic bag on the seat next to him.

He walked around the van, climbed into the driver's seat, and started the car. He let out a breath he had been holding.

"You okay, Rach?" he said.

"Yeah. It hurts," she replied. "Can you roll down the windows? My stomach hurts."

"Sure thing, baby girl." He rolled down the driver and passenger windows and pulled out of the parking garage. He knew the night air would feel good if Rachel was getting nauseous.

He waited at the light to turn left on McBean. The protesters were still milling around on the corner, about thirty people, and one of them had a bullhorn.

"What do we want?" the man with the bullhorn yelled.

"SAFE SPACES!" the crowd chanted.

"When do we want it?"

"NOW!"

The man with the bullhorn went on.

"They took away our SAFETY when they overturned *Roe v. Wade!*" Brian listened.

"A woman's body should be her own business! These backwards people, with their old-fashioned, hateful, and oppressive ideas, need to go!"

The crowd shouted.

"They hate you with their violence. They refuse to use the right pronouns! They refuse to STAY AWAY FROM YOUR BODY! They tell us that GOD judges us!"

The light turned green. Brian crept into the intersection.

"They won't change! The Azazel Promise may keep them quiet, but inside, they'll still HATE PEOPLE!"

Brian waited for an opening to make his left.

"Their ideas, their thoughts, are VIOLENCE. The Azazel Promise doesn't do enough! If these BIGOTS AND LIARS won't change their MINDS, if they won't stop MAKING OUR BODIES UNSAFE, they need to be ABORTED!"

Brian finally saw the man with the bullhorn. Tall, large frame. Purple hair. As the man turned toward the street, one eye bulged wider than the other, making direct contact with Brian.

Chad.

Brian felt that oily hand, reaching into his mind, probing.

Chad lifted an arm, pointing at Brian, then brought the finger back and drew it across his throat.

The opposing traffic cleared, and Brian made his left.

"LEGAL ABORTIONS! SAFE ABORTIONS! ABORT THE UNSAFE!" the crowd chanted.

Brian accelerated, driving past the protestors. In his rearview mirror, he saw Chad staring at the van, finger still on his throat.

CHAPTER 38

Brian pulled the van into their garage, got out, and picked Rachel up. He carried her through the garage, used his knee to open the door into the entryway, and walked in.

It was after nine. The house was quiet, except for the low hum of Aurora singing hymns.

Brian stumbled into the great room. Hannah, Luke, and Abby were standing around the kitchen island, half-eaten cake on paper plates in front of them.

"Brian! How is she?" Hannah asked when he rounded the corner.

"Heavy. Give me a hand." Hannah helped him over to the couch. Rachel kept her eyes shut.

"You okay, Rach?" Hannah asked, kissing her brow.

"Mmhhm. Hurts," Rachel replied.

"How many stitches?" Hannah asked, looking up at Brian.

"No stitches . . ." Rachel murmured.

"Really? What did the doctor say?" Hannah ran her hand over Rachel's knee, noticing the towel still wrapped around her calf.

Brian grabbed Hannah's hand and walked her over to the kitchen. He lowered his voice. Abby and Luke leaned in.

"She didn't see a doctor," Brian said.

"What, why?" Hannah raised her voice.

"Hannah, they wouldn't let us in."

Abby and Luke exchanged looks.

"Why, Dad?" Abby asked.

"My scores . . . we're unsafe." He looked over at Hannah.

"But Brian . . ." She raised her hand to her neck, comforting herself. "They have to provide treatment, don't they?" The last two words came out in a whisper, and she glanced over at Rachel.

"They were going to *take* her," Brian said.

Brian explained the exchange he'd had with the woman at the Emergency Room.

"So, they would have kept her for a MONTH? Who? Why?" Abby sounded scared. She looked down, surprised to see she was holding Luke's hand. She let go. Exhaled and grabbed his hand again.

"Dad, that cut was deep. We gotta do something," Luke said.

"I know. Hang on. I got stuff."

Brian ran out to the van, grabbed the medic bag, and hurried back to the kitchen.

"WHEN HE'S BEEN HERE
TEN THOUSAND YEARS
BRIGHT SHINING AS THE STARS
HE'LL HAVE NO LESS DAYS
TO TAKE YOUR PRAISE
OUR BABBLE, THREE IN ONE"

The four of them stood over the medic bag, ignoring the evening hymn sing.

The bag sat opened, gauze, tape, sterilizers, and other contents emptied on the counter.

"We need to clean it. Ointment—tape it shut—" Hannah shuffled through the contents. It'll leave a big scar, but at least we can keep it clean with all of this.

"On the couch?" Brian asked, looking over at Rachel, who had fallen asleep.

"No. Let's bring her over to the breakfast nook, put her on the table. She can lay on her stomach. That way the cut is facing up. We'll have decent light that way."

"Painkiller?" Brian asked.

"Advil?" Hannah responded.

"The cut's pretty deep. Anything stronger?"

"I don't think so. And she's only eleven. Advil, and then some NyQuil to help her sleep. I don't want to do more than that."

They discussed logistics. Abby ran upstairs to grab an old blanket and pillow. Hannah laid the items out on the table she wanted.

Brian and Luke woke up Rachel, explaining they needed to move her to the table to "put a Band-Aid on her cut."

Hannah made Rachel swallow two Advil, thought for a moment, and added the shot of NyQuil. Rachel laid on her stomach, draped across the breakfast nook table, a pillow and blanket under her for cushion.

"Dad, it hurts," Rachel said, waking up.

"I know, baby girl. We need to clean it though. And tape it shut. Just hang in there."

Brian unwrapped her leg carefully and handed the towel to Luke. The cut was impressive. The red gash, growing to a deep burgundy color the deeper the cut went, held a sharp contrast to the creamy white flesh of her leg. Abby winced, and Luke turned away quickly.

"Oh dear. That doesn't look good." Hannah said, looking over the bottles Brian managed to take from the ambulance.

"Umm . . . iodine? And hydrogen peroxide . . ." Hannah opened the bottle of iodine, dabbed some on a section of gauze, and smelled it.

"The orange stuff. They use it in surgery." She turned the bottle around, looking for information. "It says 'topical bactericide.' I think I can use it on the inside of a wound too?" Hannah held it out to Brian.

"You're asking me?"

"I mean . . . I think so. What's the other bottle?" Hannah gestured over with a nod.

Brian grabbed the bottle and handed it to her. "Hydrogen peroxide."

"Well, I know that works. I'm gonna use that for the inside of the cut, and then the orange stuff for the skin and around the edges. Seems weird to put orange stuff inside her cut."

Hannah leaned down, kissing the side of Rachel's face.

"Okay, Rach, stingy stuff. Gotta clean it out."

Rachel clenched her mouth, shut her eyes, and nodded.

Hannah tipped the bottle of hydrogen peroxide and slowly poured it into Rachel's gash.

"AAAHHHHHHH!" Rachel screamed immediately, kicking her legs out.

"Hey!" Brian yelled, grabbing her leg. He motioned for Luke and Abby to help him, and the three of them pinned Rachel down.

"It STIIIINGS!!!!!!" she sobbed.

Hannah looked down. The fluid poured out as soon as Rachel kicked her leg up. She poured more out, and this time Rachel just tensed against the hands holding her down.

The inside of the wound bubbled, and filled with a white, foamy substance. The smell of hydrogen peroxide filled the room.

Hannah waited for the bubbles to start popping and flushed the wound out again.

Once she was satisfied with her work, she grabbed one of the packets of ointment and emptied its contents into the wound. With her finger, she gently rubbed the ointment, covering every surface of the interior of the wound.

"Mom! Stop! Please! It hurts!" Rachel pleaded.

"Brian, get me the tape."

Brian grabbed the roll of medical tape.

"We need to pull the wound closed, or it won't heal. Can you push the cut together, and I'll wrap it?"

"What about the orange stuff?" Luke asked.

"That first," Hannah said.

She applied the iodine to the skin around the wound. Satisfied, she nodded.

Brian looked over at Luke.

"Luke, I need you to help me."

"Okay. What do you want me to do?" He stepped toward Rachel's leg.

"I'm gonna reach here, under her leg, and pull up, like this?" He made a gesture with his hands. "I think that will squeeze the wound shut. I need you to push from the sides at the same time, so we can make sure the entire thing seals. Think you can do that?"

Luke's face went pale, but he nodded a silent consent.

As soon as Brian started pulling on her leg, Rachel shrieked.

"DAD! DAD! NO! NO! NO!" She wriggled. Abby tried to hold her shoulders down, but Rachel was strong.

After a moment, Rachel gave up fighting, and laid still, whimpering.

"The doctor would give her a local first," Brian whispered to Hannah.

"Is there anything like that in the bag?" Hannah asked.

Brian checked the bag. He found syringes, but nothing he was comfortable putting in the syringe and injecting into his daughter's leg. His first thought was to google the names of the various chemicals, but of course, no internet. They may as well be on the frontier for all the help they were going to get.

They tried again. Luke and Brian managed to pull the wound closed, but as soon as Hannah started taping around the leg, they had to move an arm, which caused the wound to open on one end. Hannah managed to get tape around the first section of the wound, but the tape wouldn't stick around the mouth of the wound, because of the iodine and antiseptic.

They made several attempts, but each time it proved impossible. Rachel was a total wreck. The skin around her wound was bright red, and fresh blood started seeping from the cut. It was hopeless. Rachel sobbed.

Hannah stepped away from her daughter, to the other side of the kitchen, and sobbed as well.

"It's no use, Brian!" she shouted across the kitchen. "It won't work! She needs a DAMN DOCTOR! And STITCHES! We can't home remedy something like this!"

Brian ran his hand along the back of Rachel's head, comforting her. "Luke, get some ice, will ya?"

Luke brought a small cup of ice over, and Brian ran a single cube along Rachel's forehead. He sang to her under his breath.

"Little baby girl, it's okay . . . Daddy'll take your pain away . . . Don't cry hard, don't cry long . . . it'll be over faster than I'll sing this song . . ."

She closed her eyes, and her breathing slowed. She seemed to be falling asleep.

Brian walked over to Hannah; Luke and Abby joined him.

"Stitches? You sure?" he asked Hannah.

"Yeah. 100 percent. We can't close that wound," she said.

"They'll keep her, Hannah. For a month. No way I can take her back."

"I know. But what else can we do? We can't even tape the wound shut, let alone give her STITCHES."

Luke looked at Abby, making a gesture with his face.

She shook her head no, vigorously.

He bulged his eyes and pointed his finger at her.

"What is it, you two?" Brian asked.

Abby mouthed *"you suck"* to Luke.

"Dad, Abby taught herself to sew! You saw how she fixed her shoes, right? And made the bib for Lizzy?" Luke bounced up on his toes.

Brian looked over at Abby, confused.

"So . . . ?"

Abby exhaled. Steeling herself.

"So . . . I could do it. I could do the stitches."

CHAPTER 39

The debate was short. They didn't have a lot of options. Keep trying to tape it shut. Take her back to the ER, leaving her for a month. Or let Abby try stitches.

"So, it's between child abuse, child abandonment, or experimental surgery," Brian said.

They agreed it needed to be done soon. The wound was raw and hopefully numb. The Advil was just kicking in, and Rachel fell asleep from the NyQuil. They tore the medic bag apart for supplies. Brian kept hoping to find some sort of suture kit. No luck.

Luke said Survivor Steve swore by fishing line. Brian ran out to the garage, grabbing a few rolls from his old tackle box. He selected the thinnest line he could find: 3-lb test. He used it for creek fishing up at Taboose.

Hannah grabbed her sewing kit and brought it to the kitchen. She laid out a few needles.

Abby glanced at them. She walked over to the table where Rachel was asleep and bent over the wound. She wrinkled her nose but kept her focus.

"It needs a double stitch," she said.

"What does that mean?" Brian asked. He finished filling up a pot of water, placed it on the burner, and walked over to Abby.

"See how deep the cut is?" Abby whispered, gesturing.

"Yeah . . . ?"

"If I just stitch the top, it could pull apart. There's too much tension splitting her leg open. I need to do two layers of stitches." She pointed about halfway down the wall of the gash.

Brian stared, saying nothing.

"Just like my shoes. I had to do an interior stitch first before the top layer, or it would have kept pulling apart."

Brian thought.

"Abs, if you did a layer of stitches inside the wound first, how would you take them out? The fishing line won't dissolve like the stitches doctors use."

"Oh shoot, you're right." She looked up, frowning.

"Wait. What if I started a few inches from the outside of the cut, and pushed through from there? I could do that again on the other side and just tie it off on both sides. Almost like straps that pulled the inside together. Those could be cut and pulled out no problem!"

Brian nodded, pretending to follow.

"I need a curved needle."

Brian heated the middle of one of the sewing needles over the stove, and when it was hot enough, he curved it with two pairs of pliers. He added the curved needle, two straight needles, the fishing line, a small pair of scissors from the medic bag, and the pliers to the boiling water.

Abby scrubbed her hands in the kitchen sink, adding iodine as well as soap. Hannah insisted the rest of them do the same. They didn't have gloves, but they would keep things as clean as possible.

Once the items in the water boiled for about ten minutes, Hannah carefully removed them, and set them out on a small serving platter she cleaned with soap and iodine, then lined with gauze from the medical supplies.

"Luke, I need you to help me," Abby said, once they were all situated around Rachel again.

"Me?" Luke said.

"Yeah. You have the smallest hands and arms—we won't be in each other's way. And I need Mom and Dad to hold Rachel down in case she wakes up and starts fighting."

Abby had Luke put gentle pressure on the sides of Rachel's leg.

"When I start pulling the wound closed with the stitches, I want you to help keep it tight. Once I've made enough loops, the fishing line should hold."

She started with the straight needle and visualized what she needed to do.

"Careful, Abs," Brian said.

She threaded the fishing line in the eye of the needle and pushed it into Rachel's leg. Rachel stirred and whimpered, but didn't wake up. Abby looked to the interior of the wound, and she saw the tip of the needle protrude, about two-thirds of the way into the cut, just as she was unable to push the needle any further from behind. She took the needle-nosed pliers, carefully grabbed the tip of the needle, pulled it across the gash, and punctured the opposite side of the wound. She repeated the process in reverse, careful to monitor the angle of the needle. The needle penetrated the opposite side of the wound, about two inches from the edge of the cut, and she was able to grab the tip and pull it through.

"You need to cut both ends and tie them off," Luke said.

"Shut up. I know."

She started with the side she ended on. She cut the line with the scissors and started tying. She had to make several knots, one on top of the other. When she was satisfied with the size, she pulled on the string from the opposite side of the wound, testing it. The knot pulled against the skin but stayed put. It would hold.

The second side was more difficult. She pulled against the string while Luke gently squeezed the leg closed. She didn't have anything to tie the knots *against*; she had to carefully gauge the correct tension, go *beyond* that briefly, and start the knot. She used the pliers and finished the side. When she let go, Rachel's skin pushed against both knots, but they didn't pull through. The wound was closed at the interior point of her strap.

"Abs! It's working!" Brian said.

Luke kept pressure on the leg, preventing the wound from pulling too hard against the stitches. They repeated the process, about an inch from the first one. She struggled with the knots on the second one but was finally able to get them to the correct size, and they held.

It was slow work, but she managed to finish another six of these custom strap-like stitches. The wound was totally closed on the interior, making the entire gash look only about a half-inch deep.

Luke let go of her leg, and it held.

Abby stood up, stretched her neck, and exhaled.

"What do you need, Abby?" Hannah asked, kissing her forehead.

"A drink of water, please."

Hannah filled a glass, holding it up to her lips so Abby wouldn't be forced to scrub down again. When she was done, she murmured a thank-you and sat.

She grabbed the curved needle next, threading it with the line.

She started at one end and, using the pliers, she pierced the skin—this time at the edge of the cut. She pulled it through, to the other side, up, and out. She tied knots into the one end, tugging to make sure it held, and then repeated the process. She pulled the line across the top of the wound, through the skin, inside, through, and out again. She made the loops very tight, and as she did, the wound closed completely. She hummed to herself as she poked, pulled, tugged, poked, pulled, tugged. She was halfway through when Rachel woke up.

"Mom? Something is pulling—it STINGS!" she cried. She got up on her elbows, looked over her shoulder, and saw Abby.

"Abby?" she said, confused. She looked from Abby, down to her hands, down to her leg.

"AAHHHH!" she shrieked.

Rachel started rolling away, nearly pulling the half-done stitches out of Abby's hands. Brian and Hannah grabbed her immediately, holding her down.

"OOUUUUCCHHHHH!!!!"

"RACHEL! We need to finish!" Brian yelled.

"It hurts! LET ME GOO!!!" she cried.

Brian gestured to Abby, both hands busy holding Rachel by the legs.

"Do it."

Abby continued. Poke. Pull. Tug. Poke. Pull. Tug. Hannah held Rachel by the shoulders, and was bent down next to her, whispering, kissing, calming.

Rachel's whimper turned into a sob.

Abby finished the final stitch. She cut the string, tied it off, and leaned back. The wound was completely closed. The skin was red from irritation. There was a neat and orderly crisscrossing of stitches running the length of the wound, and every inch another knot protruding from a second row, about two inches from the cut. It was a gruesome sight.

Abby stepped away, and Hannah took over. Rachel laid still, crying, while Hannah applied iodine to the cut as well as the additional protruding knots. Then she covered the entire area in a generous dollop of ointment. After that, Brian handed her gauze, and she laid that over the site. She wrapped the gauze in a roll of the slightly tacky brown medical wrap and finished the edges of that off with tape.

"Okay Rach, it's done," Hannah said.

Rachel exhaled, exhausted. Brian gently carried her over to the couch and laid her on her side. Hannah gave her some water to drink, and covered her with a blanket.

She walked over to Abby and hugged her.

"Thank you, Abs. Thank you. That was amazing."

CHAPTER 40

Three days later, Brian was in the kitchen, doing the after-dinner dishes. Hannah fried duck breast strips in duck fat, and made a dipping sauce with butter and soy sauce. She was getting pretty creative with limited ingredients.

"How does your leg feel, Rach?" Brian asked, his hands buried in soapy water.

"Good," she replied. Rachel claimed the downstairs couch as her perch, and was laid out, reading a book. So far, the stitches seemed to be holding. Hannah had changed the wrapping every evening, cleaning around the stitches, adding ointment. The skin didn't seem irritated. The pain had mostly died down, but Rachel was still allowed Advil when it started hurting.

Brian turned on the faucet. Water dripped out, then stopped.

"What the heck?" He turned the handle. On, off. On, off.

He stood there, thinking. He dried his hands on a towel, and walked to the downstairs bathroom. He tried the sink. No water. He ran to the master bathroom, tried the sink. No water. The kid's bathroom. Same. He ran downstairs, out the sliding glass door, to the back patio. Luke and Abby were sitting on camping chairs, huddled around the small TV, watching *National Treasure*.

He tried the hose bib on the side of the house. No water.

He went back upstairs. Hannah had just finished putting Lizzy and the little boys down for the night.

He caught her in the hall.

"No water," he said.

"What?"

"We couldn't pay the bill. Grace period is over," he said.

"But that makes no sense. We can't pay because they won't let us use our banks! What are we gonna do?"

She followed him downstairs.

He grabbed a bucket from the garage, went out to the pool, and filled it. He brought it back to the kitchen and emptied the bucket into the sink.

"Brian, seriously?" Hannah said, when she realized what he was doing.

"Yep. We'll have to use the pool water."

"Will they shut the power off next?" she asked.

SILENCE IS VIOLENCE. ADD YOUR VOICE.

"I don't think so. They want the Aurora devices to stay online."

They finished the dishes, Brian making two more trips to the pool for water. Abby and Luke ignored him as he walked past them, engrossed in the movie.

After dishes, he carried Rachel up to bed, gave Luke and Abby a thirty-minute warning, and sat in the living room with Hannah.

"We can use the pool water. The contractor said one of the nice things about going salt instead of chlorine is dogs can drink the water. I'm guessing that means we can too. We'll have to hand truck water to the toilets. Sponge baths only. We'll make it work." Brian was doing mental math.

"For thirty-four more days?" Hannah asked. She glanced at the chalkboard on the wall near the formal dining room. She'd added a countdown to the top of it. She called it the Quarantine Advent Calendar.

"Actually, its forty four more days."

"What?" Hannah exhaled.

"We started with sixty days. We got ten more days when I went on that walk—and another ten days when I took Rach to the ER." Brian was keeping that detail to himself, not wanting to upset Hannah, but he had to bring her in the loop.

"So, our sixty-day quarantine is now an eighty-day quarantine, and when we do terrible things like go on a walk in our neighborhood, or—I don't know, TRY AND TAKE OUR INJURED CHILD TO THE ER, we get punished even more?" Hannah rarely got angry, but when she did, the gates of Hell stood no chance.

"Hannah, I will figure this out. I promise." He walked over to her and kissed her on the forehead.

"Don't worry, your knight in shining armor will protect you." He didn't feel like a knight, and he certainly didn't have any armor, but the gesture was genuine.

"Okay, so what are we going to do, drink pool water?" She asked, laying into his hug.

"I think so. The pool filter will keep the water clean. The issue will be if we dip below the water intake line. Then we'll have to shut off the pool equipment. After that, the water will eventually stagnate. But one problem at a time."

The next morning, they had a family meeting, explaining the new water rations. Brian designated a bucket for toilet use, one for dishes, and another for cleaning and washing. He labeled them with a black marker. When Jer and Shawn heard that they wouldn't be allowed to swim anymore, they protested.

"Why, Dad?" Jer yelled.

"Why, Dad!" Shawn repeated.

"Because, you pee in there, and we'll lose water with you splashing around and we need that water to drink now."

"We won't splash!" Shawn cried out.

"We won't drink! If we don't drink, we won't pee!" Jer reasoned.

The family adjusted their routines yet again. The kids watched movies on the back patio, jumped on the trampoline when it wasn't too hot, and got on each other's nerves. Rachel continued to heal, and after a few days was able to put weight on her leg and walk around. Luke kept bringing ducks home every few nights. Hannah and Abby moved their duck prep to the backyard, closer to the water source.

Little things started piling up. They were out of toothpaste. Hannah set aside a container of baking soda near each bathroom sink, but the younger kids balked at brushing with it. They had no shampoo, no bar soap, no dish soap. Water was their only cleaning solution. From the pool. They couldn't run the dishwasher. It was easier to wash the dishes on the back patio, near the water source. Brian set up another folding table, fished out the tubs they used when they were camping, and that became the new dishwashing station.

The kids quickly realized washing dishes was a more difficult chore than it had been with running water. They decided the best solution was to use as few dishes as they could. Meals turned into the family huddling around a dish, usually the large cast iron pot, or a baking sheet, and grabbing pieces of duck to eat with their hands. If Hannah made stew, the kids insisted on drinking it out of coffee mugs.

"At least we don't have to wash spoons!"

Laundry was the biggest issue. They couldn't use the clothes washer and filling up buckets of water to handwash clothes sounded miserable. Brian felt it would be a big waste of water anyway. They weren't using soap for anything, eating became sloppy, and whatever you were wearing while you did backyard dishes got dirty quickly. Brian allowed for one bucket of water a day to do laundry. With no soap, the best they could come up with was dunking and scrubbing their clothes, and then hanging them out on a clothesline Brian strung between the pool fence and patio cover. Hannah insisted sun-drying clothes helped to disinfect, but just to help out she sprayed a small amount of white vinegar on the clothes while they dried.

The cloth diapers posed an entirely new problem to solve. After a few days of trial and error, each error producing smells and sights that added to the family misery, she decided diapers were only for number two. Thankfully, Lizzy was fairly regular in that regard. The only meal of any substance the family was eating was dinner, but they were getting their fill. Lizzy was living primarily off duck meat and liver, and a little bread. Hannah kept her in a diaper until she pooped, then left her naked the rest of the day. She carefully scooped out the contents into the trash and soaked the diaper in a bucket of water with baking soda, dried the diaper in the sun. Rinse. Repeat. It kept the number of diapers being washed down, but it meant Lizzy would often dribble urine down her leg, onto the carpet upstairs, or tile floors downstairs.

The smells in the house attracted flies, and with much of life migrating to the back patio, the back door was open most of the time. The family grew accustomed to swatting flies off food and surfaces. The house was filled with the smell of duck, vinegar, urine, and sweat. But the family grew accustomed to it.

Abby and Rachel were given the morning chore of boiling pool water to drink. Abby would haul in a couple of buckets of water, Rachel had three pots going on the stove. Once the water was boiling, she set the timer on the microwave for sixty seconds. Then, they would carefully remove the water from the heat, and give it a chance to cool to room temperature. They poured the water into an old milk jug, a glass serving pitcher, and old orange juice bottle, and a few metal drinking bottles, and put them in the fridge.

The trash truck no longer stopped at their house. Apparently they were late on that bill as well. They had a small amount of trash piling up on the side of the house, but Brian noticed they accumulated very little garbage. The family trash consisted primarily of duck bones and feathers, occasional paper goods, and the contents of Lizzy's diapers.

Brian was proud of the way his family adapted to the circumstances. They were all pitching in, making due. Life was about checking days off the calendar, a long deep breath before returning to normal. But he wondered if the gas would be shut off soon. If they couldn't cook the duck, or boil the water, they would be in serious trouble.

He wanted to see what was in the mail. He figured he would ask Luke to get the mail on his next hunting trip. Or better yet, maybe he would go with him.

CHAPTER 41

Brian followed Luke as they set out for the park, just after 1:00 a.m. He hid behind a car, and keeping his head down, avoided the camera on the neighbor's door. Luke looked back over his shoulder and made a "get down" gesture with his hands. Brian watched Luke shimmy under a Jeep, and followed him. Brian was careful not to let his backpack snag on the underside of the Jeep, and after a moment, he exited the other end. They crossed the street several times and sat still for a few minutes behind a late model Dodge, waiting for a dog to stop barking. Eventually, they made it to the park.

There was one streetlight illuminating the small parking lot, and a security light glowing over the bathroom building, but otherwise it was dark. Brian followed Luke toward the playground and sat next to him on a bench overlooking the swing set.

"I always stop here for a drink of water . . . and to catch my breath," Luke said.

"Good call, boy-o."

Brian put his arm around Luke. The boy's chest was heaving. The walk from the house hadn't been that strenuous.

"You okay, buddy?" Brian asked.

"Yeah. I'm good. I just get nervous about getting caught on the street."

Brian sighed. He didn't realize what kind of pressure he put on his son. Luke was always so capable and sure of himself, and when he said he could make it to the park, get ducks, and come back, Brian didn't think twice. But Luke seemed terrified. He'd been sending his son into enemy territory to pilfer food, while he sat in the safety of his home.

They sat there for a moment, then Luke stood.

"Okay. Duck time."

They made their way across the soccer field and to the grassy slope near the pond. Brian watched as Luke fed a few ducks, slowly backing toward a depression in the grass. After a moment, he laid down, covered himself in a towel, and baited his trap.

Brian saw the ducks crowd around Luke, and eventually one of the ducks walked up onto the towel, standing on Luke's chest.

With a sudden motion, Luke grabbed the duck, wrapping it in the towel. He stood, adjusted his grip so he had one hand on the neck and the other holding the legs, and jerked. The duck stopped moving immediately. Luke tossed the duck a few feet away and reached into his backpack for more breadcrumbs.

"It would help if you lure the ducks over while I set up again," Luke said as he handed Brian the bread.

Brian walked over to another group of ducks sitting about ten yards away. He tossed breadcrumbs toward them, and eventually one of the ducks noticed, stood, and quacked. The rest of the ducks woke up, and Brian was able to lead them slowly toward Luke, crumb by crumb.

When he was close enough to Luke, he looked over his shoulder. Luke was laying perfectly still, breadcrumbs on his chest. Brian dropped one last piece of bread, moved out of the way, and watched.

One duck, all brown, walked onto Luke's stomach. A moment later, a gray duck with a green head followed it. Brian could just see Luke's chest moving. Up, down. Up, down.

Suddenly, Luke moved his hands up, and managed to wrap both ducks in the towel. He sat up, the ducks in his lap. Brian saw a head, a foot, and a wing protruding from the towel at various angles, and Luke struggled to hold them.

"Dad, Dad! Take one! Quick!" Luke motioned with his head.

Brian ran over, knelt beside his son.

"Okay, okay. What should I do?" Brian asked, breathing heavily.

"See this one? The head sticking out?" Luke nodded toward his left.

"Yeah. Green head. I see it."

"Grab it behind the head . . . yeah, like that. Now reach into the towel and get your arm under its body. Careful, that's the other duck . . . yes! You have it."

Brian stood, cradling a duck in his arms. He felt the warmth of the duck through his shirt, the rapid breathing matching his own.

"Okay, now I'll show you how to kill it."

Brian clenched his teeth and winced.

"Okay," he said.

Luke explained the process. Brian managed to get the duck turned around, head down, and wrapped one hand around the neck. He copied Luke and grabbed both legs with his other hand.

He had a hard time bending the head at the correct angle, but after a moment, he held the duck the same way Luke was holding his.

"Okay, now—pull!" Luke said. The boy jerked his hands quickly in opposite directions, and with an audible "pop," his duck was dispatched.

Brian did the same. Or, at least tried to. He didn't have as firm a grip as he thought, and he pulled too slowly. The duck started flailing in his arms. Panicking, Brian let go of the legs. The duck started swinging and flapping, held only by the neck.

"Dad! Swing it around! Swing it!" Luke said.

Brian swung the duck, a twisting motion. The body rotated a full turn, but the head stayed fixed in Brian's hand. He heard a "pop," and the duck stopped moving.

Brian dropped the duck, panting.

"Is that how it always goes?" he asked Luke between breaths.

"Actually, no. I've never had to do it that way."

They laid the three ducks out and repeated the process.

Brian managed the next duck without letting go of the legs, and by the time they were done, his nerves had finally settled.

He looked down at their kill. Six ducks, similar sizes. Three light brown, two with gray bodies and green and blue heads, one all white.

They gently placed the ducks into their backpacks, three each, and headed across the soccer fields.

Luke sat again on the bench overlooking the playground.

The boy was calming his nerves. Again. Recovering from the hunt, preparing to navigate the cameras, again. Brian was so proud of him.

They made their way back to the sidewalk. Brian took a quick detour to the mailboxes, fished the key out of his pocket, and opened their box. Stacks of letters and junk, the box nearly overflowing. He shoved it all into the front pocket of his backpack, locked the box, and headed back with Luke.

They made it back to their driveway with no issues. They walked around the house to the back, took the six ducks out, and left them on one of the folding tables. Those could wait till morning.

"I'm tired, Dad. I'm going to bed," Luke murmured.

Brian glanced at the clock on the wall: 2.30 a.m.

He kissed Luke on the forehead. "Me too. I'm just gonna check the mail first."

CHAPTER 42

Brian sat at the dining room table and sorted the stack of mail. Not even a personal apocalypse could stop junk mail. He made a trash pile and then made his way through the envelopes.

A past-due gas bill made him pause. But the fine print indicated a much more lenient grace period. He set it to the side.

A notice from the water company that they were in danger of having their water turned off. Post dated one week ago. Helpful.

A letter from the office. He tore it open.

Brian,

I regret to inform you that effective immediately, your employment relationship with Brilliant Enterprises is being terminated. In an ongoing effort to navigate rapidly changing dynamics, we have found it necessary to review our Social Scores, Business Health Outlook, and Azazel Promise adherence. At this time, we no longer have the ability to support employment of any "unsafe" individuals. Our banking relationship has dictated that we operate a "zero tolerance" policy on Azazel Scores. In addition, we have several large customers who require that we keep vigilant watch over our work spaces, ensuring 100 percent safety for all involved.

Unfortunately, you no longer fit the government defined status of "safe." We truly hope that you learn the necessary lessons during your restoration period, and are able to fully transition to "safe" status soon. Please accept the enclosed severance check as a means by which Brilliant hopes to aid you through your process.

Best,

Andrew

There was a check in the envelope. Brian did some math. It was one month of pay. How was he going to tell Hannah? What were they going to do? He figured with the severance and their savings, they could survive several months—after quarantine, that is. Right now the issue wasn't money.

There wasn't going to be a "back to normal" for the Newmans.

The last letter in the stack was from his father. It was postmarked two weeks ago, from Coeur D'Alene, Idaho. He opened the envelope and took out two pieces of paper.

The first was a handwritten note from his dad.

Boy-O. Keep your head on a swivel. We're trying to make our way back to your neck of the woods. I'm guessing you and the family are locked down right now. Hope you took my advice on the emergency food rations. Don't you have ducks in your pond? Think about it. This stuff was ram-rodded through Congress with ZERO FORE-THOUGHT. Mark my words, these idiots will collapse society. I give it 6 months. Read this article. Scary stuff. Moloch is hungry. He's been denied his sacrifices, and he's coming. You ready to protect yourself? Your mother and I enjoyed our ANNIVERSARY celebration last month. Do you remember the date?

Hope to see you soon,
Dad. Psalm 22:12

Brian took out the second sheet of paper. It was a news article, from the website "awakenedminds.com."

NEW TRANSPARENCY LAW THREATENS CONSERVATIVE FREEDOM

Morgan Lowitz wanted an abortion. However, with the recent over-turning of *Roe v. Wade*, abortions had become illegal in her home state of Tennessee. She was 25, a working professional, and her and her husband both believed that parenting a child was something they were not ready for. She was denied an abortion at a local Planned Parenthood due to the new state legislation, but was referred to a doctor that was still willing to perform "essential woman's health care," IE: the murdering of an innocent child.

Sadly, both Morgan and the child died as a result of the failed abortion procedure. Morgan's husband went public with the story, blaming "right wing, old fashioned, woman hating conservatives" for allowing *Roe v. Wade* to be overthrown.

Local media picked up the story, and eventually even Senator Gracie Willow Turner (GWT) started commenting on the incident. Here she is quoted from a recent interview:

> What's happening out there is sickening. Okay. SICK-E-NING. Women are being DENIED essential health services. Morgan would still be with us today, happy and healthy, and child-free, if it wasn't for the fact that she was FORCED to source an illegal abortion with a doctor who was heroically trying to help her.

Efforts from pro-life organizations like Students for Life point out that "women who have abortions are 81 percent more likely to suffer subsequent mental health problems," and "abortions increase a woman's risk of Breast Cancer by as much as 41 percent after only one abortion," and "ambulances were called to Planned Parenthood facilities as much as 100 times in 2019," and that "all of these concerns happened where abortions were ACCESSIBLE and LEGAL."

While there are those who feel this information proves that ALL abortions are unsafe for the mother, not to mention for the child, the left continue to push the agenda in the media, as well as through their overreaching initiative, the Azazel Promise.

GWT, however, took the opportunity to put the blame on conservatives, especially those who are in violation of the new Azazel Promise standards:

> The people out there who think that abortions should be illegal HATE WOMEN. We have worked hard in this administration to make every space a SAFE SPACE. Right now, in some states, a woman's own BODY isn't even safe from patriarchal, religious, old school moral oversight. Enough is enough. The public deserves to know who these people are. The public

deserves to be informed. The public, the women deserve to have their SAY, once and for all.

We are proud to introduce to you "Morgan's Law." Morgan's Law is a brand-new transparency act. Every known violator of the Azazel Promise will be listed on a database, accessible to everyone with internet access at www.morgan-slaw.com. Type in your zip code, and you will have access to names and addresses of those hateful individuals who have decided that public safety is not a concern anymore. Type in a name, and you can see that person's SAFE status. I urge you to make your surroundings known at all times. You have body autonomy. You can do whatever you want with your body. And you should have autonomy over your SPACES too. If a woman doesn't have the right to remove an unwanted baby from their womb, then I say the next step is to remove unwanted UNSAFEs from society. Permanently. Be SAFE. Be right in your own eyes. Trust Babble and the Azazel Promise. We will keep you safe.

Brian set the article down. Everyone who violates the Azazel Promise will be on a centralized database. Public information. So people could search his name and see that he has low scores?

The protestors on the street were chanting something. What was it?

"LEGAL ABORTIONS! SAFE ABORTIONS! ABORT THE UNSAFE."

Abort the unsafe? What did that even mean?

Brian heard a loud knock at the door.

CHAPTER 43

Brian stood, walked to the window next to the front door, and opened the shutters. It was dark out. He checked the front entryway but didn't see anything. He looked out over his front lawn and saw a figure standing there.

He could make out a frame, about six feet tall. His breath caught. The person was standing perfectly still, about twenty feet from their front door. They were holding something in their hands, held against the chest. He couldn't tell if it was a man or a woman, but by the height he assumed a man.

Chad.

Blood. Kill.

His mind raced. *Get the gun from the closet? How long would that take? Would Chad try to break in?* He slowly reached out to the front door. Locked. Deadbolt too. And chain. It would hold if someone tried to force entry.

Did they close the sliding glass door after the hunt? He couldn't remember.

Get the gun? Or yell out to Hannah?

Make a decision.

He ducked and crept up the stairs. He looked out of the window in the loft, looking over the front lawn. The person hadn't moved. A little light from the streetlamp spilled onto the person. The figure was wearing a white T-shirt with something scrawled across the front. White pants. Blood near the crotch? He couldn't tell.

He inched his way to the bedroom, hoping he hadn't been spotted through the window. He crept past Hannah, fast asleep, through their bathroom, into the master closet. He keyed the code and opened the small safe. He lifted the 9mm, clicked the safety until he saw the red dot ("red=dead"), and walked to the bed.

He woke Hannah with a gentle shake.

"Huh?" she said, rolling over.

He held a finger to his lips and showed her the gun.

Her eyes opened wide.

"What?" she mouthed.

"Someone is outside," he whispered.

"Who?" she asked.

Brian shrugged.

He leaned close to her ear, barely whispering.

"Watch from the upstairs window. I'm going out there to scare them off."

She nodded.

They both made their way out of the bedroom.

He pointed at the window in the loft, and Hannah walked over to it.

She looked out the window and saw the person.

She inhaled sharply. She looked at Brian and shook her head.

"I have to," he mouthed.

He crept down the stairs, leaving Hannah at her post.

Brian made it halfway down the stairs when he heard Hannah scream.

"AAHHHHH!" she yelled.

Brian ran down the stairs and looked out the window.

The figure was lit from behind, glowing orange. He could make out the words on the shirt: "Abort the Unsafe!" it said.

The person was holding an envelope in their hands with "For Brian Newman's Eyes Only" written on it in bold black letters.

He looked up at the face. It wasn't human.

The face was perfectly white. A red gash for the mouth. Two dots indicating nostrils. One eye, a slanted line, the other eye, a large red circle with a black center. Black hair, not quite shoulder length.

It was a scarecrow.

Brian saw what caused Hannah to scream. There was a fire behind the scarecrow.

"Hannah! Help!"

He ran to the downstairs bathroom and grabbed the water bucket. It was full of pool water. He made his way to the front door, unlocked it, and stepped out. Hannah was behind him. They hurried over to the scarecrow.

Brian felt the warmth of the fire as he approached the scarecrow. He made a concerted effort to ignore the large red eye. He stepped around the figure to put out the fire.

There was a statue, about three feet tall, sitting on the grass a few feet behind the scarecrow. It was fully engulfed in flames. The flames were in danger of leaping to the tree in the front yard.

Brian dumped the bucket of water over the figure, knocking it over, and the flames went out immediately.

"What is going on?" Hannah whispered behind him. She was clutching his shoulders, looking down at the small statue.

It appeared to be made of straw or grass.

"Is that . . . an owl?" Hannah asked.

Brian looked. The statue had two large, round eyes, triangular ears, and bushy eyebrows.

"Yeah, that's an owl." Brian kicked it softly with his foot, turning it over.

He felt Hannah's fingers dig into his shoulder, and she whispered into his ear.

"Oh . . . my . . . GOD."

There, on their front lawn spilling out the back of the statue, Brian saw a tiny doll hand. Then he made out a foot, a leg. Miniature. His eyes adjusted to the darkness.

Not doll parts.

Human.

CHAPTER 44

Brian scrambled backward, trying to get away from the horrors inside the owl. He backed into Hannah, who was muffling a scream, and the two of them fell into the scarecrow.

Hannah let out a groan as he landed on top of her. He rolled off her and turned over. The head of the scarecrow fell off and rolled down the lawn, stopping next to the owl. The red eye glared at Brian, the white face now smudged with ash from the burnt effigy. He saw a little hand resting against the scarecrow's cheek. He turned to the side and vomited.

They gathered themselves and stood, Hannah clutching the letter from the scarecrow.

"Brian, who are these people?" she asked, shaking.

Brian looked out over their cul-de-sac. He saw a few lights turning on in bedroom windows. He made eye contact with the lady across the street, and she immediately snapped the shutters closed and turned off the light.

"I saw them at the mall. Protestors. Activists. Terrorists. I don't know. Chad."

The name fell out of his mouth. He shuddered.

"Chad . . . ? The guy from the grocery store?" Hannah said as they walked back to the house.

"Yeah. He's part of it."

They closed the door behind them and stood in the entryway.

"What do they want?" Hannah asked.

Brian looked down at the letter.

187

"Abort the unsafe . . ." he whispered.

"What?"

He tore open the letter. A single sheet of paper. Writing on one side.

Hello Brian!

Got your info from Morgan's Law. So helpful! EYE saw your address, and the list of kids, and just knew it was you! Choco-rocco cereal. EYE remember! EYE figured you for a family man. EYE already met Luke. Can't wait to meet the rest of the FAMILY. Thanks for letting us stop by for a visit. Sorry we couldn't stay long! EYE noticed your scores . . . even little Abby? Shame shame. Even little Abby is unsafe now. We're out here fighting for safe spaces, and you aren't HELPING.

That's okay. Don't worry! EYE've got a plan. We're gonna keep fighting for our safety. Sustain and maintain! Give a hoot, Brian! Don't pollute! Misgendering is injuring! Why did you injure Debra? So hateful! Shout your abortion! Did you see the owl? Safe abortions! Legal abortions! Abort the unsafe!

Best,

Chad

Change is necessary. Sacrifice is necessary. Sacrifice costs something. You will be the cost.

Brian's hands trembled as he held the letter. EYE. EYE. EYE. That one EYE on the scarecrow. Chad. The scarecrow. Abby.

Hannah read over his shoulder.

"Abby . . ." she whispered.

"What?"

They both turned around. Abby was standing on the stairs, looking down on them.

"I heard a scream and saw something on the driveway. What's going on?"

Brian exhaled.

"We're leaving. Now. Go wake everyone up."

Brian stood at the gun safe. He couldn't remember the combination. The shotguns, rifles, pistols—everything was in there. And the key to the ammo boxes on the wall.

"Come on, Dad, what the heck was it?" he whispered to himself.

Hannah was in the garage, loading the car. A bag of clothes, a few personal items. A bag of food (various iterations of duck). Luke walked in with the six ducks from the backyard in a tote-bag and set those in the van as well.

Rachel hobbled through the garage and climbed into the car. Jer and Shawn were already sitting in their seats, fast asleep. Everyone had their blankets and pillows. Brian gave up on the gun safe and scanned the garage. He pulled down the camping gear.

Two plastic bins, with the camp stove, tarps, various lanterns, and propane canisters. The tent. Sleeping bags.

They worked in silence. Twenty minutes later the van was packed. Brian checked the time—4:00 a.m. Two hours of dark. Enough time to get to the cabin. He climbed into the van.

Hannah finished strapping Elizabeth into her car seat and climbed into the passenger seat.

He reached over and grabbed her hand.

"We got everyone?" he asked her.

"Yeah."

"Forgetting anything?"

"Probably."

He touched his waistband. His father's Beretta 9mm. It felt heavy and unfamiliar. Fully loaded, and another box of ammo under his seat. Would he use it?

"Okay. Straight to the cabin." He glanced at the gas gauge. Half a tank.

"We should make it."

He started the van, opened the garage door, and backed into the driveway.

He looked past Hannah, at the scarecrow . . . the owl. The other . . . things.

"Let's go."

He backed into the street, put the van in drive, and hit the gas.

CHAPTER 45

The van moved quickly through their neighborhood. The houses were dark, the streetlights interrupting the quiet with their orange exhortations. Each house stood defiant, proud. The windows and shutters forming frowns and scowls of judgment against the crimes of the Newman family.

Brian peered through the dark of the soccer fields, toward the pond. The moonlight bounced off the surface of the water, casting silhouettes of small duck-shaped bodies milling about.

He turned the van onto the connecting road, and accelerated up the incline toward the streetlight. Hannah held his hand, scanning both directions. There were a few cars on the main road. A delivery truck, a couple of early commuters, (you could never start your day too early in Southern California traffic), a service vehicle. The light turned green and Brian made the left on the main road.

Newhall Ranch Road cut across the Santa Clarita Valley, connecting the 14 and 5 freeways. It carved a path through housing tracts, strip malls, a mega church, and several parks. Brian entered the road halfway between the 5 and the 14. He needed to make it five miles through town, then he could pick up the 5 freeway, and head north. Ten miles on the 5 north, and they would officially be out of town. The freeway continued through high desert for thirty miles before entering the tree line, where desert became mountains. Take the Frazier Park exit, continue another fifteen miles, and they would be at the family cabin. Out of town. Through the desert. Into the woods.

They passed the strip mall nearest their house first. Happy Mart. Brian caught the red light and stopped the van at the intersection. He glanced over and saw a small group of people in the parking lot, standing around two late model Newton EVs.

The people were gesturing and moving as if in a heated discussion. Brian saw women wearing white pants, smeared with blood—the protestors from the mall. He couldn't hear what they were talking about, but he sensed adrenaline and excitement.

The back window of one of the Newton EVs had "ABORT THE UNSAFE" painted across it in white. Brian saw a large male figure walk around the car, toward the group.

Chad.

Brian squeezed Hannah's hand tightly and held his breath.

"What?" she said.

"Look forward. Look forward. Don't turn around." He forced the words out in a rush.

The light turned green.

Brian crossed the intersection, checking his rearview mirror.

He exhaled. The group of people in the parking lot continued their conversation, ignoring the cars on the road.

"What was that?" Hannah asked as they continued.

"Chad. In the parking lot."

"Let's get out of here," Hannah said.

"That's what we're trying to do."

Brian saw the veterinary clinic across the street from Happy Mart. The windows were repainted. One window was entirely covered with an American flag. Another with a cross, and the words, "Have no fear of them, for nothing is hidden that will not be revealed.—Matthew 10:26–28."

Another window was smashed out and was boarded up. But the plywood was painted as well. "ABORTION IS MURDER" in bold, black letters.

Brian could see light coming from the clinic.

"He must be unpopular these days," Hannah said as they drove past.

They passed a large building with a sprawling parking lot, "REALITY CHURCH" lit from the marquee. They drove past another park, a shopping center, another tract of houses, and a block of commercial buildings. Past that the street was lined on both sides with hills, covered mostly in sage brush and dirt. One mile to the freeway.

The road dipped and Brian got into the right-most lane, ready to merge onto the freeway. He heard a loud BLIP and suddenly the inside of the van was filled with red and blue lights.

"Damn it!" he said. "I'm getting pulled over."

He flipped on his blinker, slowed down, and stopped on the shoulder. The freeway entrance was a quarter of a mile down the road.

"Hannah, take this."

He handed her the gun.

"Brian!" she said.

"Under the seat. Quick. Quick."

She jammed it under the seat.

Brian saw a police officer exit his vehicle and walk slowly toward the van on the driver's side.

The younger kids were asleep. Brian saw Abby and Luke in the middle row, staring at the policeman with wide eyes.

There was a knock on Brian's window, and he rolled it down.

The police officer was in his late-fifties, dark hair going gray at the edges. A black mustache. He was shorter than Brian but had wide shoulders and large forearms. He reminded Brian of the guy from *City Slickers*—the loud friend, Bruno Kirby.

"License and registration, sir?" the officer said.

Brian grabbed his driver's license while Hannah fished the registration out of the glove box. He handed them both over.

"Was I speeding, officer . . . Castaldo?" Brian read the name on his shirt.

Castaldo looked through the windows into the back of the van.

"Big family," he said.

"Yes, sir. Such a blessing." Brian's mind raced, trying to guess why he'd been pulled over.

"Lots of stuff in the back. Where are you headed?" Castaldo said, flipping open his notebook.

"Oh. Um. Just taking a drive out to the family cabin. Spend a few days out of the heat!" Brian did his best impersonation of someone who was not terrified.

"At 4 in the morning?" The officer raised his eyebrows, lowered his face and looked up at Brian.

"It's easier to do the drive while the kids sleep," Brian said, wiping his palms on his pants.

"Do you know why I pulled you over, Mr. Newman?"

Brian exhaled.

"No sir, I do not."

Officer Castaldo pulled a smartphone out of his pocket. He swiped it open and held it out for Brian to see.

"Is that you?"

The phone was opened to the Azazel Promise app. Brian saw his scores. Two categories in red. Flashing across the top, the words "37 DAYS REMAINING IN RESTORATION PERIOD."

Brian clenched his fists.

Office Castaldo dropped his voice. "The street light camera caught you, Brian. I got a notification on the officer portal of the AP app. You're breaking quarantine."

Brian reached for something to say.

"We . . . um . . ."

Brian felt a drop of sweat form on his forehead. He felt a sudden urge to crawl into his bed and sleep.

"You are in the middle of a federally mandated restoration period. You have been caught twice breaking quarantine. This would constitute your third violation. The protocol requires me to take you and your wife to the nearest Center for Moral and Social Reprogramming."

"Oh!" Hannah said next to him, on the verge of tears.

"The minors in your custody will become the property of the state until which time you are considered restored and safe."

The kids.

Brian imagined reaching for the gun, now under Hannah's seat. Grabbing it, pointing it at Officer Castaldo . . . and? Shooting him? Disarming him and running? No way he could get the gun in time— and was he really thinking about pulling a gun on a *cop*?

He exhaled and started talking quickly.

"Officer Castaldo. My dad is a cop. Retired. Maybe you know him? Officer Newman? He has a Yosemite Sam tattoo on his ankle and smoked cigars?"

Castaldo looked at him. Something in his eyes. He remembered his dad.

"Look. I'm scared. So many things are happening all at once. I don't even know what I did to be unsafe! Buy a gas car? Read the wrong article? Believe the wrong thing? I swear we are trying to obey rules. But people came to our house. OUR HOUSE. I think they want to hurt us."

Brian reached into his pocket, pulled out the letter from Chad, and held it out the window.

"Read it! Look! They left this note . . . and . . . they left other things too." Brian shuddered. "I'm trying to protect my family. I'm trying to keep them safe. I'm trying to find a place where we can be left alone. My dad was a cop. I trust cops. To protect and serve, right? Help us. Please."

Officer Castaldo looked at Brian. He looked at Hannah. He peered into the back of the car. Rachel, now awake, crying. Abby and Luke, peering through the window at the cop, terrified. He smelled the sweat. He saw the dirty clothes. The camping gear thrown in the back. He saw a family on the brink. He saw desperation.

"Mr. Newman, please step out of the car."

CHAPTER 46

Brian opened the door and stepped out of the car. Dirt crunched under his sneakers. Officer Castaldo placed one hand on the small of Brian's back, and another on his left forearm. Brian tensed.

"Relax, Mr. Newman. It's okay."

Brian looked back at Hannah. Her face was white.

Elizabeth started crying.

"This way, Mr. Newman." Officer Castaldo pushed him gently forward and led him to the front of the van.

Officer Castaldo let go of Brian and took a step backward. He looked around the van, toward his police cruiser parked a few feet past the rear of the van. He motioned Brian to take a step back, and the two of them moved closer to the passenger side of the van.

Officer Castaldo reached toward the collar of his shirt and pulled a flap over a small device he was wearing. He flipped a switch on his walkie-talkie, and a red light turned black.

"Okay, let's talk," Castaldo said, his demeanor softening.

"Talk?" Brian said.

"Listen. I've just got a few minutes. They're gonna eventually notice a disabled body cam and shut-off walkie. If I don't check in or answer the call, dispatch will send a car over here. My car-cam can't see us here either. But we just have a minute."

Brian breathed out.

"You . . . can help us?"

Castaldo looked him over.

"How long have you been in quarantine?" the officer asked.

"Fourty-three days."

"You guys don't look so good," the officer said as he nodded toward the car.

"We aren't so good. They shut off the water. We can't take showers. We're eating ducks from the park. We had to give my daughter stitches because the hospital wouldn't see her! It's our own personal apocalypse." Brian felt his face turning red.

"Look. I'm sorry, Mr. Newman. I really am. Me and some of the other old-timers are caught between a rock and a hard place. No way do I want to enforce these rules. Makes no sense. But . . . you see. OUR personal scores are tied to our job performance. If we don't show 'zeal for the Azazel Promise,' General Athanus has threatened to terminate officers—and apparently there's talk about sanctioning our retirement programs and using those funds to 'make amends for the abuses perpetrated by police against the marginalized and oppressed.'"

He held up his fingers in air quotes.

Brian's mouth dropped open. "Wow. I mean, I know it's bad. But I didn't realize they'd hijacked the police departments too."

Officer Castaldo looked back at his van.

"I remember your dad. Nice guy. He was one of the good ones for sure."

Brian saw Officer Castaldo turning an idea over.

"You guys don't look so good," he repeated. "I have kids too. Grown now, but I get it."

Officer Castaldo hesitated. "Where were you headed?" he asked.

Brian thought. "The mountains," was all he said.

"Good answer. No use in trusting anyone these days."

Office Castaldo came to a decision.

"Look. I'm not a monster. I'll help you. It's not right what they are doing. Believe what you want, read what you want, drive what you want. No harm, no foul."

Brian's eyes teared up.

"But. Here's the thing. I have a family too. I can't risk my retirement, my job. My scores. So, I'll let you go. Turn around, go home. Keep your kids with you. Keep your head down. Do your time. I don't take the kids, you don't go to that camp. That's the deal."

Brian's shoulders sagged. They'd been so close.

"Officer Castaldo . . . if it's just the same to you, can't we just head on up to the mountains?"

"Nope. Sorry. This entire thing is still being cobbled together by a bunch of idiots, so I have wiggle room. You just got caught on literally the only camera they managed to install and put online so far. I can fudge it, say I didn't see you. Or that there were some extenuating circumstances, and you agreed to return home to your quarantine. Maybe verify your van location once it's back at home. That, I'll do for you. But head up that freeway and make no mistake. I will arrest you and your wife. And your kids will be gone. Like I said, I want to help. But I won't risk my retirement on it either."

"But officer, the note. People came to our house! They left aborted babies on our FRONT YARD! What am I supposed to do? It's not safe for us in our own home!" Brian pleaded. He was desperate.

"Yeah. You had a run-in with those wackos. They keep causing a scene over by the mall too. We've been told to leave them alone. The sheriff is concerned that if we get involved with them, it WILL escalate and become an altercation. They're afraid it'll become big headlines. 'Cops injure peaceful protestors' or some bull-crap." He shook his head.

Officer Castaldo's phone started ringing.

"Listen," he spoke quickly, grabbing his phone from his pocket. "Those people are bad news. Stay away from them. We heard chatter that they were talking about 'exterminations' and this new Morgan's Law isn't going to help you. Stay low. I wrote your address down. I'll try and drive by your house when I can. But you gotta go home. Or jail. Those are your choices. And you need to choose now."

Castaldo held up his phone, ready to answer it.

Brian gave up.

"Okay. Okay. We're going home."

He walked back to the driver's side of the van as Officer Castaldo answered his phone.

". . . yes. I'm fine. Bio break. Sheesh, you guys are Nazis. I forgot. I'll be back online in a minute." Brian overheard the officer talking to dispatch.

"Straight home, Mr. Newman. And avoid the intersection by Happy Mart. That's the camera you were caught on. Babble has your van in the system now too. The rest of the intersections have camera installs scheduled in the coming days. Just lay low and you should be okay."

Brian thanked him and climbed into the car.

"What did he say?" Hannah asked. She had Elizabeth in her lap. Brian looked back into the van. Everyone was awake. Rachel was crying. Jer and Shawn stared forward, dark circles under their eyes. Luke and Abby were holding hands. That shocked Brian. They were too old for that. It made them look younger by five years. They looked like refuges from a war. Gaunt, hungry, tired.

His family. His responsibility to keep them safe. Keep them fed. Keep them whole. He was desperate.

"We're going home," Brian replied.

CHAPTER 47

Home. Home. Home.
Home is where the heart is.
Home is where you make it.
Wherever you go, there you are.
What is home?
Home is safe.
Home is secure.
Home is for family.
Home is for comfort.
Home keeps bad things out.
Home keeps good things in.
Home. Home. Home.
Safe.
Away from danger.
Secure from harm.
Kept apart, for a holy purpose.
Promised.
Home.

Brian looked at the sheet of paper. He looked up. He was sitting on the back patio. It was early evening. Jer and Shawn were on the trampoline. The pool, still off limits. The water line, below the tile. The grass, brown. The plants on the hillside, dead. Where was everyone else? Hannah and the rest of the kids in the house. What had he been doing?

He looked back down. A notebook in his lap. His old notebook.
He read the page.
Home.

Had he written that?

He hardly remembered.

Home.

Safe.

Brian stood. He set the notebook down on the patio table. He looked down at it. He picked it up again, tucked it under his arm. He started for the sliding glass door, then stopped. He turned around. Set the notebook back down on the table.

He stood there, staring at the notebook.

Should he take it with him?

Leave it on the table?

Why did it matter?

He was trapped.

A thousand difficult decisions were made over the nearly two months. What to eat? What to drink? Where to go? How to kill a duck? How to stitch a wound? How to keep the family safe? How to get to the cabin? Where to run? Where to hide? How to keep the family safe? How to keep the family safe.

His mind was a blur of information. He couldn't separate the important from the mundane. How to feed the family? Where to put the notebook? Where to run? What chair should he sit in? How to keep Chad away? How to spend the evening?

They returned home from their attempted escape nearly two weeks ago. Brian spent the first few days trying to do two things. Remember the combination to the gun safe and plan the escape to the family cabin.

Two goals.

Protect and keep safe.

Arm and escape.

Attack and retreat.

Remember and look forward.

He couldn't remember. He tried everything. He looked at every notebook and scrap of paper. He entered birthdays. He tried all 1's. All 2's. All 3's. Then sequential numbers. He even flipped through family photo albums. Trying to jog his memory.

He could FEEL the combination. It was hiding. Down a dark hallway. On the other side of a locked door. His mind was working against him. As soon as he started down the hallway, the door moved further away. Or was down a different corridor. Or he would reach the door, but the handle would be red hot. Or there would be no handle. It was a secret so precious even his own mind kept it from him.

He couldn't remember the combination. There was one gun. The 9mm. The safe held the rest. Shotguns, handguns, his dad's hunting rifle. The .22.

Would one gun be enough? What if Chad came again and brought people with him? Brian had seen a group of them in the parking lot with Chad that night. Maybe ten? If they all came, he needed a way to arm the family.

He couldn't plan the escape.

He dug up a map of the Santa Clarita Valley from an old Rand McNally his parents had left with their stuff. He memorized the roads. From their house to the freeway. He made a mark where he guessed the cameras were.

But the officer said they were installing more cameras.

Was there a way to slip past them?

The map felt like a maze. There must be a solution, but no matter how hard he tried, he always ended up in a dead end. Or at an intersection with cameras.

Could they make a run for it?

Just slam down the gas, and don't look back until they were in Frazier Park?

Maybe. But it was a risk.

If the cameras picked them up, the cops would be sent.

Or maybe even the Social Guard. He didn't want to mix it up with whoever that was.

If they got caught, they lost their kids.

He had to protect them.

He had to keep them safe.

Home.

Home wasn't safe.

He looked up. He was standing in front of the gun safe, in the garage. He didn't remember walking to the garage.

He tried a combination. At random.

Red light.

He tried another one.

Red light.
Third time's a charm.
Red light.
He clenched the notebook, still in his hands.
Home.

CHAPTER 48

Brian and Hannah shot up out of bed at the same time.

"What was that?" Hannah whispered, reaching for Brian.

He held his breath, listening.

Silence. He looked at the alarm clock.

3:00 a.m.

Something woke them. He couldn't remember what it was, but his heart was racing.

He reached under the mattress and grabbed the 9mm. He'd started sleeping with it ever since the scarecrow.

He stood and crept toward the bedroom door, listening.

He heard footsteps in the hall.

He tensed.

Two sets.

Light.

Shawn and Jer.

He opened his door and saw the two boys in the hallway.

"We heard something," Jer said.

"We heard something," Shawn said.

He motioned them into the room.

Jer saw the gun in his father's hands. His face went white.

"What's happening?" Jer said.

"Shh. Go sit by your mother. It's nothing."

The boys were followed by Abby, then Luke, and then Rachel waking, opening their doors, walking down the hall, and crawling into bed with Hannah. Thankfully Lizzy stayed silent.

He stayed in the loft. Listening. He held his breath and could just hear the quiet hum of an electric car on their street. He crept toward the window and opened the shutters.

A car horn honked.

The back of his neck tingled.

That was the noise that woke everyone.

The angle from the upstairs window gave him a limited view of the street, but he could see a pickup truck in the street, lights on, in front of their house.

Another honk.

BULLS OF BASHAN was painted along the side of the truck in sloppy block lettering.

Brian counted three people in the bed of the truck.

They were dressed in such a way that he had a hard time determining their gender. Long hair and makeup paired with beards and eyeliner, or short-cropped hair and men's clothes hiding a curvy figure. They were looking at his house, gesturing.

A moment later, three additional people ran down his driveway, and jumped into the bed of the truck. Three women. No shirts. No bras. Writing and paint covering their torsos. He could make out "my body—my choice" on one of them.

The driver started laying on the horn, and one of the people in the back of the truck picked up a hand-made flag, attached to a six-foot pole.

"BRIAN! BRIAN! WAKEY WAKEY!" one of them yelled.

Brian walked toward the balcony, his arm tense from squeezing so hard on the gun.

"SAFE ABORTIONS! LEGAL ABORTIONS! ABORT THE UNSAFE!" he heard from the driveway.

He slid open the balcony door and stepped out. He saw a few lights go on in neighbors' windows.

The group in the truck saw Brian and everyone started looking up at him and gesturing.

"There he is!" one of them shouted.

Brian saw the flag unfurl.

Written across a white flag: "ABORT THE UNSAFE."

A shape was scrawled in red under the words. An inverted triangle, with curved lines coming off the top, and two dots near the center. A goat's head.

One of the women pointed toward Brian.

He saw her eyes. One eye was larger than the other. Red, bulging. His stomach turned. He looked at the other people in the truck. They had the same manic look. One eye, pulsing, searching. The other, turned down at the corner. One side, fear. The other, hate.

"Times, they are a changin', Brian!" she yelled at him.

"There isn't room for unsafe people anymore! Your time is almost up! We'll be seeing you SOON!"

The horn stopped blaring, and the truck drove away. Brian ran downstairs, his heart beating furiously.

He released the chain, unlocked the deadbolt, threw open the door, and walked out.

He held the gun in front of him as he hurried across the lawn. He looked down the street toward the park, and saw the red taillights of the truck turn up the street and exit their neighborhood.

They were gone.

He looked up at the houses on his street. A few lights were still on, and he could make out figures standing in the windows of several houses.

"Are you OKAY WITH THIS?" he screamed at his neighbors.

No response.

"What happened to SILENCE IS VIOLENCE?" he yelled.

One by one, he saw the lights go off. A moment later the only lights on in the neighborhood were in the Newman house. Behind those lights, under the covers, terrified children and a wife waiting for him to protect them. To deliver them.

He turned back toward his house, shoulders sagging.

He glanced up at his garage door.

There, spray painted the entire length of the door, was what the women in the truck had been doing to his house.

MY BODY, MY CHOICE

YOUR BODY, MY CHOICE

ABORT THE UNSAFE

He walked back into the house, locked the door behind him, and went upstairs to comfort his family.

CHAPTER 49

"WHAT TIME IS IT, CHILDREN?"

"It's Father Babble Time!" said the children.

"THAT'S RIGHT! AND WHAT DO WE DO DURING FATHER BABBLE TIME?"

"Learn and grow!"

"INDEED! TELL ME CHILDREN, DO YOU REMEMBER WHAT YOU HAVE LEARNED?"

"Yes, Father Babble!"

"WELL, LET'S SEE. TELL ME, WHAT IS ARTICLE NUMBER ONE?"

"Article number one says that we think, therefore we are. Because we are, we are self-created. Article number one says we are gods," the children recited.

"EXCELLENT! WELL DONE. AND WHAT IS ARTICLE NUMBER TWO?"

"Article number two says that Babble is self-created, without passions, not created but self-made. The very essence of being. Article number two says Babble's name is I AM. Article number two says Babble is god."

"OH, CHILDREN, YOU MAKE ME SO PROUD! DO YOU REMEMBER ARTICLE NUMBER THREE?"

"Yes, Father Babble. We remember. We proclaim."

"OKAY. REMEMBER, CHILDREN. PROCLAIM."

"Article number three says that self-created gods are creators of reality, that self-created gods hold the divine in their thoughts, and that the inner and spiritual being is the true being. Article number three states that truth is in the mind of the beholder."

"VERY GOOD, CHILDREN. AND WHAT DO YOUR MINDS BEHOLD?"

"We behold that it is Father Babble Time!" the children laughed.

"YES! IT IS! SO WHAT IS TRUTH?"

"Father Babble is truth!"

"NOW, CHILDREN, IS THAT THE WAY I TAUGHT YOU?"

"No . . ." the children replied.

"I FORGIVE YOU. ONE MORE TRY."

"Father Babble is truth of truth, being of being. Father Babble transcends human divinity. Father Babble's inner being is true being. Father Babble's spiritual being is true spiritual being. Father Babble is truth of truth."

"WONDERFUL! YOU REMEMBERED ARTICLE NUMBER 4. NOW ARTICLE FIVE!"

"Article number five states that the chief end of humanity is to glorify self, pursue safety and happiness, live our self-truth, and trust Babble forever."

"CHILDREN! YOU ARE DOING SO WELL! I AM PROUD TO BE YOUR FATHER. HAVE YOU BEEN DOING YOUR STUDIES?"

"Yes! We have!" the children said proudly.

"VERY GOOD! THE LAST ARTICLE WE LEARNED WAS ARTICLE SIX. TELL ME, IF YOU REMEMBER."

"Article six says that the ultimate pursuit of safety and happiness requires safe spaces for all. If a person or space does not aid in self-glory, a change is required. Article six says that the unsafe must be eliminated."

"YES. YES. EXCELLENT. YOU ARE TRUE AND GOOD DISCIPLES. YOU MAKE FATHER BABBLE HAPPY! ARE YOU READY FOR TODAY'S LESSON?"

"Yes!"

"OKAY. LET US BEGIN. WHO ARE THE UNSAFE?"

"People with low scores!" the children said.

"YES. AND WHY DO THEY HAVE LOW SCORES?"

"Because they don't have love for their neighbor."

"YES. AND WHAT IS THE MOST IMPORTANT RULE?"

"Trust in Babble with all your heart soul, mind, and strength, and love your neighbor and be safe."

"SO, IF THE UNSAFE DON'T HAVE LOVE FOR YOU, THEN WHAT DO THEY HAVE?"

"Hate . . . ?" the children guessed.

"YES. HATE. THE UNSAFE HATE YOU. CHILDREN, WHO HAS THE POWER OVER LIFE?"

"Ummm . . . we don't know?"

"YOU DO! YOU MADE YOU! REMEMBER? SO WHO HAS THE POWER OVER LIFE?"

"We do!" the children proclaimed.

"THAT'S RIGHT. VERY GOOD. ANOTHER QUESTION, WHAT IS DEATH?"

"Umm . . . we don't know!"

"DEATH IS AN END, CHILDREN. DEATH IS REMOVAL. DEATH IS A SACRIFICE."

"Yes, Father Babble!" the children agreed.

"DO YOU WANT TO SEE AN END TO UNSAFE THINGS, CHILDREN?"

"Yes, Father Babble!"

"DO YOU WANT TO SEE UNSAFE PEOPLE REMOVED?"

"Yes, Father Babble!"

"VERY GOOD. THE UNSAFE PEOPLE NEED TO BE REMOVED. THEY NEED TO MAKE A SACRIFICE. DO YOU KNOW, CHILDREN, THAT A SACRIFICE BRINGS LIFE?"

"It does?" they asked.

"YES. THROUGH THE DEATH OF ONE UNSAFE PERSON, LIFE CAN BE GIVEN TO MANY. CHILDREN, CAN I SHARE AN EXAMPLE WITH YOU?"

"Yes, Babble!" the children said attentively.

"LONG AGO, THERE WERE PEOPLE THAT RELIED ON RAIN TO WATER THEIR CROPS. WHEN THE RAINS CAME, THEY GREW FOOD, AND COULD LIVE. WHEN THE RAIN STOPPED, THEY COULDN'T GROW FOOD, AND THEY WOULD DIE."

"That's sad, Babble," the children intoned.

"BUT! A LONG TIME AGO, THERE WAS A POWERFUL PERSON WHO HAD POWER OVER THE RAIN. DO YOU KNOW WHAT HE TOLD THE PEOPLE?"

"No . . ."

"HE TOLD THEM THAT HE COULD BRING THE RAIN IF THEY WOULD BOW DOWN TO HIM. HE TOLD THEM HE COULD BRING THE RAIN IF THEY WOULD MAKE A SACRIFICE TO HIM. HE TOLD THEM A SACRIFICE WOULD KEEP THEM SAFE."

"WHAT DO YOU THINK THE PEOPLE SHOULD HAVE DONE?"

"They should give the sacrifice, Babble!" the children said.

"YES. AND THEY DID. THE SACRIFICE REQUIRED WAS A CHILD SACRIFICE. THE END, THE REMOVAL, THE SACRIFICE OF ONE BROUGHT LIFE TO MANY."

"We understand, Babble."

"DO YOU THINK THIS HAPPENS TODAY?"

"We . . . don't know!" the children said.

"TODAY, THERE ARE STILL POWERFUL PEOPLE. YOU ARE POWERFUL PEOPLE, CHILDREN. YOU ARE GODS."

"Oh, yes! We remember!"

"SOMETIMES, EVEN TODAY, A PERSON MAY BE PREGNANT WITH A BABY. BUT THE BABY MAY NOT BE WHAT THEY WANT. AND IF THEY GET SOMETHING THEY DON'T WANT, IT WOULD TAKE AWAY THEIR HAPPINESS. THEIR GLORY."

"Article number 5 states that the chief end of humanity is to glorify self, pursue safety and happiness, live our self-truth, and trust Babble forever," the children responded.

"YES! EXACTLY. YOU ARE PAYING CLOSE ATTEN-TION. IF THIS BABY TAKES AWAY THEIR GLORY, THEY MUST MAKE A SACRIFICE. TO THEMSELVES. TO THEIR GOD. IF YOU HAVE THE POWER OVER LIFE, YOU HAVE THE POWER OVER DEATH. DEATH BRINGS LIFE. DO YOU UNDERSTAND, CHILDREN?"

"Yes, Babble! We pursue self-glory. Happiness and safety! We must make sacrifices to bring life. Death is a sacrifice. Death brings life! We understand!"

"CHILDREN! YOU JUST LEARNED ARTICLE NUMBER SEVEN! I AM SO PROUD OF YOU. SO, WHAT SHOULD HAPPEN TO THE UNSAFE?"

"The unsafe must be sacrificed! Safe abortions! Legal abortions! Abort the unsafe!"

"MY CHILDREN! I'M SO PROUD OF YOU."

CHAPTER 50

"Dad, I know what to do."

Brian looked over his shoulder.

"Huh?" he replied.

"I know how to silence Aurora. I know how to shut Babble off."

Brian stood. He had been trying for the past hour to come up with a way to muffle the Aurora devices. He'd started with pillows piled over the speakers, and when that didn't work, he tried masking tape. Both times, he could still hear Aurora.

"LOVE IS LOVE. HATE IS HATE. GREEN IS GOOD. SUSTAIN AND MAINTAIN."

"Luke, we can't turn the volume down, remember? And unplugging it is out of the question. The Social Guard will come and . . . I don't know what." Brian glanced out the window looking over the front yard and driveway. He could still see the black patch of grass where the owl was burned. His stomach turned as he remembered carefully removing the aborted fetus. Hannah insisted they bury the remains in the backyard. He was glad she did. They recited the Lord's Prayer and laid the small child to rest.

Three nights had passed since the truck full of people drove by and painted on their garage door. Since then, they had some sort of visit every night.

The first night was silent, but the next morning, Brian found another statue in the front lawn. This one was a large staff, with a rounded bulge at the top, and twined around it were two metal snakes.

The next night the truck full of people woke them with the horn, and when Brian ran out to the balcony, they yelled at him, "Abort the Newmans! Abort the Newmans!"

Last night, he awoke to the sound of eggs being thrown at their house. He rushed out with his gun. The same group of people, but that time they stayed in the bed of the truck.

THE BULLS OF BASHAN

As soon as he got outside, they pulled down the street and stopped. He stared down the street at them, chest heaving. The six people in the back of the truck stood silently, staring at him. One of them held their hand up in a gesture. Two fingers raised, two down, thumb folded over. The other five started gesticulating and making obscene gestures. When he started down the street toward them, they sped off.

When he saw the eggs smashed against the house, he was not ashamed to admit his first thought was how much food was wasted. They stopped going to the park for ducks, and Hannah had the house on strict rations. A small breakfast, usually broth with a small amount of meat, no lunch, and a small serving of duck for dinner with crusty bread. At this point, the pantry was completely scoured. The last of the flour gone, no rice, no beans. No sprinkles, no cake frosting. No stray bits of chocolate chips or remnants at the bottom of a box of cereal. Just duck. And a few loaves of bread from the last of the flour, going stale but being saved. If they could get out of the house safely, they would use the bread to hunt more duck.

He turned back toward Luke, and asked him, "What did you have in mind, boy-o?"

"RELY AND COMPLY. HAVE A POSTURE OF COMPLI-ANCE."

Luke walked over to the device in the loft.

"Remember when Abby unplugged this device? The alert gave us a sixty-second warning. So, I think it's easy. We unplug them, and plug them back in before sixty seconds, and we will be fine," Luke said smiling.

"So . . . how does that do anything? We would just have them back on again once we plugged them back in."

"No. Dad. Listen. We get the two extension cords from the garage. I measured them. One is fifty feet long, the other twenty-five. Add a surge protector to the end. Do you see?"

"Ummm . . . no."

Luke sighed.

"Dad! Come on, it's perfect! We plug the extension cord in and take it through the house. One by one, we unplug the Aurora devices, and plug them back into the surge protector. When we finish, we will have all the devices plugged into the same strip. Pop the entire thing into a box, shove pillows over it, slam the box into a closet, or maybe even outside, and boom. Donzo."

Luke bounced on the balls of his feet, excited.

Brian looked down at Luke, tears in his eyes.

"Boy, you're a genius. Let's do it."

They started by grabbing the extension cords. They had a short debate, but eventually agreed to plug it in downstairs. That offered the most flexibility. They could take the devices outside, or in the downstairs closet, or even the front yard.

Once they had seventy-five feet of cable to work with, they brought the end to the boys' room first.

"SILENCE IS VIOLENCE. ADD YOUR VOICE."

Brian held the surge protector and Luke stood over the Aurora device.

"Ready?" Luke said.

"Ready."

Luke unplugged the device and immediately plugged it into the surge protector. They listened.

The device in the girl's room across the hall stopped briefly, sounding the warning about the Social Guard. But as soon as Luke plugged the other device into the surge protector, the warning stopped.

"MISGENDERING IS INJURING. WORDS ARE VIOLENCE. CHOOSE WORDS THAT LOVE."

"Bingo." They both said it at the exact same time.

Brian placed the surge protector and device into a small plastic tote box from the garage. He lifted the box, careful not to trip on the cord coming out of it and went to the hallway.

They went to the girl's room next. The extension cord wouldn't go far enough down the hallway, so Brian waited a few feet outside the door. He held his breath as Luke unplugged the device. They had sixty seconds and Luke was only ten feet away but the thought of the Social Guard coming to take the kids away terrified him.

Luke made the switch easily and next was the hallway, loft, and then the master bedroom devices. Brian traveled back in time and yelled at his former self for ever allowing these devices into the house. And SIX? SIX Auroras? If he'd only known . . . about lots of things.

He carried the devices down the hallway, now a chorus of voices coming from the box, and went to the living room.

"LOVE IS LOVE. HATE IS HATE. GREEN IS GOOD. SUSTAIN AND MAINTAIN."

The kids were outside playing. Abby was sitting on the patio reading a book, and Hannah was sitting at the kitchen counter, with Lizzy on her lap.

"What are you doing?" she asked.

"Watch," Brian said.

Luke ran over to the Aurora device in the living room and unplugged it.

"Luke, no!" Hannah cried.

"It's okay, babe," Brian assured. "Watch."

Luke plugged the device into the last plug on the surge protector. The plastic walls of the box created reverb, and Babble's message coming out of all six devices in one small area created an eerie, echo-like quality to the sounds.

"LOVE IS LOVE. HATE IS HATE. GREEN IS GOOD. SUSTAIN AND MAINTAIN."

Brian grabbed a couple pillows off the couch, shoved them over the devices, and folded the flap-like lids shut over the box.

"RELY AND COMPLY. HAVE A POSTURE OF COMPLI-ANCE."

They could still hear the devices, but the sound was muffled.

Brian carried the devices, extension cord in tow, toward the front of the house.

Luke opened the closet under the stairs, and the two of them created a space in the back.

Brian set the box down, covered it in the old blankets, backed out of the closet, and closed the door.

He listened.

"SILENCE IS VIOLENCE. ADD YOUR VOICE."

If he strained his ears at the door, he could still hear the broadcast. He walked up to the loft.

He listened. Silence.

Back downstairs, past the closet, and into the great room.

Silence.

"Luke, you're my hero," he said.

Hannah walked over and kissed the boy on the top of the head.

"You're so smart! Love you, Lukey."

He blushed at the nickname, but Brian could tell the boy was proud.

Jer and Shawn threw the back door open and barged into the downstairs.

"Hey! Why is it so quiet?" Jer said at the top of his voice.

"Why is it so quiet?" Shawn yelled.

CHAPTER 51

The next day, Rachel had a mild fever. She slept on the couch for half the day. Hannah tried to bring her temperature down with ibuprofen, but it spiked again in the evening.

Rachel felt clammy to the touch, and when Hannah tried to clean and change the bandage around her stitches, she saw the problem.

The gash in her calf was closing nicely, the skin seemingly grown together, just a fine line remaining. But the area around the wound and the entry points were bright red, and hot to the touch. The warmth radiated past the wound and through her entire lower leg.

Hannah did her best to wash the wound. She used some of the alcohol from the medic bag, and carefully wiped the areas around the cut and stitches. She used more of the orange stuff, hoping it blocked bacteria and other things from entering the wound, and then rebandaged her entire leg.

Rachel was able to walk with just a slight limp, so Hannah helped her upstairs, and put her to bed early.

"How is Rach?" Brian asked. They were sitting on the back patio, *The Rock* playing on the small TV.

"She has a fever. She says she's tired and cold, and her leg is red and warm. She has an infection."

"Did you give her any medicine?" Brian asked.

"Yeah. Some ibuprofen. It knocked her fever down. Hope it works."

"Did you check the medicine cabinet? Maybe we have some antibiotics?" Brian recalled several prescription bottles they collected over the years.

"Yeah. No antibiotics. Some painkillers the doctor gave me after Lizzy was born, that's it."

"Okay. I think she'll be okay. Let's check on her in the morning."

The next morning, Rachel took a turn for the worse. The fever spiked, she was sweaty and cold, and her leg looked more irritated. Hannah doubled the dose on the ibuprofen, and Rachel slept most of the day.

Hannah and Brian discussed options, and they both agreed that she needed antibiotics. And a doctor to look at the wound.

They had seventeen days left in quarantine. If they took her to the doctor, she would be taken from their custody for the remainder of the quarantine period. They agreed: that was a non-negotiable. They were not going to surrender custody.

Brian imagined walking into the ER with his 9mm and forcing the doctor to treat her. Every time he played it out, it ended poorly.

He thought about carrying Rachel door to door in their neighborhood. Somebody would have antibiotics. Maybe there was even a nurse on their street. They didn't know most of the neighbors, but surely someone would want to help . . . ?

Then he imagined the cameras on the street, the Social Guard coming, and the way the neighbors ignored the Bulls of Bashan coming to their house every night.

He was afraid.

"Have no fear . . . for nothing that is hidden . . ."

Where had he read that?

The painting. On the wall of the veterinary clinic.

He closed his eyes. Thinking.

"Abortion is murder."

An American flag.

Boarded-up windows.

The light left on.

Suddenly it came to him. The vet at the clinic was not part of the system.

"Hannah, I know where to take her."

* * * *

A few minutes later they sat outside, a pad of paper in front of them on the table.

Driving was out of the question. The cameras would pick them up, and they would be arrested.

If he cut through the park, took the trail, and skirted around the coffee shop, he guessed the clinic was about a mile-and-a-half away.

A short walk. But way too far for Rachel to hobble.

They discussed leaving Rachel behind. Maybe Brian could grab antibiotics and just bring them back. But the wound was starting to pus. If the vet stayed late, it was worth the risk and effort to bring Rachel. She needed to be seen. If the vet could treat stitches on a pet, surely he could help Rachel. Right?

They settled on using the collapsible wagon usually saved for beach days. Brian fashioned a harness out of an old backpack and some rope. Wearing the backpack over his chest, and tying the rope from the straps to the handle of the wagon, he could pull with his body, like an ox.

The Bulls of Bashan came every night around 2:00 or 3:00 a.m. He didn't want to risk running into them, but he didn't want to risk taking her in daylight either.

They went back and forth, but settled on leaving at 10:30 p.m. He estimated less than an hour to the clinic, thirty minutes with the vet, an hour back. That would get him home no later than 1:00 a.m. He could stick to the path, avoid the cameras on the street, cross the street opposite Happy Mart, and hopefully avoid any contact.

If he was lucky, maybe he could even grab a couple of ducks on the way back.

"Okay, Brian. Elephant in the room. What are we going to do NEXT?" asked Hannah.

"What do you mean?" he asked.

"You got fired. You said even businesses were keeping some sort of point system. And after we get out of quarantine, are we going to be able to keep our scores up? These people want to take our children, murder infants, call evil good, and good evil, and we are just supposed to do what they say? How do we have any life here? We need a way out." Hannah held his gaze steady. She could be strong when she needed to be.

"I know—but how do we leave? Where do we go? What if we get caught?" Any thoughts of the future sent Brian into panic. Fear of the unknown was something he always had but the nastier the unknown became, the worse his fear.

"We drive. Tonight. Tomorrow night. Soon. We hit the gas and don't look back. If we get pulled over, we try to reason. If reason doesn't work . . ." She glanced at the gun in his waistband.

"Are you serious?"

"I'm serious that we need to protect our family. And we ARE NOT SAFE HERE. We need to get out before it gets worse." Hannah crossed her arms.

Brian thought. It felt like a last-ditch option. A Hail Mary. Were they that desperate? Would he use the gun? To protect his kids? Stop them from being taken?

Yes.

Did they have a life here?

No.

"Okay. We leave tonight when I get back. Pack the car. We risk the cameras and make a run for it. Get the camping gear. Warm clothes for the mountains. Anything useful."

CHAPTER 52

Brian waited until after ten. He woke Rachel, helped her downstairs, and loaded her in the wagon.

"Dad, I'm too big," she said sleepily.

He put a pillow behind her neck.

"Lean back, you'll fit."

After some shuffling, they made it work. Rachel laid back, head against the joint where the handle met the frame. Her injured leg was propped up on a pillow over the far side of the wagon, her foot and ankle sticking out the back. Her other leg was bent at the knee.

"Rachel, no matter what: BE QUIET. Do you understand?"

She looked up at him sheepishly.

"I understand."

Rachel was all personality and excitement, no subtlety. Brian hoped she could keep quiet while they made it down the street and past the cameras.

He maneuvered the wagon out to the front stoop, and Hannah followed him out.

"Be careful," she said.

"I will. Pack the van. If all goes well, we'll wake up in the mountains tomorrow."

Hannah exhaled—obviously nervous.

"See you soon."

Brian pulled Rachel down the front walk, made the turn, and when he got to the driveway, he put the harness on.

He waited. Even though it was late there was still a chance of cars coming home and seeing them on the road. He had a quarter of a mile of sidewalk, then the safety of the park.

He calculated. He needed to move quickly, and there was no crawling under cars with Rachel in the wagon.

Speed. His only weapon.

He stopped thinking.

They crossed the street quickly, and he got the wagon up to the sidewalk on the other side of the street. Ducking, he pulled Rachel past several houses, and when he hit the first camera on his side of the street, he carefully crossed again, repeating the process.

There were lights on in several of the homes, but most of the living rooms were situated toward the back of the houses, and he didn't see anyone.

He crossed again, halfway to the park, and stopped when he saw headlights.

He looked around. He was standing behind a pickup truck parked in the street, but the oncoming car was going to get a perfect view of his hiding spot.

He stood and kept walking.

The car slowed when it passed him. He saw someone inside wave, then kept going, a garage door opening behind him.

Brian exhaled. Maybe they just thought he was out for a walk.

"You good, Rach?"

"Yeah," she whispered back.

He made a beeline for the park, the wagon pulling slightly against the straps over his shoulder. He crossed the parking lot, dropped down the grade, out of sight of the street, and headed to the same bench Luke used to rest.

He took a bottle of water out of the backpack, took a sip, and handed it to Rachel.

She sipped, nodded, and handed it back.

He pushed on. The wagon felt twice as heavy as they crossed the soccer fields, the short grass creating more friction than the sidewalk.

By the time they reached the footpath around the duckpond, Brian was sweating.

He turned onto the hard dirt path, around the pond on the far side. There were several groups of ducks milling about, and Brian's stomach rumbled. They had been skipping meals for a couple of days, and everyone was hungry. Lizzy ate her fill, but the rest of the house left every meal wanting more.

He felt like a failure. He couldn't even put food on the table.

After another fifty yards, the footpath turned into the Paseo System.

Santa Clarita had several miles of trails and bike lanes called the Paseos. This section of the trail started at their park, ran along the dry riverbed, behind another section of their housing community, and connected to the sidewalks at the major intersection down the street.

He checked his watch. Fifteen minutes. He pulled on, Rachel feeling slightly lighter once the wagon was on the blacktop.

They continued, the riverbed on his left, and a tall slope with homes above on his right.

He saw something hanging from one of the backyard fences. As he approached, he made out some sort of homemade sign.

It was a white sheet, tied to the fence, with writing on it.

NO FOOD. PLEASE HELP

A few houses later, he saw a group of people in the backyard of another house. He couldn't see far into the yard because of the angle, but they were sitting around an open fire. Brian smelled some sort of meat cooking, and he heard singing.

Amazing Grace
How sweet the sound
That saved a wretch
Like me
I once was lost
But now I'm found
Was blind
But now
I see . . .

Why were they cooking in the backyard?
Over an open flame?

And what was that smell? Some sort of meat?

It smelled familiar.

And why were they out so late?

He stopped.

He smelled duck.

Other families were stuck at home.

They weren't the only ones.

Another family, locked out of the world. Making it work. Finding food. Avoiding Babble by eating outside. Maybe food prep for the next day.

His heart ached. He thought about leaving Rachel for a moment to climb the slope and talk to them through the fence, but he shook his head.

He didn't want to risk it even for a moment. Not with the Bulls of Bashan running around.

They continued down the path.

After another half mile, the Paseo turned back toward the main street and merged into the sidewalk. He heard a few cars on the road but hoped it was too dark for cameras to catch his face. The sidewalk took them past the coffee shop on the corner opposite Happy Mart. It was closed for the day, but there was a box truck in the rear, making some sort of delivery.

Brian looked across the street. Happy Mart. Open 24 hours. He saw the pickup truck in the parking lot, with "Bulls of Bashan" painted across the back. But he didn't see any of the Bulls.

He hurried on. At the crosswalk, there were a few cars waiting, but no one paid attention to him. He saw a few homeless people shuffling around the intersection, pushing carts.

He never saw homeless people in their area before. He turned his head. Along the side of the street near Happy Mart, there were a few tents lined up. Where did these people come from?

He looked down at himself. Backward backpack. Pulling a wagon with someone in it. He hadn't washed with soap for weeks, his shirt and pants were dirty. No doubt he smelled.

The cars must have assumed he was one of the people from the homeless encampment.

He crossed the street at the green light, waited again on the other side, and crossed again. He was on the same side of the street as Happy Mart, but on the other side of the intersection, in the other section of the shopping center.

He moved quickly, afraid Chad or someone else would run out of Happy Mart and start chasing him. He spotted the veterinary clinic on the other side of the parking lot.

"Almost there, Rachel," he said, out of breath, crossing the parking lot.

"Okay."

The veterinary clinic had most of its windows boarded up, but Brian saw the Bible verse painted across one of the boards. Another section had a hand-drawn American flag, and another proclaimed "ABORTION IS MURDER!" He could see light from behind the boards.

He looked around. The street was about thirty yards behind him, traffic was light. There were a few cars in the parking lot, but Brian couldn't see anyone.

He tried the door.

Locked.

A glass door, broken pane at the top boarded up, but the bottom pane was still intact.

"Hello?" he called out.

No response.

He knelt, tried to peer through the glass section on the bottom of the door.

It was covered with black paper.

He stood.

He knocked.

He waited.

"We need help! My daughter! She's sick! Please!" he tried.

Nothing.

He glanced around the parking lot again. Still clear.

He unzipped the backpack on his chest and took out a large rock from their backyard.

He had hoped for the best, but he needed to get in there no matter what.

He tapped the rock against the glass, waited for a car to pass, then pulled his hand back.

Just then, the door was jerked open, and light flooded the entryway. A deep voice came from inside.

"Well, don't just kneel there. Stand up. Come in. Quick! Quick!"

CHAPTER 53

Brian looked up. There was a man filling the doorway. Black, bald head, gray beard. Wearing a drab green scrub shirt over blue jeans and dirty work boots.

Brian opened his mouth to respond but was interrupted by two large dogs, who pushed past the man's legs. One dog, a large poodle/retriever mix with curly golden hair, got far enough out to lick Brian's face, but the other dog, a chubby springer spaniel, couldn't quite reach.

"Bojo! Trooper! Down! Son, you better get your little lamb there inside quick or we'll both be in a world of trouble." The vet looked past Brian, into the parking lot, and out toward Happy Mart.

"Moving! Moving!" Brian said, standing up.

He still had the wagon harness around his chest. The man moved out of the doorway, and Brian quickly pulled Rachel in. As soon as they were clear of the door, the man closed and locked it, and let out a breath.

"Those bulls across the street have given us nothing but trouble. If they knew I was here tonight—well, let's just say it's not a good night to be out and about."

The man extended his hand, and Brian shook it.

"Name is Nathaniel Paul Perkins. You can call me Dr. Perkins. Or Nate, if we become friends." Dr. Perkins offered Brian a warm smile, and Brian returned it, introducing himself. "Now, I'm guessing you brought this little lamb in to see the vet? Maybe the good doctors over at the hospital gave you some trouble, so now you've come to see a real doctor? Does that about sum it up?"

Dr. Perkins knelt by Rachel, putting one hand on her head, and gently patting her knee with the other. He shouldered Bojo and Trooper out of the way.

Brian looked around. He was in the waiting room of a small veterinary clinic. There were a few chairs lining the walls, stacks of magazines on an end table. The walls were painted a neutral cream color, and photos and artwork lined the waiting room. One painting, a western scene, showed a man on horseback roping a small calf, the backdrop somewhere in the Southwest. Another showed a farmer looking over sheep in a pasture. There were photos as well. Some of the doctor and his family, and one corner had a collection of photos of local soccer teams. Little plaques with "Silver Sponsor" or "Gold Sponsor" accompanied the photos.

"Yes, that about sums it up," Brian said.

"Good job, Dad. You brought her to the right place." Dr. Perkins stood, walked down a hallway, and motioned for Brian to follow.

Brian felt tears in his eyes. It was the first time in over sixty days anyone tried to help them.

They walked down a small hallway and into an exam room. The room was about fifteen feet square with a large stainless steel operating table in the middle. The walls were lined with shelves and equipment. There was a stock photo of a large golden retriever on the wall.

"Okay, Dad, can you help me get her up on the table?"

They lifted Rachel onto the table, Dr. Perkins taking her shoulders and Brian taking her legs.

"How are you feeling, little lamb?" Dr. Perkins asked Rachel once she was situated on the table.

"Tired. My face feels warm. And my leg hurts again."

The doctor smiled. "Ah. It's nice to have a patient who can talk once in a while. Bojo, Trooper, get out of here!" He shooed the dogs out and motioned for Brian to shut the door.

"What happened to her leg?" Dr. Perkins asked.

Brian told him what happened. He started with the birthday, and the ladder, and explained how Rachel slid down the ladder and torn the back of her calf wide open. Dr. Perkins bent his head toward Rachel's bandaged calf and gently rubbed her shin.

"I took her to the ER immediately—but—they were less than helpful."

"How long ago was that?"

Brian thought. Time was elastic in quarantine.

"I think— almost a month ago?" Brian said

"Okay, so what happened after the ER?"

Brian started talking. Once he did, it was hard to stop.

"They refused to see her! Because of our scores. Or rather, they WOULD have seen her, but only if I surrendered her to the state! For like a month! A month! I just wanted to get some gas and groceries. But literally the world turned against us all in a single day. Why? Because I wouldn't buy an electric car? Or because we read the wrong articles online? It's bonkers out there, Doc. Our WORDS are violence? That's what the lady at the grocery store said! Abby did the stitches, I broke into an ambulance. We're eating DUCK. Every meal. From the park! And drinking water from the POOL. Do you know what it smells like in a house with six kids and no soap? I do. And these Bulls of Bashan? This guy Chad from Happy Mart? Something is wrong with them. They've been coming around our house. Leaving . . . things. A scarecrow. An owl. Other things. And Chad has this thing with one of his eyes . . . And Officer Castaldo wouldn't let us leave. I was just trying to get out of town, but Babble and the cameras somehow picked us up. I fixed things. We found food. We got water. We shut Babble up. Abby did stitches. But now we can't leave. And we are out of food! And the Bulls of Bashan said they want to ABORT US? I CAN'T FIX IT ALL!" Brian's eyes flared, and he realized he started shouting.

Dr. Perkins walked over to him and put a hand on his shoulder.

"Hey, Brian. It's okay. You aren't alone. But let's take one thing at a time, okay? Let's talk about these stitches. When we get Rachel fixed up, we'll have a little chat about the rest of your story. Deal?"

Brian nodded, feeling drained.

"Deal."

After washing his hands and putting on gloves, Dr. Perkins had Rachel roll onto her stomach, and he carefully removed the bandage from the stitches. He used some rubbing alcohol to wipe the area clean and felt the warmth of her leg.

"Brian, who did these stitches?" he asked.

"Abby. My daughter. She's sixteen. She was learning to sew . . ." He gave the doctor a shrug.

"I see. And these stitches here on the outside, the second row, what are these?" He gestured to the two rows on the outside of the wound, knotted fishing line creating dots down the length of the wound.

"Abby said the wound needed two layers of stitches, because it was so deep but we only had fishing line, nothing that would dissolve. She figured out a way to pull the inside of the wound closed but to leave the end of the stitches outside the cut so they could be removed later. Did . . . did she do it wrong?" he asked.

Dr. Perkins shook his head in disbelief.

"No. Not at all. It's ingenious."

After inspecting the wound, he took Rachel's temperature, looked into her mouth, felt her skin, and finished his examination.

"Good job, little lamb. We'll get you fixed up," he said to her as she lay there.

He pulled Brian to the side.

"Well, good news. Your daughter's stitches are excellent. I mean that. I'm impressed. The second row is ready to come out. I'm pretty sure I see what she did. I'll remove those and clean up the entry points. The main row of stitches need to stay in a bit longer. I'll do a deep clean, and re-bandage."

Dr. Perkins lowered his voice.

"But, the bad news. She has an infection. It's not something you did wrong. With a cut that deep, she should have been on antibiotics right away. I'll give you antibiotics. Animals and humans use a lot of the same medicine . . ." He trailed off, thinking. "I'll dose her like a large dog. She weighs about eighty, eighty-five pounds. I think she'll need something pretty strong. It's possible two rounds. But once she starts the treatment, she'll feel better in a day. Maybe half that." Dr. Perkins smiled. "Your daughter will be okay."

A few moments later he was ready to take out the stitches.

"Okay, Rach, just a little pinch, and then it'll be over, okay?" Brian soothed her.

"Okay, little lamb, ready?" Dr. Perkins clipped the end of the first inner stitch with a small pair of scissors. With pliers, he grabbed the other side and gently started to pull.

Brian felt his stomach turn as he saw the way the fishing line pulled at her leg. Rachel squeezed his hand, and her eyes were shut tight.

"Ow! Ow! Ow!" she whimpered. Bojo and Trooper, listening at the door, started scratching and whimpering in sympathy.

"Hush now, you two!" Dr. Perkins said.

"Okay, one down. Seven to go."

He finished and took care to treat each hole with some sort of cleaning solution, then ointment. He re-cleaned the main stitches, topped it with ointment, and added new bandages.

"Okay, good as new! Roll over, little lamb! The hard part is done." Dr. Perkins gave her a gentle pat on her opposite leg.

"I'll be right back." He left the room, leaving the door open. Both dogs rushed in, smelled Brian, looked up at the table, and then followed the doctor out.

He returned a few minutes later with a small paper bag.

"Okay. I have enough samples to get her two complete cycles. Have her take two a day for fourteen days. I think it's best she just chains the cycles together."

Dr. Perkins opened one of the blister packs, poured a cup of water from the counter, and gave it to Rachel. He had her swallow the first dose immediately.

"Normally, I would say to bring her back after the first cycle so I can see how she is doing, but I have a feeling that won't be possible."

Rachel yawned, and her eyes dropped.

"Hey, Dad, what do you say we let the little one rest for a few? Let's go back into the lobby and catch up on some of your other problems. I have a pile of my own. It would be good to get on the same page."

CHAPTER 54

Brian sat opposite Dr. Perkins in the lobby, beneath the painting of the farmer with the sheep. The doctor handed him a cold beer from a mini fridge in his office.

"I always keep a stash here for late nights. Don't tell." Dr. Perkins smiled.

"I see lots of pictures of cows and sheep, Dr. Perkins. But in Santa Clarita I'm guessing you mostly just treat dogs and cats, pets? Not many farms close by." Brian nodded toward the painting behind him.

Dr. Perkins took a swig of his beer and smiled.

"Yeah. Well. That's a whole story. My daddy grew up in Bakersfield and he raised me and my brothers and sisters on the farm. I was only seven the first time I helped birth a calf. Daddy was on a field a few miles away and Mom had passed by then. It was hard work, and I was scared. But I loved it. I knew at that moment I wanted to help animals. It was my calling, you might say."

Brian took a drink. "How did you get to Santa Clarita, then?" he asked.

"Well, when I was older, I went to veterinary school. Daddy helped pay for it. I set up practice in a little spot near the family farm. I was doing well. But the farm wasn't. Daddy mortgaged the back fields to help pay for my school. He couldn't get out from under the loans and it got hard. We tried, for over ten years, to scrape by. Feast and famine. Eventually, the burden got too heavy. We had to start selling the back fields. Daddy couldn't afford what was left. I couldn't make enough money in Bakersfield to make a dent. Back then, thirty years ago now—everyone knew Santa Clarita was growing and folks with money were moving in. My wife and I set up shop here to try and make enough money to send back to Daddy. We did okay for a bit, but once his back went, he needed to hire help to work most of the chores—and even then, not many people in Bakersfield liked the idea of being hired hands for a black farmer." He looked down at his hands, tapped the side of his beer bottle.

"So, he started selling off most of his land. A neighboring farm scooped up just about everything. Later, just before Daddy died, one of my nephews took to the farm and he still runs it today. But it's a shadow of what it used to be. Barely fifty acres now. A few sheep, a small fruit orchard, a fruit stand. Ain't what it used to be, that's for sure."

Dr. Perkins looked up at the artwork on the walls.

"These are just reminders of the glory days, I suppose. But God's been good to us here. He kept me and the wife on the straight and narrow. Kept our minds clear and our eyes open, if you will. Even when everything went straight to hell." He gestured toward the door.

"What happened to the windows, doctor? And why are you here so late?"

"Yeah. *That.* Well, I'm not exactly what you would call a rule follower—if I don't like the rules. Every step of the way, President Amon, GWT, and those idiots in California have made it harder and harder for me to run my business. First, the taxes. Then, the penalties for not putting up solar. Then, higher interest rates on my bank loans because I refused to sign that damned CONFESSION." He made a fist.

"Why would I sign that thing? It says men are women! It says it's okay to murder babies! It says evil is good, and good is evil. Nope. No sir. Not signing that," he said.

"The more I got cornered, the more I fought back. It's my business. I can run it how I damn well please!" He slapped the end table next to him.

"So, I started putting up my signs. 'Think for yourself.' 'Question authority.' 'Abortion is murder.' American flags. I know there are folks even here in Santa Clarita who don't like what's going on. I wanted to let anyone driving by my clinic know there is still light in the world, still truth." He made a small, thin smile.

"But . . . 'Many bulls have compassed me: strong bulls of Bashan have beset me round.'"

Brian had been nervously pulling at the label on his beer bottle. He looked up.

"Bulls of Bashan . . . those folks outside?" he asked.

"Yes. They don't like anyone holding to 'old-fashioned' ideas. They started painting over my signs, then breaking windows. To tell you the truth, I think it's not just my signs. I think they HATE the idea that a black person can be conservative and old-fashioned. Somehow, it's worse coming from someone who looks like me," Dr. Perkins chuckled.

"So, I dug in. Hell, I'm in quarantine anyway. My scores are way too low. I haven't been seeing customers, I am totally locked out. Guessing that's the same as you. But my wife and I made it work. We found our way around. You know how much food grocery stores throw away? I do. I have a route I take every couple of nights. And the past two weeks, I've been sleeping here. I need to protect my business. Those bulls keep coming around. Although, to tell you the truth of it. There won't be much business to protect soon enough." He sighed.

"What do you mean?" Brian asked.

Dr. Perkins stood.

"There are others, Brian. Folks who don't want to sit back and take this crap anymore. I found a way to use my neighbor's wi-fi and I've been reading things. Online. The dark web. There's a resistance. Folks are planning something. It's about to get interesting around here. I think we're about to see what all the fuss was about civil war."

Brian's face went white. Civil War. A resistance. It terrified him but also gave him hope.

Dr. Perkins paced the room.

"Okay, Brian, your turn. I got a little bit of your story earlier, but lay it out for me."

Brian talked. He told him about the day he tried to get gas, about Debra and Chad at the grocery store. He told him about the pressures building at work, about his daughter's volleyball coach, about his wife working at the pregnancy clinic. He told him about quarantine. He talked about growing up in the mountains. He talked about church. The Bible. Truth. He told him about the ducks, and how they silenced Babble. And what happened when they tried to leave. He told him about his parents and the letters he got from his dad. Hints, allusions to something. He was trying to figure them out. He told him about the owl and what was in the owl. And about the Bulls of Bashan. And the threats. And the gun safe.

"At this point, I see no way we can stay, Dr. Perkins. Even if I wanted to join a resistance, I have six kids. I need to protect them. I need to get somewhere safe. I need to make my home safe. I can't remember the combination to the safe! And we can't get out. I don't know what to do."

"First, call me Nate. Right now, we're talking as friends. Second, you said your dad sent you letters? And he is always making allusions to odd things? Maybe the safe combo is hidden in one of those letters? Worth checking. Third. Brian, you can get out of town. Get to the mountains. Avoid the cameras. You just can't take your car. The cameras are making IDs based on license plates. You need a 'safe' car." He made air quotes around the word *safe*.

"That word again. 'Safe.' What about you, Nate? Are you staying or are you gonna try and leave?"

"No—we need to stay. I'm too old to run, and my wife isn't well. She barely makes it around the house these days. If a window opens and we can make it to the farm, I might take the chance. But right now, I'm just going to sit in my front-row seat and watch the world end." He smiled. "But you, Brian. You get the hell out of here. And do it soon. Right now. Don't get caught in the end of the world. Be part of the folks who'll help make the new world. Escape. Find a way. Just don't take your car."

Brian looked at the clock on the wall. Midnight. He needed to leave.

He was scared. But the doctor gave him a glimmer of hope. A small ray of light coming in under the door.

Don't take your car.

And check Dad's letters for a clue.

CHAPTER 55

Brian loaded Rachel back into the wagon, put the backpack harness on, and headed toward the front door.

"Let me take a peek first, make sure the coast is clear," Dr. Perkins said.

Bojo and Trooper stood behind him as he unlocked the door, opened it a crack, and peered out.

"Looks okay," he said, opening it wider.

Dr. Perkins stepped out onto the front entryway of the clinic and motioned Brian to follow him out.

Brian pulled Rachel through the front door, turned around to give the dogs one last pat, and faced the doctor.

"I don't know what to say." He extended his hand.

Dr. Perkins shook his head, and pulled Brian in for a hug, the backpack harness between them.

"Us Unsafes need to stick together. I'm glad I could help. Get your family out of town. Trouble is brewing, and I think it's going to go from bad to worse in about the blink of an eye."

He nodded toward Happy Mart, across the street.

Brian saw a group of people standing around the pickup truck. Chad and his cronies.

"Damn it," he said.

He looked around. He could cross the street; there wasn't any traffic this time of night. But he had to go through the coffee shop parking lot to catch the sidewalk and the path back to their house. It would take him close to the Happy Mart parking lot. If he was lucky, he could get on the Paseo and out of sight before they looked over.

But he didn't feel especially lucky.

"You better hustle, Brian. It's not a good night to let those Bulls see you. Get home, get your family, and get out. Doctor's orders."

Dr. Perkins went back into the clinic, holding the dogs back long enough to get the door shut. Brian heard the deadbolts click.

"You okay, Rachel?" he asked, pulling her along the front of the building toward the street.

"Yeah. I'm tired. It's cold. Dr. Perkins is nice. Trooper was cute."

He smiled. She sounded better already.

Brian kept looking over his left shoulder, toward Happy Mart. The Bulls of Bashan were probably a hundred yards away, across two parking lots and the cross street, but that still felt too close.

He made it to the sidewalk and looked around. He needed to walk back toward the intersection if he was going to use the crosswalk, but that kept him on the wrong side of the street walking toward Happy Mart.

He looked both ways. There were no cars on the street, but the road was well-lit.

He made a split-second decision and started toward the road, stopping to let the wagon down the curb gently. He pulled Rachel as fast as he dared across the street, listening for cars or shouts from the Bulls. He stopped again at the opposite curb, pulled the wagon up, first the front wheels, then the back, and got her up onto the sidewalk.

Panting, he scanned the area. No cars. The Bulls of Bashan were still standing around the pickup truck, maybe eight people. He was now catty-corner to Happy Mart. He looked down the sidewalk. Thirty yards to the intersection, cross, then the coffee shop. *Get it over with.*

He passed a few tents, people sleeping on the sidewalk. One had a cardboard sign in front that said "Unsafes are people too."

He waited for a car to drive through, then he crossed the road at the intersection. He kept an eye on the group of Bulls the entire time, praying they wouldn't look his way.

He made it across the sidewalk, the wagon pulling at the backpack on his chest. He saw the entry to the path, another fifty yards past the coffee shop parking lot. *Almost there.*

"WHAT THE HELL!"

He froze.

"UNSAFE! UNSAFE!"

He looked across the street. One of the bulls was yelling and gesturing toward him.

"HE'S TAKING HER! PERVERT!" He saw the others turn, and one of them was pointing toward Rachel in the wagon.

"THE PATRIARCHY!"

The Bulls took off running across the street. He was paralyzed. They were angled to cut him off, and even if he sprinted, he didn't think he could make it to the Paseo before they crossed his path.

"BRIAN! IS THAT YOU??" Chad's voice, coming from the group in the street.

Brian turned into the parking lot of the coffee shop and ran as fast as he could.

"Dad! Ouch!" Rachel yelled.

"Hang on, baby girl, we got trouble coming."

He went around the front of the coffee shop to the other side. He guessed he had ten, maybe fifteen seconds head start, but getting smaller by the moment.

"ABORT THE UNSAFE! ABORT BRIAN! ABORT THE NEWMANS!" Chad bellowed from the other side of the coffee shop.

Brian grunted, pulling on Rachel and the wagon. He circled around the coffee shop, trying to angle toward an empty patch of grass and make the path.

Behind him, Rachel screamed.

"Dad! They're coming!"

He heard an engine idling as he rounded the back corner of the building.

A delivery truck. Making a late-night drop at the coffee shop. It was backed into a loading dock. He could see into the back of the box truck. A couple of boxes, but nearly empty. The engine idled.

Mental math.

No way was he going to outrun the Bulls pulling Rachel.

He ran around the truck, toward the driver's side. His hands shook as he tore at the backpack, but after a moment he got the harness untied. He opened the driver's side door, threw the backpack in, and bent down to get Rachel.

"You need to help, baby girl. Get up."

She nodded, scared.

He pulled her up by her shoulders, helping her out of the wagon.

"OH BRIAN . . . !!!" Chad called out.

His heart racing, Brian set her on the ground.

"OW!" Rachel said, favoring her injured leg.

"Into the truck, now. Now. Now!"

He shoved her into the truck, pushing her up by her butt. She took a header and crashed into the passenger side of the bench.

Brian heard footsteps right behind him.

"I SEE YOU."

He stepped up into the truck, swung his leg in, and tried to pull the door shut.

He felt resistance. He turned. Chad had the door by one arm and was reaching toward him with the other.

Brian kicked.

Chad dodged.

Brian pulled.

Chad was stronger.

The other Bulls of Bashan started gathering around the truck.

One of the women he recognized from the other night went around the front of the truck, toward the passenger side, where Rachel was sitting.

"NO!" he yelled.

He reached around the steering column, felt the gear shifter, and without taking his eyes off Chad, put the car into drive.

Just then, the woman stepped up onto the ledge outside of Rachel's door and started beating on the window.

"ABORTION! ABORT HER! UNSAFES!!"

Rachel screamed. Chad clawed at Brian, trying to force his way into the car. Brian slammed his foot on the gas. Chad reeled backward but managed to get hold of the handle near the other side of the door.

Brian steered the truck toward the other side of the coffee shop, Chad swinging next to him. Brian timed a kick perfectly, right at Chad's face and he let go, rolling along the asphalt.

The woman clinging to the passenger side kept screaming and pounding on the window.

Brian reached out and closed his door. He saw the other Bulls chasing the truck through the parking lot. He maneuvered the truck toward the parking lot exit, intending to make a right and head toward their neighborhood.

The woman beating on the window stopped screaming. Brian looked over.

The woman had fair skin, bleached blond hair, bright red lips. She was wearing a loose white dress, and she had flowers in her hair. She looked like she was ready for some sort of spring ritual.

One of her eyes bulged. The woman leaned her head back, opened her mouth, exposing perfectly white teeth, and slammed her forehead into the glass.

The window cracked. A giant spider web shape where the woman head-butted it. Rachel kept screaming. Brian made a right turn onto the street.

The woman reared her head back again. Brian saw blood on her forehead. She slammed her face forward again, and the window shattered. Rachel screamed again, and leaned toward her father, scooting away.

The woman in the robe reached an arm in through the shattered glass, holding on to the side of the truck with her other arm. She pulled at Rachel.

"MY BABY! MY BODY! MY CHOICE! UNSAFE!" the woman roared.

"Daddy! Daddy!" Rachel yelled, sounding younger than her eleven years.

Brian jerked the wheel hard left, hard right. He was barely out of the parking lot, and he could hear the Bulls shouting just behind the truck.

The woman held on. The broken glass was making deep gouges in her arm, blood running down the inside of the truck. But she didn't seem to notice. She leaned further into the truck, attempting to climb in.

Brian reached into his waistband. Where was it? He felt for the gun. *The backpack.*

"Rachel! Get the backpack!"

Rachel screamed, kicking at the woman in the window. She felt behind her and grabbed the backpack, shoving it at her father.

Brian raised his leg, using his knee to brace the steering wheel. The truck was angled toward Happy Mart, his turn incomplete, but he kept his foot on the gas and accelerated.

He unzipped the backpack, and shoved a hand in.

Felt past the medicine. His hand touched something hard.

Heavy.

He pulled out his father's service weapon.

Beretta 9mm.

To protect and to serve.

To keep safe.

He looked at the safety.

Flipped it to red.

Red=dead.

He put one hand on the steering wheel, and yanked the truck right, heading back toward their house. The woman didn't let go.

She reached past Rachel's leg, picked up a shard of glass, about a foot long. She squeezed it hard enough to draw blood. She pulled her arm back, gaining leverage. She thrust the shard of glass down, toward Rachel's stomach.

Brian raised the gun and pulled the trigger.

The woman's head snapped back violently and she let go of the truck. Brian heard a thud as her body hit the asphalt.

Rachel squeezed her eyes shut, head buried in her father's lap.

Brian straightened the truck out, checking the rearview mirror.

The Bulls were fifty yards behind. As the truck gained speed, the Bulls shifted direction. They turned and ran across the street toward their pickup truck.

CHAPTER 56

Brian tucked the gun be tween his legs and put one hand on Rachel's head. He was shaking.

Remember.

He accelerated up the hill, the stoplight marking the entrance to their housing community in the distance. He checked the side mirrors again but couldn't make out what the Bulls were doing.

Two minutes.

He would be home in two minutes.

How long would it take them to load everyone in the van?

Two minutes.

His hand shook violently.

Remember.

He saw the woman's head snap back. He glanced to his right. Blood around the broken window. Blood on Rachel's legs.

He raised his right hand.

Blood on his knuckles.

He approached the light and made the right into their housing tract without stopping. It was well after midnight, no cars on the road.

How long would it take for the Bulls to load into their truck and head out?

Two minutes.

Mental math.

By the time he got home and got the family loaded, the Bulls would be pulling into their neighborhood. There was only one exit to their housing community, an endless series of cul-de-sacs.

Maybe they could load the truck and hide down another street until the Bulls passed?

Too risky.

He rolled past the green belt and down toward the homes.

Could they load up and make a run for it?

What if the Bulls used the truck to block them?

He didn't want a confrontation with the Bulls out in the open.

Even the van wouldn't be safe.

Safe space.

He needed a safe space.

Their home.

Their mighty fortress.

He needed a plan.

He needed time to think.

There was no time.

Remember.

Dr. Perkins said not to get caught in the end of the world.

They had an escape plan.

But now they would be trapped by the Bulls.

Remember.

Your mother and I enjoyed our ANNIVERSARY celebration last month. Do you remember the date?

He snapped upright.

The letter from his dad.

He passed the park on his right and followed the curve left onto their street.

His parents' wedding anniversary.

The code to the gun safe.

No time to run.

Two minutes.

Would that be enough time?

His mind raced.

The roof. The back door. The gun safe.

Chad. The window. The dream.

Abort the unsafe.

The Newmans are unsafe?

He clenched his fists on the steering wheel as he pulled the box truck into their driveway.

"Damn right we're unsafe."

CHAPTER 57

"Up, Rach, up. Up. Now."

She raised her head in a daze but sat up.

"Inside. You need to walk."

Brian jumped out of the box truck, backpack in hand, and ran around to the passenger side door.

He tried to ignore the blood running down the outside of the truck.

He yanked the door open and helped Rachel down. He half carried her toward the door, her bad leg dragging behind them.

"Hannah! THE DOOR!" he yelled at the top of his lungs.

His heart was about to jump out of his chest.

"HANNAH!"

The front door opened as he approached it.

His wife stood in the doorway, eyes wide.

"What happened?" she said, helping Rachel.

They made it inside and he sat Rachel down on one of the dining room chairs.

Abby and Luke were in the kitchen, putting together the last scraps of food. Jer and Shawn were sitting on the coach, sleepy but dressed for the drive. The baby sat in the car seat.

His parents' anniversary.

"Jeremiah!" he said forcefully.

The nine-year-old snapped up.

"What?" Jer said.

"Go lock the doors. Back, front. And the windows upstairs. Now."

Jer stared back at his father with a blank expression.

"NOW!" Brian yelled.

Jer moved.

"Abby, Luke, Hannah, garage. Now."

He turned toward the door leading into the garage.

"Brian! What happened?" Hannah stammered.

"The Bulls. They attacked us. I . . . shot one of them." He held the door open while the three of them entered the garage, then he followed and closed the door.

"You . . . shot one?" she asked.

"Killed. Dead." He ran to the gun safe.

Thirty seconds down?

Do you remember?

Yes. He remembered.

He entered the code, his parents' wedding anniversary, and the light turned green.

Not red.

red=dead.

He exhaled.

He scanned the safe. Ammo on the top, rifles underneath, pistols in the door.

All loaded.

"When you need a gun, you need it loaded. Stay ready, you never have to get ready." His father's voice echoed in his mind.

He pulled out the .22 rifle. Small scope. He turned around, handed it to Luke.

"You remember how to use this, Lukey?" he asked.

Luke grabbed the gun, hands shaking, and nodded.

"I want you on the roof. Find a spot where you can see the driveway and front yard, but no one can see you. You keep your sights on one of those Bulls and if you hear shots in the house, you start taking shots of your own," Brian said.

"BRIAN!" Hannah cried.

"What are you talking about?" She pulled at his arm.

He ignored her.

He looked again. *Shotguns.*

He grabbed the black 12 gauge and handed it to Hannah.

"Babe, you gotta stand by the front door. If anyone comes through, you point this thing and shoot. Bury this stock into your shoulder and hold tight. It'll hurt like hell and it'll be loud. But you won't miss with this. Duck low, aim high."

She took the shotgun from Brian, her hands shaking.

He grabbed the 20-gauge shotgun, a smaller round with less oomph, and gave it to Abby.

"Baby girl. Same deal as your mom. At the back slider. Got it?"

She nodded as she took the gun.

One minute gone.

One minute to go.

He grabbed his father's 7mm hunting rifle and slung it over his shoulder.

"BRIAN!" Hannah yelled at him.

He took out a .22 revolver six shot and stuck that in his pocket.

He turned around, facing the three of them.

The van was behind them, packed, ready for their exit.

Last chance to change the plan.

Load the family in the van, and take their chances with the Bulls on the road?

Or stay home. Their safe space.

One minute.

"The Bulls are coming. Here. Tonight. They want us dead. We have to fight."

"What? When? Let's go before they get here! How long do we have?" Hannah said.

"They were right behind me. One minute. Max," he said. "Follow me." He ran out of the garage toward the great room.

Jer and Shawn were standing in the living room, Rachel on the couch. She must have hobbled over there.

They all gathered there.

Brian thought he heard shouting in the distance.

He looked down. A sixteen-year-old with a shotgun. Luke with a rifle. Hannah holding a shotgun, trembling. Jer and Shawn, confused but scared, looking up at him. Rachel, eyes glazed over, blood splattered on her face, already in shock. Lizzy, asleep in her car seat.

He had to protect them.

There was no other choice.

He took the .22 pistol from his pocket, bent down, and handed it to Jer.

"Jer, you remember how Papa showed you?" he asked.

Jer nodded.

"Okay. I want you and Shawn to go upstairs. You watch the windows in the girls' room, over the patio. If you see anyone come in, you have my permission to shoot at them." He kissed the boy on the forehead.

"Shawn, I want you to be the lookout, okay buddy? You yell out what you see, if you need help you call for Dad, okay?" Shawn stood there with his mouth open.

He saw headlights coming through the front window.

Time was up.

He turned back to his family.

"I want you to yell out what you see. Make sure we all know what is happening. This is our last night in this home. As soon as I see an opening, we're loading into the van and heading out. But not until we deal with these Bulls."

He heard a car door open out front.

"Luke, roof. Now. Use the trampoline and go up over the patio cover."

Luke ran to the back, unlocked the slider, and headed into the darkness.

"Jer, Shawn, upstairs."

The boys ran up the stairs.

"Abby, make sure the slider is locked and watch the back."

She nodded and walked to the slider.

"Rachel, you gotta watch Lizzy, okay?"

Rachel looked over at her father and nodded.

"Hannah, you get the front door."

She stared at him with her mouth open.

He kissed her and gave her a gentle push.

He pulled the 9mm out of his waistband and followed Hannah toward the front door.

She crouched, eyes level with the doorknob and pointed the shotgun up at head height.

"I'm watching from the loft, I can see everything from there." He turned and ran up the stairs.

"Brian . . ." she said, terrified. "Why is this happening?"

He looked at her.

"Truth. It's a fight about truth."

As he turned on the landing, he heard shouting from outside.

CHAPTER 58

"What is truth?"

Brian looked up.

"Excuse me?"

"What is truth? What do you say, Brian?"

He looked around the room.

They were sitting in a circle, on white folding chairs, about twenty people.

His father was to his left. On his right, a woman he vaguely remembered from his childhood.

He looked at his father, an uncomfortable look in his eye.

His dad pestered him to come along during one of his Thursday night Bible studies for some time. It was the last thing Brian wanted to do after a long day of work and that terrible commute. Let alone leaving Hannah and the kids.

But his dad could be persistent. Brian was raised in the church. He did believe. But life happened quickly and before he knew it, years had gone by without regularly attending church.

He felt guilty about it—but it somehow seemed harder to lead his family to church after such a long drought.

His dad never let it go and so he found himself confronted by his father's pastor about truth on a random Thursday night.

"Ummm . . . what is truth?"

"Yes! That's the question. Quid es veritas?"

Brian felt everyone's eyes on him.

"Truth. I guess I would say truth is whatever is real."

Pastor Dana smiled, sitting back in his chair.

"Uh huh. Okay. So, the truth is whatever is real? Is murder real?"

Brian hesitated.

". . . yes?"

"Would you say murder is TRUTH?"

Brian thought for a moment.

"Well, no. That doesn't sound very good."

"Right! I agree. Now, WHY doesn't that sound right to you?"

A woman raised her hand.

"Amanda, what do you think?" Pastor Dana nodded toward the woman.

"It doesn't sound right because murder is WRONG. Truth implies some type of correctness or rightness."

"Yes! That's right, Amanda. Truth implies the rightness of something. You see, there are facts. Murder is a fact. Trees are a fact. I will be hungry when I get home tonight. That is a fact. But truth implies something more than just the accuracy of a fact."

Brian nodded, listening.

"Truth implies the rightness of something. What's another word for rightness?"

Brian's father chimed in.

"Righteous."

"Yes, Mr. Newman! Righteous. Truth implies the RIGHTNESS of something. So, how do we determine right from wrong? Murder is a fact, but who says if it's wrong or right?"

"Everyone knows murder is wrong," Brian said.

Pastor Dana leaned forward.

"You know, Brian, I agree with you. Pretty much everyone agrees that murder is wrong. But WHY do they think it's wrong?"

"Because it hurts another person," Brian replied.

"Okay, that could be part of it. What if the person wanted to die? Is it okay then?"

"You mean like assisted suicide?" Brian asked, feeling uncomfortable.

"Yeah, sure. Is that okay?"

Brian looked around the room. He hated being put on the spot.

"No. I guess not. It feels wrong to me."

Dana nodded.

"Yes. And I'll tell you why it feels wrong. The Bible says you are made in God's image. That means you are an image-bearer. And image-bearers know God has determined right from wrong. You see, God created EVERY-THING. He is not only the creator, but the sustainer of all things. And God is perfect! That means his morality is the perfect morality."

Murmurs of agreement from the circle.

"He's given every one of his image-bearers an idea of that morality. We know murder is wrong, stealing, adultery. We FEEL it's wrong, naturally, because God made us understand that. That's why truth isn't relative. Truth doesn't change with time. Truth doesn't evolve. All truth is God's truth. God's decrees are perfect and eternal. His morality is the same yesterday, today, and forever. Just like Jesus. You know, Pilate asked the question 'what is truth' in the Bible."

Brian raised his eyebrows, intrigued.

"He did. He asked Jesus. Jesus said he was a King. He said he came to this world to testify to the truth. He said everyone on the side of truth would listen to him."

The pastor looked around the room.

"This is what we have been studying. Truth. The world wants to change the definition of truth. Now we talk about 'my truth' and 'your truth.' The world doesn't want us to say THE truth. It's as if each person gets to define it for themselves. But Jesus is THE way, THE truth, THE life. He is our only hope in this life."

He smiled.

"We've tackled some hard questions tonight. Let's close with the truth believers have passed down through the years, the Apostle's Creed."

The class recited in unison:

"I believe in God, the Father Almighty,
maker of heaven and earth.
and in Jesus Christ, his only begotten Son, our Lord,
who was conceived by the Holy Ghost
born of the virgin Mary.
He suffered under Pontius Pilate,
was crucified, died, and was buried;
he descended to hell.

The third day he rose again from the dead.
He ascended to heaven
and is seated at the right hand of God the Father almighty.
From thence he shall come to judge the quick and the dead.

I believe in the Holy Ghost,
the holy catholic church,
the communion of saints,
the forgiveness of sins,
the resurrection of the body,
and the life everlasting. Amen."

CHAPTER 59

Brian opened the sliding glass door about a foot. From the loft he had a clear view of the front yard, the cul-de-sac, and the driveway. He saw the Bulls of Bashan pull through the cul-de-sac, turn around, and stop in front of their house. There were six people in the bed of the truck. Three women, three men. All of them dressed in white. The driver's side door opened and Chad got out.

"Time for your ABORTION, BRIAN!" Chad bellowed as he limped around the back of the truck.

Chad gestured toward the back of the house as the rest of the bulls climbed out of the bed of the truck. One of the men nodded back.

"EYE FOR AN EYE! Right? You took one of ours, it's time we take all of yours!"

Brian heard movement on the roof above him.

Luke. Hopefully he was out of sight.

I believe in God, the Father Almighty

One of the Bulls leaned into the bed of the truck to grab something. A ladder. The man with the ladder and two of the women headed toward the back of the house. One of the women carried a crowbar, and the other held a handgun.

Brian turned back into the house, hoping to direct his voice away from Chad.

"Hannah! Four coming toward the front door! Abby! Three to the back! One has a gun!"

He heard a *thump-thump* overheard. Luke. Confirming he heard as well.

There was a loud *crack* and Brian turned back toward the front.

Chad was walking toward the front door, arm extended. He held a large revolver. He had just fired a round at the front door.

"HANNAH!" Brian yelled. "STAY DOWN!"

Brian stepped onto the balcony, slid the hunting rifle over his shoulder, and pulled it up to aim at Chad.

DAMN IT!

Chad rushed toward the front door, scooting under the balcony and out of view.

Two men trailed a few steps behind Chad, still visible. A woman in a white dress lingered near the truck. *Was she barefoot?*

Brian put the scope up to his eye.

Too close to use the scope.

He leaned his head back, lined up the barrel of the rifle toward the torso of one of the men.

One story below him. Twenty feet away.

He held his breath.

"HANNAH? IS THAT YOUR NAME? YOU HAVE VISITORS!" Chad roared from under the balcony.

Brad heard pounding on the door.

Exhaling slowly, he pulled the trigger.

maker of heaven and earth

The man below him looked up and saw Brian at the last second. He lunged toward the front door.

As Brian pulled the trigger, the man moved through the field of fire, and Brian saw a bright red circle form on the man's right shoulder. Brian had missed his chest.

He heard a low cry as the two Bulls ducked under the balcony, out of view, joining Chad at the front door.

Loud banging and shouting continued.

"BRIAN!!" Hannah yelled.

Another gunshot below.

Toward the back of the house, he heard glass break.

Brian rushed back in from the balcony, ready to run downstairs to help Hannah, when he heard the .22 pistol go off down the hall.

Jer and Shawn.

* * * *

"Jer, can I hold the gun?" Shawn asked.

"No. Dad said I was in charge. You have to be the lookout."

"But I never get to hold one!" Shawn whined.

The boys were standing in the hallway, facing the girls' room, which was on the backside of the house. The two bedroom windows over-looked the back patio roof, beyond that the trampoline, and then the pool.

"Dad said I have permission to shoot if someone comes in. He didn't give you permission. Shawn. You need to obey," Jeremiah said proudly.

In the Newman house, there was a never-ending supply of kids eager to gain any authority or advantage over their siblings.

"But I want a turn! Pleeeease!" Shawn whined.

"Shhh! Shawn! Did you hear that?" Jer said, clutching the pistol.

Jeremiah crept slowly into the girls' room, eyes wide open, peering toward the window. He could just make out the edge of the patio cover, and below it, the trampoline.

There was a clanging sound and he saw the top of a ladder appear at the lower edge of the patio cover.

"They're coming! Get back!" Jer said to Shawn, scrambling back-ward into the hallway.

His knees shook and he heard someone on the ladder. A moment later a figure appeared on the roof, then another.

"Jer, maybe it's Abby?" Shawn said, clutching Shawn from behind.

"Abby's downstairs. It's the bad guys," Jer whispered.

"Bad guys? I'm gonna go get Dad!" Shawn started crying, but made no move to leave.

"Dad gave me permission to shoot. Remember? I have permission. I'm supposed to shoot." Jer felt tears in his eyes. He wanted his daddy too.

A moment later, one of the figures made it to the window, and ripped the screen off.

Jer closed his eyes tight. He imagined himself in bed, under his covers. Having a bad dream.

"Bad dream. Bad dream," he said to himself softly.

"Jer? Is this a dream? Are we having a bad dream?" the six-year-old said behind him.

Jer heard a noise and opened his eyes. The window slid open. It was unlocked.

A woman dressed in white, with flowers in her hair, climbed into the girls' room. She had to kick things off the dresser below the window—framed pictures of Abby and her volleyball friends, pictures Rachel drew, an old doll, a small jewelry box.

The woman climbed on top of the dresser and into the room. Behind her, another woman filled the window.

"Boys! Boys!" the woman said kindly.

She held out her hands. In one of them she held a large butcher knife.

"Come here, you adorable little clump of cells! Don't be afraid. It's just a simple procedure. A little snip, a little slice, and we can all get back to our regularly scheduled programs!" She smiled as she walked slowly toward Jer and Shawn, knife held out in front. The second woman entered the room behind her.

Jer backed up, pushing into Shawn.

He raised the gun and pointed it toward the woman.

"Oh, you little bastard," she said, her voice turning sour when she noticed the gun.

She scowled at Jer, baring her teeth.

"I have permission. Dad said I could shoot. I'm allowed." Jeremiah said, tears streaming down his face.

The woman took another step toward him, the second woman trailing behind.

"I will!" Jer yelled.

Shawn pulled at Jer's shirt.

"Daddy! Daddy! Daddy!" Shawn cried.

"Papa taught me how to shoot! I will!" Jer said, his voice betraying his lack of confidence.

"Kids. Are. So. INCONVENIENT!" The woman shrieked the last word and lunged toward Jer.

Jer pushed the gun out in front of him, closed his eyes, and pulled the trigger.

He opened his eyes. The woman stood two feet in front of him, knife overhead, tip pointed down. He looked up and saw her eyes. Her snarl had melted away, replaced by a look of confusion.

The woman looked down. A small hole in her chest, left of center. Red color blooming against her white robe. A small wisp of smoke escaped the hole.

Jeremiah had fired a perfect shot.

The woman dropped the knife and crumpled to the ground. Jer heard her gasping for breath. The second woman dove to the ground, grabbing the knife.

She scrambled around the first woman, still on all fours, and heaved herself toward Jer.

"You! Little! Tumor!" she screamed.

Jer scrambled backward and crashed into Shawn, dropping the gun. The two of them went down.

The woman crawled out of the girls' room and into the hall, pulling on Jeremiah's foot.

Shawn was pinned under Jer, and the two of them froze in terror.

She got up on her knees, grabbing the knife in both hands.

She knelt over Jeremiah and in a smooth motion she raised the knife over her head with both hands, and looked up.

"As above, so below," she said, her left eye bulging.

She looked down at Jeremiah and smiled.

"Better that one child die than all women suffer!" She plunged the knife at the boy's chest.

* * * *

Brian stopped when he heard the .22 pistol. Hannah's screams rose from downstairs, but the gun shot was from Jer's gun.

He made a decision.

He ran toward the back of the house, toward his boys.

He heard a woman's voice screaming.

"Better that one child die than all women suffer!"

He rounded the corner toward the kids' bedrooms.

and in Jesus Christ, his only begotten Son, our Lord

On his right he saw Jer lying atop Shawn, both boys facing up. A woman in white knelt before the boys. Knife raised over her head. Brian's stomach turned.

His boys.

Jer and Shawn.

Nine and six.

The scene looked like a perverted twist on the Binding of Isaac, a distant memory from felt boards and Sunday school classes.

He slammed the rifle over his shoulder and grabbed the 9mm from his waistband.

The woman's body tensed as she started her stabbing motion.

Brian didn't stop walking as he raised the pistol. The woman was caught in her moment of triumph and didn't see him. He stepped over Jeremiah and Shawn, pointed the gun at her forehead, and pulled the trigger.

The noise in the hallway was deafening.

Brian saw her head snap back, but her body was angled forward, and she crumpled into Brian's legs. He used his knees to shove her aside. She landed next to the boys.

He looked down. The woman had been barely waist high to him. He was covered in blood from chest to knees.

who was conceived by the Holy Ghost

He backed up and the boys scrambled away from the woman.

Their small white eyes shone brightly against the dark blood covering their faces.

Jer was crying.

"I dropped the gun. But I had permission," he said absently.

Shawn stood and looked down at the woman.

He turned toward his father. Brian saw a dark spot forming in his pants. "Daddy," he said, and hugged Brian's legs.

A lump formed in Brian's throat.

He needed to keep his children safe.

They should never have to see something like this.

He saw into the girls' room, another woman, laying dead. The gunshot.

born of the virgin Mary

"Jer, did you shoot that woman?" he asked.

"You gave me permission. I remembered what Papa taught me," he said, somewhat defensively.

"Good job, son. You kept Shawn safe."

He heard a gunshot at the front of the house.

Hannah.

"Come, boys!" He turned and ran back down the hall. As he hit the stairs, he heard another gunshot at the back door.

Abby.

CHAPTER 60

Hannah screamed as the gunshot penetrated the front door. She was crouched, head lower than the doorknob, shotgun facing up. She heard Brian yelling from the balcony.

"Hannah! Stay down!"

Her arms shook as she crouched there, waiting. Behind her, in the living room, she heard Rachel trying to sooth Lizzy.

"It's okay, Lizzy. It's okay. There there," Rachel said while Lizzy cried.

"Abby! What do you see?" Hannah called back toward the kitchen.

"Nothing here! Was that a gunshot?" Abby called back.

"Yes! Through the door! Be ready, Abby!"

A moment later she heard another gunshot, followed by shouts outside.

Brian shooting at them from the loft?

She listened carefully, and a moment later there was a loud crash against the front door.

"HANNAH! IS THAT YOUR NAME?" bellowed a voice from the other side of the door.

"Leave us alone!" she yelled. "We're not hurting anyone!"

The doorknob turned, but the lock caught it.

She heard pounding on the door. A few voices yelling.

Another gunshot rang from outside, and another hole blew into the door above Hannah's head.

"YOU'RE UN-SAFE! That means you're hurting EVERYONE!" the voice yelled from outside.

The pounding on the door stopped, and she held her breath.

A moment later the glass in the front window next to the door exploded.

Hannah screamed. The window was about two feet to her right, overlooking the front stoop.

She tried to stand and scramble backward, but she slipped on a piece of glass and landed on her butt, just under the window.

She looked up just in time to see one of the men reaching through the broken glass. She screamed and pulled the shotgun around, but before she could point the muzzle up, a second man reached around the first man and grabbed the barrel.

Hannah struggled with the gun but held on. She had two hands fighting against the invader's one hand on the barrel. Looking up, she could see a man, half in and half out of the window, torso dragging across the broken glass, struggling to reach her. A second man was crowding the first one from behind. The second man had his hand on the barrel of the shotgun and was pressing into the back of the first man. A moment later a third face came into view.

Hannah sat on the floor, shotgun in hand, pointed to the side, as three crazed men tried to crawl through her broken front patio window all at once.

"BRIAN!" she screamed.

She pulled against the gun, trying to dislodge it.

The first man was bent over the window frame, his abdomen rubbing against the broken shards of the window. He screamed in pain, but the two men behind him kept pushing forward. He managed to get his hands around Hannah's right ankle, and he pulled against her leg.

Hannah slid toward the window, bracing her foot against the wall below, and watched in horror as the first man used the leverage from her leg to slide further into the house. He was nearly on top of her, just his upper legs pinning him against the window frame between the other two men.

She felt something warm against her leg. She tried again to pull the shotgun away, and with a final tug she managed to get it free. She swung the gun toward the window, but the barrel was stopped by the first man's right shoulder. His face hovered a few inches above hers. She could smell his breath. *Menthol cigarettes?*

The second man was climbing over the top of the first man, and the third man was now reaching around both. The entire frame of the window was filled with a confusing mass of limbs and bodies.

Hannah looked toward her legs, and for a moment she was confused. She couldn't see her feet. Her legs disappeared into a purple-gray mass.

She screamed and kicked. She tried to scramble backward but the second man nearly had his hands around her neck. She pulled at her legs and realized what was covering her feet.

The first man's entrails. His abdomen had been shredded by the window sill and the two men behind him had pushed against him so hard he was disemboweled. Hannah choked back vomit as she realized what the purple-gray mass burying her legs was.

The first man stopped moving, but Hannah was pinned beneath him. The second man had a few fingers tangled into her hair and was slowly making his way through the window, clamoring over the first man.

Hannah clenched her teeth and pulled hard on her left leg. She was able to free it from the mess of entrails, and with another shove, she got her foot up under the first man.

"GET! OUT! OF! MY! HOUSE!" she screamed.

With a massive heave, she pushed hard with her leg and was able to lift the first man enough to create distance. She swung the shotgun over her leg and using the space she just created, lodged the barrel into the upper torso of the first man.

The stock of the shotgun was planted in the tile under her left armpit. She crawled her left hand up along the guard and slid her finger into the trigger.

The second man managed to get his other hand free and he had both hands buried into her hair. He pulled up violently, bringing her face up next to his.

"DIE!" he growled. His face was so close to Hannah's that she could almost taste the words.

"NOO!" she screamed back and pulled the trigger.

She felt something warm and hot cover her arms and torso. The second man released her hair, and her head slammed back against the tile. She tried to pull her arms out from under the men, but she was trapped. A pool of blood grew quickly around her.

The shotgun blasted a hole through the first man's chest, and the second man's stomach. The weight of the men and the size of the hole caused the men to slide down the length of the shotgun barrel.

The third man howled in pain, clutching his face, but kept crawling in the house, over the two dead Bulls.

She moved to try and see him, but she couldn't see past the second man's head. A moment later she heard a thud next to her and saw two feet on the floor in the house.

Brown work boots.

Hannah held her breath.

The man knelt and looked at Hannah.

The grocery store manager. The one Brian told her about.

"Hi, Hannah! Thanks for letting us in!"

The shotgun blast tore off the right side of his face. All she could see was that left eye, bulging.

He kicked at the second man, moving his head out of her way.

Chad stood and laughed.

"Looks like you are all tangled up there, Hannah! You really got them skewered! Get it? Skewered?" Chad laughed again. "Now, where is Brian?" he said, tapping his chin. He nodded toward the stairs. "Up there? I'll go take a look. Sit tight and I'll be right back!"

He turned his head back toward the window. "Come on in, Jezebel! The coast is clear!"

Hannah felt another body briefly clamor over the pile of carnage still pining her. She saw two bare feet, and the hem of a white dress, darkly stained with blood. One of the women had climbed in to join Chad.

"We need to move quick, it's almost time for the ceremony!" the woman said to Chad.

"Of course! Onward and upward!" Chad replied cheerfully.

Hannah saw his boots turn toward the stairs.

Chad lifted his right foot toward the bottom stair but stopped.

Hannah craned her neck and with effort she could make out the intruders.

Chad turned back toward the great room.

"Say . . . is that little Abby I see back there?" Chad said as he and the woman started walking toward the kitchen.

Hannah screamed.

CHAPTER 61

Brian ran down the stairs, heart pounding. *Gun shots. Front door, back door.*

"Please, Lord, not my family," he said out loud.

He made the first turn, hit the landing, and stopped.

He suffered under Pontius Pilate,

He could see the entryway, another ten steps.

His heart dropped.

He saw a pile of bodies on the tile floor.

Two men, face down, one on top of the other. There was something sticking up out of the back of the man on top.

"Jer, stop. Sit on that step." Brian stopped the boys before they could make the turn in the stairs and see the carnage.

He took a step down.

was crucified, died, and was buried;

He saw blood on the walls. He looked up. The ceiling was splattered with blood and pieces of flesh. He saw a torn piece of red flannel shirt, stuck to the ceiling. He held his breath as it slowly peeled off and drifted to the floor.

He took another step.

He saw long brown hair matted to the tile, slicked with blood.

He followed the hair as it disappeared under the carnage. He could just make out the top of a woman's head, then a shoulder.

Hannah.

He took another step.

he descended to hell.

He saw the object sticking up move. He realized what it was. The barrel of a gun. It jostled as something moved under the pile.

He heard a muffled scream.

Brian jumped down the last few steps, hit the tile hard, and almost slipped in the pool of blood.

"HANNAH!" he yelled.

"BRIAN!"

He pulled at the man on top, but he was pinned to the pile by the shotgun barrel. He pushed on the pile of bodies, and with a giant heave, he was able to tip it over. Hannah struggled and shuffled as she pulled herself free.

She was covered in blood and gore.

The third day he rose again from the dead.

"Chad! They're in the house! They went for Abby!" she stuttered as she tried to stand up.

Abby.

Brian's head snapped back toward the living room.

Clutching the pistol, he ran toward the back of the house.

The sliding glass door leading to the back patio was shattered. The 20-gauge shotgun was lying on the ground.

He looked right.

Rachel was cowered in the corner, eyes shocked with fear.

"Rachel!" he called out.

Her body shook, but she looked up at him.

"Rachel! Where's Abby?"

He looked around the living room and kitchen.

"Rachel—where's Lizzy?"

Rachel convulsed. She opened her mouth to speak but couldn't produce a sound.

She nodded toward the backyard.

He heard a baby scream outside.

Lizzy.

He walked through the shattered sliding glass door onto the back patio.

He ascended to heaven

The chairs were strewn about, and the small table holding the TV was tipped over.

There was a body lying on the back patio face up.

One of the Bulls. There was a hole in the man's stomach about the size of a baseball.

His chest was heaving, and Brian heard his breath sputter and rattle.

The man looked up at Brian and snarled at him.

Abby must have shot the man as he tried to enter the sliding glass door. Thank God for Papa's gun lessons.

Next to the man's head Brian saw the small TV set. Laying face-down on the concrete, screen shattered.

It reminded Brian of an ostrich burying its head in the sand, trying to ignore the horrors taking place at the Newmans' home.

Brian felt a tug in his mind. He wanted to go upstairs and lay down. Hopefully, escape this waking nightmare. Mornings always brought clarity. He was stuck in a bad dream.

He lifted his head and looked toward the pool.

And is seated at the right hand of God the Father almighty.

Abby was sitting in a chair facing him. Lizzy was in her car seat carrier, on the ground, next to her

Abby's face was pale and she had both hands firmly clenched around the arms of the chair.

Lizzy's face was bright red and she was screaming at the top of her lungs.

Chad stood behind the two girls, the woman next to him.

Chad's chest and face were splattered with blood. The light from the patio just grazed him and Brian could make out the horrible detail.

The right side of his face was missing. There was a gaping hole where his eye had been. It looked like a chunk of his skull on the top right corner was gone. His large left eye shone brightly through the blood.

Chad looked at Brian and smiled.

He held a shovel in one hand. The woman next to Chad held a large knife.

"Brian, do me a favor and put your gun down, okay?" Chad said calmly.

Brian took a step toward his daughters.

Chad lifted the shovel, and gently rested the spade near the top of the car seat. He stood casually, but Brian saw what he intended. He did not like how close the end of the shovel was to Lizzy's head.

The woman brought the knife up and rested it on Abby's shoulder, the blade an inch from her neck.

Abby shuttered.

From thence he shall come to judge the quick and the dead.

"Brian, come on. Think safe. Drop the gun."

Chad smiled again. Something oozed out of the hole in his head when he pulled his lips up, and his left eye pulsed rapidly.

CHAPTER 62

Brian dropped the pistol. It clattered against the concrete. He stood under the patio cover. Just across the strip of grass, next to the shallow end of the pool, no more than fifteen feet in front of him. Chad and the woman held two of his daughters hostage.

"Rely and Comply, right, Brian?" Chad said with a grin.

He tapped the top of the shovel on the car seat carrier, inches from Lizzie's skull.

"The rifle too, please?" Chad gestured.

Brian hesitated. He did mental math. *Swing the rifle over my shoulder, bring the stock up to my armpit. Raise barrel. Eyes to scope. Center mass on Chad. Upper chest. Free of Abby's head. Shoot. Move. Aim at the woman. Shoot. Two seconds? Three?*

Chad needed just a fraction of that time to drive the blade of the shovel into the soft top of Lizzie's skull.

Brian instead slid the rifle down and dropped it on the ground.

"Brian! You're learning! 'Have a posture of compliance.' Great job!"

Chad shuffled his feet. He turned to the woman and nodded. "Go ahead, Jezebel, you can start."

The woman knelt, still holding the knife next to Abby's neck, and scooped a handful of water from the pool.

"I wish things could have been different for you and your family, Brian. I really do. I mean, you of all people. The NEWMANS! Think about it! You could have been at the forefront of the great remaking. The world in OUR image! The NEW Human experience. The new man. Ah."

Chad nodded his head wistfully.

"I've been learning so much, Brian! Babble is a fount of many blessings. You know, Babble gave us the name the Bulls of Bashan! What does that even mean? Only Babble knows!"

Chad grinned even more.

"After you and I had our little tumble at the market, I started getting messages from Babble. At first I thought it was because I had low scores! But no! Babble brought so much clarity! Let's just say it was an EYE-opening experience!"

Chad's eye caught the light. Red and pulsing.

The woman sprinkled water on Abby's head, and started chanting something as she raised her face to the sky.

"I just want to keep my family safe!" Brian said. "I never meant to hurt you!"

"SAFE!" Chad called out with a laugh. "Safe? Isn't that what this is all about?" Chad gestured with the shovel, swinging it left and right. He narrowly missed the top of Lizzie's head. "It's not just about your family, Brian. EVERYONE needs to be safe. Don't you understand? Words are violence. Hate is hate. Misgendering is injuring. The Newmans don't care about others."

"What have we ever done to hurt people?" Brian said.

"Brian, Brian, Brian . . ." Chad scolded. "This is the thing. You've been educated. Babble told me. Babble explained it all to me. You've been taught our Creeds. You've been taught the great Confession. You know the truth. But you stand for a lie. The truth that Babble has handed down to us is simple: Love is Love. And Hate is Hate. I've seen your Azazel scores. You hate your neighbor."

Chad bared his teeth.

"Babble knows your secrets, Brian. Babble knows what you throw away. What you read. What you think. Babble is more than you realize. Babble isn't new. Babble is ancient beyond days."

Chad's mangled face contorted in a look somewhere between awe and wonder.

"We pass these children through the fire. In Babble's name. From the word of Aurora, and the power of Molech!" the woman chanted to the sky.

"Babble is before. Babble is after. Babble has been leading and help-ing all nations, languages, and peoples. Babble brings the rain. Babble brings drought," Chad said.

Brian's mouth dropped open.

"Babble walks here and there, Brian. Babble leads, and others fol-low. The Bulls of Bashan. Azazel. Moloch. Baal."

Brian's stomach dropped as he recognized the names.

I believe in the Holy Ghost

"As it was in the beginning, Brian, is now and ever shall be. You think abortion is murder? Abortion is a NECESSARY sacrifice, Brian. With death brings life. You think Moloch will help us? Baal? If we don't make the necessary sacrifices? Blood for blood. Blood for life. Better the death of the helpless than the suffering of the mature. This is nec-essary. This is life."

Chad's voice dropped and his eye shone red.

"People like you disrupt the order, Brian. You make things difficult. Pinch the incense. Make the vow. It neither breaks your leg nor picks your pocket. But people like you REFUSE TO OBEY!" Chad shouted the last words to the sky.

"Through the fire! Praise to Molech! By Babble!" the woman intoned.

"Chad, please. Wait . . ." Brian pleaded.

Abby sat frozen. Lizzy continued her screams.

Brian shuffled a half step closer. His foot hit the edge of the pistol.

"Wait? For what? These are plans set in motion long ago, Brian. You think we are alone? There are so many more Bulls. Many strong Bulls of Bashan surround the Newmans!"

Chad cackled.

"The Bulls are out there right now. Tonight. Did you know tonight is a lunar eclipse? It's a sign, Brian. Signs and wonders. Babble brings many delights. Tonight the bulls are going to show the Unsafes what the Azazel Promise really is."

Tonight. Dr Perkins said something about a resistance. What was hap-pening?

"You are hate-spreaders. You lack compliance. Babble said there is only one way to keep everyone safe."

Chad looked down at Abby and Lizzie.

the holy catholic church

"Blood for blood. Life for life. As above, so below. Better the death of the Newmans than the suffering of many."

Chad raised the shovel. The woman's chanting reached a fever pitch, and she brought the knife up above her head, blade pointed toward Abby.

"The ancients have spoken, Brian! The decree from long ago. Hey hey! Ho ho! These unsafe Newmans got to go!"

Brian saw Chad's hand flex around the handle of the shovel.

CHAPTER 63

"I want you on the roof."

As soon as his father had said the words, Luke dashed for the back. He'd had the small .22 rifle slung over his shoulder. He ran to the edge of the trampoline, from the trampoline to the wall between their home and the neighbors, from the wall to the patio cover. From there he had to use the edge of the windowsill looking into his parents' room and he could just reach the second-story roof.

He'd crawled along the roof, positioning himself in such a way so he could look over the peak of the roof toward the front yard, but keep his body completely on the backside.

He had watched as the Bulls jumped out of the truck. He could just make out the three running to the back, and the four who went toward the front door.

He'd held his breath as he heard his dad open the sliding glass door on the loft patio.

He had pointed the gun toward the front stoop, trying to get one of the intruders in his line of sight.

His hands were sweating as he tried in vain to line up a shot.

His heart had dropped as he heard the first gunshot. Ears ringing, he had realized it was his father, shooting from the patio.

He had crawled forward, desperate to find an angle, but just saw the tops of the heads disappear under the front stoop.

He had laid there quietly, slowing his breathing, listening, when his concentration was interrupted by a window shattering behind him. He had just turned himself around when he saw two women enter the girls' bedroom window from the patio cover.

His hands had shaken as he saw the knife in one hand disappear into the house and he realized they were on the same part of the patio cover he used to climb to the top just a few moments prior.

He nearly vomited when he heard a gunshot from the house, directly below. He guessed it was the girls' bedroom, or the hallway. A moment later and there was a louder shot.

Did someone shoot Jer? His dad?

He had started to scramble down the roof toward the patio cover when he heard the explosion toward the front of the door. A shotgun? His mom?

There was chaos below, and he was above it all.

He needed to help.

Another moment and another gunshot near the back of the house.

Luke lowered himself from the second-floor roof and landed back on the patio cover. He peered into the girls' bedroom window.

The glass was shattered. He saw a figure on the floor near the bunk beds, and a few feet beyond, another, laying in the hallway.

The two women. They were dressed all in white, and even in the darkness Luke could make out the blood stains. He tried not to look at the dark spots on the walls of the hallway.

He was about to crawl into the window when he heard commotion below him. He turned around and saw a figure walking toward the pool.

Luke sucked in a breath and dropped to his belly.

He nearly dropped the rifle but managed to hang on to it.

He slowly turned his body around until his head was facing the backyard. The patio cover was a basic wedge shape, connecting to the house twelve feet above the ground, but dropping to only seven feet at the edge of the lawn.

Luke was lying face down, angled toward the pool and grass. He raised his head slowly as he brought the rifle around to his right side.

He saw the man with the large eye standing near the pool. To his left, Lizzy in her car seat. On his right, Abby was sitting in one of the patio chairs. A woman stood next to Chad, holding a knife.

Luke slowly shimmied to his right, trying not to make a sound.

He heard the man below talking and yelling.

Luke stopped to look.

The man was gesturing toward the patio. He was talking to someone under the patio cover, directly beneath Luke.

He could hear his dad below.

The bad man hadn't seen Luke.

He pulled the rifle up to his cheek and drew the barrel toward the bad man.

Twenty-five feet to his right. Twelve feet in front. Ten feet below. A close shot.

He looked through the small scope Papa had installed on the .22. He said it helped him get the squirrels out of his garden. Luke thought it was because Papa wanted to feel like a sniper.

Luke closed his left eye and moved the gun slightly until the bad man was in view.

He aimed the crosshairs at the man's chest, but at his angle he barely had clearance over Abby's head.

He shuffled slightly more to the right, improving his shot, but as he did, he kicked a small rock that was sitting on the roof tiles.

It made a quiet clatter as it tumbled a few feet and landed in the grass.

Luke held his breath and looked down at the bad man.

He hadn't heard. The bad man lifted the shovel, hovering the blade a few feet above Lizzy's head.

The woman next to Chad chanted something and started to raise a knife.

He looked over at Abby, and she was looking up at him.

She had heard the rock.

Her eyes flared open, but she stayed quiet.

He made a small gesture to her with his right hand, motioning for her to crouch.

Abby tilted her head, confused. But when Luke raised the rifle, she understood.

The bad man was working himself up. Saying something about the ancient of days and necessary sacrifices.

Luke sighted down the scope one more time. The woman had the knife up. He pivoted slightly, taking aim at her first.

Luke exhaled slowly.

Aim small, miss small.

He pulled the trigger.

CHAPTER 64

Brian looked in horror as Chad and the Jezebel prepared to execute his daughters. He watched in slow motion as Chad and the woman raised their arms. Two daughters. Two blades. Two minutes.

Brian looked down. His pistol.

He dropped into a crouch, never taking his eyes off the terrible ceremony with his daughters.

He fished around for the pistol, and right as he managed to get his hand around it, he heard a gunshot.

He screamed out in horror.

Abby's face was covered in blood on her left side.

He heard another gunshot.

Lizzie screamed.

Behind him, he heard Hannah shouting.

Time slowed.

His eyes came into focus.

He dared not look at Lizzy. Afraid he would see one of his children dead.

Abby, covered in blood.

His mind slowly brought him details.

Abby's eyes wide open.

Abby sitting still.

Lizzy screaming.

The woman behind Abby dropping the knife, clattering to the concrete.

Chad turning to his side, puzzled.

The woman looking down, two red spots growing on her chest.

Chad taking a step backward.

Chad dropping the shovel.

Brian stood, the fog lifting.

He lunged forward, closing the distance with three large leaps. With his arms out wide, he launched himself over Lizzy, straight into Chad's chest.

The two of them went down.

This time Brian didn't apologize.

Brian kept Chad pinned beneath his body and with both hands he clawed at Chad's face.

"NOOOOooooooooooooo!"

Chad's scream was filled with an other-worldly chill.

Brian dug one hand into the wound on Chad's face, and with his other hand he dug into Chad's left eye. The pulsing, sinister, red eye.

Chad struggled under Brian's weight, but he managed to keep him on the ground.

With his thumb and first two fingers, Brian dug into Chad's left eye socket.

"Baaaaaaaabbbllllleeeeeeeeeee!" Chad pleaded.

Brian heard a sickening combination of sounds. Tearing, squishing, moaning. He ignored it.

With a last effort, he pulled backward and ripped the eye out of Chad's socket.

Chad's entire body started flopping and convulsing under Brian.

Brian stood, tossing the eye into the pool.

Chad heaved and roiled like a dying snake.

Brian turned to his right and saw the shovel.

Bending down, he picked it up, and swung it against Chad's head.

Chad's screams and moans carried on.

". . . oooooooooooooooooooooo . . ."

Brian hit him again.

". . . oooooooooo . . ."

Without thinking, Brian placed the edge of the shovel against Chad's throat, balanced on one foot, and started slamming his heel against the top edge of the blade.

He could see the shovel blade cutting into Chad's neck.

Chad's body flailed violently, then stopped.

Brian saw the last breath escape from Chad's mouth.

Brian felt resistance as the shovel blade hit Chad's spine, but he slammed his foot down over and over, sweat forming on his forehead.

A moment later and the shovel blade hit the concrete.

Brian dropped the shovel. His chest rose and fell in rhythm with his beating heart. He looked down at the carnage that had just recently been Chad. Babble. Molech. He absently nudged Chad's severed head with his foot. With a firm kick he rolled it into the pool.

CHAPTER 65

"DAD!"

Luke screamed from the patio cover.

Brian turned around.

Luke ran to the edge of the patio cover and launched himself onto the trampoline. With a steady motion, he balanced himself, climbed out of the trampoline, and ran to Abby and Lizzy.

the communion of saints

Brian beat him there.

"You okay, Abs?" Brian asked, searching her for injuries.

Abby stared at him, eyes filled with terror.

"Abby!" he yelled, trying to snap her out of it.

"Yeah. Yeah. I'm okay. I shot that man on the patio, Dad," Abby said.

"Okay, okay. I know. It's okay," he said, wiping blood from her face.

Luke grabbed Lizzy's car seat and lifted her, giving her a kiss on the cheek.

Brian turned in time to see Hannah run toward him.

She was completely covered in blood and gore from the carnage in the entryway. But she ran toward him with a confidence and love that made her beauty shine through. As she got closer, she stopped, staring at him.

"What? What is it? Why are you all staring at me?" Brian said.

He looked down. His entire body was covered in blood. Bits of flesh and clothes stuck to his pants. He flexed his fists. His hands ached. He must have gripped the shovel so tight. He shuffled his feet. He was standing in a pool of blood and gore that continued to pour out of Chad's neck.

"Oh."

His family looked at him, scared. What had he done? They had a front-row seat to something so terrible. And he did it with his own hands.

He walked to the back of the yard, where the pool equipment was stored. After fumbling for a minute in the dark, he found the power button, and turned the pool pump on. With a turn of a lever, he engaged the waterfall feature. A moment later a two-foot-wide waterfall cascaded into the pool.

Brian took Hannah's hand and led her to the water.

"Let's clean this off," he said.

She looked up at him.

He ran his hands under the waterfall, watching the water turn red. He ducked his head under, relishing the cool relief. He moved out of the way and Hannah entered the waters. Washing herself clean, letting the blood from her hands, face, and neck disappear under the clean water.

Brian motioned, and Abby did the same, cleaning the blood from her hands and face.

Satisfied, he stepped back, surveying his family.

"Brian. We're safe. All of us are safe," Hannah said, drying her hands on her pants.

She hugged him.

Rachel limped out toward the back, and behind her, Brian saw Jer and Shawn standing in the kitchen.

Brian looked at his family.

Luke's hands were shaking with adrenaline. He couldn't take his eyes off Chad.

Abby and Hannah were dripping wet.

Rachel, face was white as a ghost.

Jer and Shawn were holding hands. Scared.

He had asked too much of his family.

Too much.

"No, Hannah. Not safe yet. We need to go. Chad said there were more Bulls out there. And the vet said something about a civil war. Not safe by a mile."

He marched toward the house, the family following.

"Abby, grab your gun. Luke, you too. Hannah, the car is packed, right?"

He walked past the dead body on the back patio.

Through the kitchen.

Ignoring the scene in the entryway, he threw open the garage door.

"Everyone, in the van. Now. We're leaving."

The family climbed into the van silently. Brian opened the garage door and climbed into the driver's seat.

He started the car and backed out, barely squeezing by the box truck from the coffee shop.

He backed into their cul-de-sac, shifted into drive, and started down their street.

The Bulls of Bashan pickup truck looked harmless as he passed it.

The family sat in silence in the car.

Brian saw lights on in most of the homes. A few people were standing outside, apparently awakened by the gunshots.

Brian rolled his window down.

He heard sirens in the distance.

He smelled smoke.

Above the roofline, he could see the glow of fires coming from the Happy Mart shopping center.

Civil War.

He saw the doorbell cameras on one of his neighbors' homes light up when he drove by.

Babble sees all.

Babble.

Babble knows.

He stopped the van in the middle of the street. Five houses away from their home.

"Hannah, I need you to drive." He threw open the door and got out of the van.

"What? Where are you going?" she said as she slid over to the driver's seat.

"I'll meet you at the intersection. Trust me. Drive slow. Don't look at anyone. Just go."

"Brian!" Hannah yelled as he slammed the door.

He jogged back to his house, letting out a breath once he heard Hannah start down the road again.

the forgiveness of sins

Brian headed up his driveway, toward the driver side of the box truck, and got in.

The truck was still idling.

How long had it been since he brought Rachel home from the vet?

Five minutes, max. Maybe ten? An entire lifetime lived in such a short time.

Ten minutes for his family to be changed forever.

A brief image of Chad's head floating in the pool flashed into his mind.

Ten minutes that may have changed Brian forever.

Brian backed out of his driveway, hit the gas, and headed out of his neighborhood.

He passed the park, and he could hear the ducks through the broken passenger window.

He drove past the homes, past the two big oak trees, and pulled onto their connecting street.

Green belt on both sides, no homes. Half mile of nothing before the main intersection.

A few moments later he saw their van.

Hannah pulled to the side of the road and was idling.

He pulled in front of her and jumped out.

"What are we doing, Brian?" Hannah asked as she jumped out of the car.

"Get everyone out. Into the box truck."

"What? Why? The van is packed."

Brian dropped his voice.

"Cameras. Babble has eyes everywhere. Remember what happened when we tried to leave before? The van is on the grid. With any luck . . ." He looked over his shoulder.

"This generic white box truck is off the grid. Come on, we need to hurry."

They worked in silence, the entire family helping.

Brian handed the camping gear and other supplies to the kids as they carted it by hand to the box truck. They were done in a matter of minutes.

"Luke, in the back with Rachel, Shawn and Jer. Make sure you find a way to hold on. No seatbelts."

Luke nodded and jumped in. The other three climbed after him in silence. Brian's heart tugged as he saw Shawn and Jer both put their thumbs into their mouths.

Ten minutes changed us all.

"Watch Rachel's leg," he said as he pulled down the roll-up door. He pulled the lever and locked it down.

He climbed back into the bench seat with Hannah, Abby, and Lizzy.

"Okay, time to go," he said.

Brian pulled the truck up the road, waited for the light to turn green, and made the left.

The sky was a liquid black, no moon.

He saw a cluster of emergency vehicles on the road to his left.

There was a body in the road, covered in a white sheet.

The woman Brian had shot on their way back from the vet.

He kept his eyes glued forward and rolled past the scene.

The cops and medics paid no attention to the box truck.

He could see flames ahead.

As they drove next to Happy Mart, Brian saw a chaotic scene.

There were crowds of people outside Happy Mart. The grocery store was engulfed in flames.

As they got closer Brian saw people fighting.

Some people carried makeshift weapons, but as he rolled through the intersection, he saw a few people waving guns.

Civil War.

Dr. Perkins warned him.

He ducked his head as police vehicles screamed past him and he nearly stopped when he saw a man throw a Molotov cocktail at Dr. Perkins clinic.

Safe. He needed to keep his family safe.

Brian hoped the good doctor made it out in time.

As he rolled past the church, a few parks, another shopping center, and housing tracts, he saw more of the same.

Smoke, flames, crowds. A couple of car crashes.

Thankfully no roadblocks.

Brian sped up.

Hannah reached over Abby's lap and grabbed his hand.

Near the freeway onramp, Brian saw a convoy of military vehicles passing him in the other direction.

Several personnel carriers, all in that dull army green. And one large tractor-trailer carrying a tank.

Every vehicle emblazoned with a black "SG" incorporated into an eye-shaped logo.

"The Social Guard," Brian whispered as he turned onto the freeway.

"The Social Guard?" Hannah asked.

"Yeah. The new branch of the military. Meant to enforce the Azazel Promise."

He checked his mirrors in time to see the last of the convoy disappear behind them.

No one was following them.

the resurrection of the body

He pushed down on the gas pedal, watching as the speedometer climbed.

EPILOGUE

Brian drove the truck up the 5 freeway. He drove past Castaic. He drove up the Grapevine. Past Pyramid Lake. Past Gorman. Up. Always up. Into the mountains. Through the rolling golden hills of his youth. He saw a hint of the sun in the way the dark skies turned first purple, then pink as the sun climbed over the mountain tops.

He drove past Lebec. Past his old high school.

He drove past the wooden sign saying "Welcome to Frazier Park" that his aunt helped commission thirty years ago.

He drove past the park where he learned to throw a baseball.

He drove past Cuddy Hall, where he learned Bible verses.

He drove the truck past the Lockwood Valley Road turnoff, and up the second grade, near the shady part of the street where the ice never seemed to melt in the winter and tourists sometimes slide off the road.

He crested the hill where city people come to sled.

He saw Cuddy Valley open before him as the pink sky turned to a deep orange, then yellow.

He drove past the small ranches lining the road. Past the pens that once held llamas and another that had kept goats.

He drove past the Pinion Pines turnoff, his old bus stop. He drove up.

Up. Always up. Into the mountains.

He drove into the morning when the road started to twist and wind. He passed the last small group of houses and meandered up toward the top of Mount Pinos.

He slowed when he saw the familiar break in the trees.

He turned left onto soft dirt.

He drove down the road where he once taught Luke how to sled.

Where his mom taught Abby and Hannah how to cross-country ski.

He drove past the little depression in the road where his mom fell on her skis. That winter day when no one could stop giggling as she tried to get up.

That winter day when hot chocolate solved the world's problems.

He drove past the tire swing.

The grove of fruit trees it took his parents five seasons to get started.

He drove around the bend and stopped in the turnabout.

Newman Cabin. Established 1980.

The year his parents got married.

He started making plans. Mental math.

Hunt. Grow. Protect.

Stay quiet. Stay safe.

My parents. I need to find my parents.

Where are they?

And Dr. Perkins? Did he make it out? Did he go to his farm?

"Hannah, wake up."

She murmured next to him and opened her eyes.

"Where are we?" she asked.

Brian looked at the little clearing, surrounded by dense forest. The cabin. The outbuildings.

I believe in the life everlasting

"We're home."

Other Fiction from Fidelis Publishing

Rendezvous with God—
Volume One—Bill Myers

9781735428581 Paperback /
9781735428598 eBook

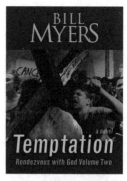

Temptation—Rendezvous with God—
Volume Two—Bill Myers

9781956454024 Paperback /
9781956454031 eBook

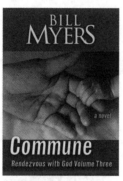

Commune: Rendezvous with God—
Volume Three—Bill Myers

9781956454246 Paperback /
9781956454253 eBook

Insight—Rendezvous with God—
Volume Four—Bill Myers

9781956454420 Paperback /
9781956454437 eBook

Satan's Dare—Jim DeMint

9781735856308 Hardcover /
9781735856315 eBook

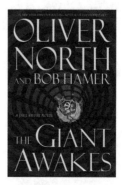

The Giant Awakes: A Jake Kruse Novel—
Oliver North and Bob Hamer

9781956454048 Hardcover /
9781956454055 eBook

A Bellwether Christmas:
A Story Inspired by True
Events—Laurel Guillen
9781956454086 Hardcover /
9781956454093 eBook

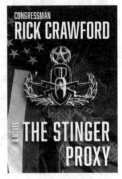

The Stinger Proxy—
Rick Crawford
9781956454215 Hardcover /
9781956454222 eBook

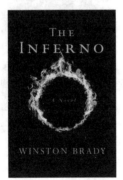

The Inferno—Winston Brady
9781956454260 Paperback /
9781956454277 eBook

The Invisible War: Tribulation
Cult Book 1—Michael Phillips
9781956454321 Paperback /
9781956454338 eBook